DICK FRANCIS

WHIP HAND

PUBLISHED BY POCKET BOOKS NEW YORK

This book is for
MIKE GWILYM
Actor
and
JACKY STOLLER
Producer
with gratitude and affection

POCKET BOOKS, a division of Simon & Schuster, Inc.
1230 Avenue of the Americas, New York, N.Y. 10020

Published by arrangement with Harper & Row, Publishers
Library of Congress Catalog Card Number: 79-3408

ISBN: 0-671-46404-3

First Pocket Books printing March, 1981

10 9 8 7 6 5 4

Printed in the U.S.A.

Prologue

I dreamed I was riding in a race.

Nothing odd in that. I'd ridden in thousands.

There were fences to jump. There were horses, and jockeys in a rainbow of colors, and miles of green grass. There were massed banks of people, with pink oval faces, undistinguishable pink blobs from where I crouched in the stirrups, galloping past, straining with speed.

Their mouths were open, and although I could hear no sound, I knew they were shouting.

Shouting my name, to make me win.

Winning was all. Winning was my function. What I was there for. What I wanted. What I was born for.

In the dream, I won the race. The shouting turned to cheering, and the cheering lifted me up on its wings, like a wave. But the winning was all; not the cheering.

I woke in the dark, as I often did, at four in the morning.

There was silence. No cheering. Just silence.

I could still feel the way I'd moved with the horse,

the ripple of muscle through both the striving bodies, uniting in one. I could still feel the irons round my feet, the calves of my legs gripping, the balance, the nearness to my head of the stretching brown neck, the mane blowing in my mouth, my hands on the reins.

There came, at that point, the second awakening. The real one. The moment in which I first moved, and opened my eyes, and remembered that I wouldn't ride any more races, ever. The wrench of loss came again as a fresh grief. The dream was a dream for whole men.

I dreamed it quite often.

Damned senseless thing to do.

Living, of course, was quite different. One discarded dreams, and got dressed, and made what one could of the day.

Chapter 1

I took the battery out of my arm and fed it into the recharger, and only realized I'd done it when ten seconds later the fingers wouldn't work.

How odd, I thought. Recharging the battery, and the maneuver needed to accomplish it, had become such second nature that I had done them instinctively, without conscious decision, like brushing my teeth. And I realized for the first time that I had finally squared my subconscious, at least when I was awake, to the fact that what I now had as a left hand was a matter of metal and plastic, not muscle and bone and blood.

I pulled my tie off and flung it haphazardly onto my jacket, which lay over the leather arm of the sofa; stretched and sighed with the ease of homecoming; listened to the familiar silences of the flat; and as usual felt the welcoming peace unlock the gritty tensions of the outside world.

I suppose that that flat was more of a haven than a home. Comfortable certainly, but not slowly and lovingly put together. Furnished, rather, on one brisk unemotional afternoon in one store: "I'll have that, that, that, and that . . . and send them as soon as possible." The collection had jelled, more or less, but I now owned nothing whose loss I would ache over; and if that was a defense mechanism, at least I knew it.

Contentedly padding around in shirtsleeves and socks, I switched on the warm pools of table lights, encouraged the television with a practiced slap, poured a soothing Scotch, and decided not to do yesterday's washing up. There was steak in the fridge and money in the bank, and who needed an aim in life, anyway?

I tended nowadays to do most things one-handed, because it was quicker. My ingenious false hand, which worked via solenoids from electrical impulses in what was left of my forearm, would open and close in a fairly viselike grip, but at its own pace. It did *look* like a real hand, though, to the extent that people sometimes didn't notice. There were shapes like fingernails, and ridges for tendons, and blue lines for veins. When I was alone I seemed to use it less and less, but it pleased me better to see it on than off.

I shaped up to that evening as to many another—on the sofa, feet up, knees bent, in contact with a chunky tumbler, and happy to live vicariously via the small screen—and I was mildly irritated when halfway through a decent comedy the doorbell rang.

With more reluctance than curiosity I stood up, parked the glass, fumbled through my jacket pockets for the spare battery I'd been carrying there, and snapped it into the socket in my arm. Then, buttoning the shirt cuff down over the plastic wrist, I went out into the small hall and took a look through the spyhole in the door.

There was no trouble on the mat, unless trouble had taken the shape of a middle-aged lady in a blue head scarf. I opened the door and said politely, "Good evening, can I help you?"

"Sid," she said. "Can I come in?"

I looked at her, thinking that I didn't know her. But then a good many people whom I didn't know called me Sid, and I'd always taken it as a compliment.

Coarse dark curls showed under the head scarf, a pair of tinted glasses hid her eyes, and heavy crimson lipstick focused attention on her mouth. There was embarrassment in her manner and she seemed to be trembling inside her loose fawn raincoat. She still appeared to expect me to recognize her, but it was not until she looked nervously over her shoulder, and I saw her profile against the light, that I actually did.

Even than I said incredulously, tentatively, "Rosemary?"

"Look," she said, brushing past me as I opened the door wider. "I simply must talk to you."

"Well . . . come in."

While I closed the door behind us, she stopped in front of the looking glass in the hall and started to untie the head scarf.

"My God, whatever do I look like?"

I saw that her fingers were shaking too much to undo the knot, and finally, with a frustrated little moan, she stretched over her head, grasped the points of the scarf, and forcefully pulled the whole thing forward. Off with the scarf came all the black curls, and out shook the more familiar chestnut mane of Rosemary Caspar, who had called me Sid for fifteen years.

"My God," she said again, putting the tinted glasses away in her handbag and fetching out a tissue to wipe off the worst of the gleaming lipstick. "I had to come. I had to come."

I watched the tremors in her hands and listened to the jerkiness in her voice, and reflected that I'd seen a whole procession of people in this state since I'd drifted into the trade of sorting out trouble and disaster.

"Come on in and have a drink," I said, knowing it was what she both needed and expected, and sighing internally over the ruins of my quiet evening. "Whisky or gin?"

"Gin . . . tonic . . . anything."

Still wearing the raincoat, she followed me into the sitting room and sat abruptly on the sofa as if her knees had given way beneath her. I looked briefly at the vague eyes, switched off the laughter on the television, and poured her a tranquilizing dose of mothers' ruin.

"Here," I said, handing her the tumbler. "So what's the problem?"

"Problem!" She was transitorily indignant. "It's more than that."

I picked up my own drink and carried it round to sit in an armchair opposite her.

"I saw you in the distance at the races today," I said. "Did the problem exist at that point?"

She took a large gulp from her glass. "Yes, it damn well did. And why do you think I came creeping around at night searching for your damn flat in this ropy wig if I could have walked straight up to you at the races?"

"Well . . . why?"

"Because the last person I can be seen talking to on a racecourse or off it is Sid Halley."

I had ridden a few times for her husband way back in the past. In the days when I was a jockey. When I was still light enough for flat racing and hadn't taken to steeplechasing. In the days before success and glory and falls and smashed hands . . . and all that. To Sid Halley, ex-jockey, she could have talked publicly forever. To Sid Halley, recently changed into a sort of all-purpose investigator, she had come in darkness and fright.

Forty-fivish, I supposed, thinking about it for the first time, and realizing that although I had known her casually for years, I had never before looked long enough or closely enough at her face to see it feature by feature. The general impression of thin elegance had always been strong. The drooping lines of eyebrow and eyelid, the small scar on the chin, the fine noticeable down on the sides of the jaw, these were new territory.

She raised her eyes suddenly and gave me the same sort of inspection, as if she'd never really seen me before: and I guessed that for her it was a much more radical reassessment. I was no longer the boy she'd once rather brusquely issued with riding instructions, but a man she had come to in trouble. I was accustomed, by now, to seeing this new view of me supplant older and easier relationships, and although I might often regret it, there seemed no way of going back.

"Everyone says . . ." She began doubtfully. "I mean . . . over this past year, I keep hearing . . ." She cleared her throat. "They say you're good . . . very good . . . at this sort of thing. But I don't know. . . . Now I'm here, it doesn't seem . . . I mean, . . . you're a jockey."

"Was," I said succinctly.

She glanced vaguely at my left hand, but made no other comment. She knew all about that. As racing gossip goes, it was last year's news.

"Why don't you tell me what you want done?" I said. "If I can't help, I'll say so."

The idea that I couldn't help after all reawoke her alarm and set her shivering again inside the raincoat.

"There's no one else," she said. "I can't go to anyone else. I have to believe . . . I have to . . . that you can do . . . all they say."

"I'm no superman," I protested. "I just snoop around a bit."

"Well . . . Oh, God . . ." The glass rattled against her teeth as she emptied it to the dregs. "I hope to God . . ."

"Take your coat off," I said persuasively. "Have another gin. Sit back on the sofa, and start at the beginning."

As if dazed, she stood up, undid the buttons, shed the coat, and sat down again.

"There isn't a beginning."

She took the refilled glass and hugged it to her chest. The newly revealed clothes were a cream silk shirt under a rust-colored cashmere-looking sweater, a heavy gold chain, and a well-cut black skirt: the everyday expression of no financial anxieties.

"George is at a dinner," she said. "We're staying here in London overnight. . . . He thinks I've gone to a film."

George, her husband, ranked in the top three of British race horse trainers and probably in the top ten internationally. On racecourses from Hong Kong to Kentucky he was revered as one of the greats. At Newmarket, where he lived, he was king. If his horses won the Derby, the Arc de Triomphe, the Washington International, no one was surprised. Some of the cream of the world's bloodstock floated year by year to his stable, and even having a horse in his yard gave the owner a certain standing. George Caspar could afford to turn down any horse or any man. Rumor said he rarely turned down any woman; and if that was Rosemary's problem, it was one I couldn't solve.

"He mustn't know," she said nervously. "You'll have to promise not to tell him I came here."

"I'll promise provisionally," I said.

"That's not enough."

"It'll have to be."

"You'll see," she said. "You'll see why. . . ." She

took a drink. "He may not like it, but he's worried to death."

"Who . . . George?"

"Of course George. Who else? Don't be so damned stupid. For who else would I risk coming here on this damn charade?" The brittleness shrilled in her voice and seemed to surprise her. She took some deep breaths, and started again. "What did you think of Gleaner?"

"Er . . ." I said. "Disappointing."

"A damned disaster," she said. "You know it was."

"One of those things," I said.

"No, it was *not* one of those things. One of the best two-year-olds George ever had. Won three brilliant two-year-old races. Then all that winter, favorite for the Guineas and the Derby. Going to be the tops, everyone said. Going to be marvelous."

"Yes," I said. "I remember."

"And then what? Last spring he ran in the Guineas. Fizzled out. Total flop. And he never even got within sight of the Derby."

"It happens," I said.

She looked at me impatiently, compressing her lips. "And Zingaloo?" she said. "Was that, too, just one of those things? The two best colts in the country, both brilliant at two, both in our yard. And neither of them won a damn penny last year as three-year-olds. They just stood there in their boxes, looking well, eating their heads off, and totally damn bloody useless."

"It was a puzzler," I agreed, but without much conviction. Horses that didn't come up to expectations were as normal as rain on Sundays.

"And what about Bethesda, the year before?" She glared at me vehemently. "Top two-year-old filly. Favorite for months for the One Thousand and the Oaks. Terrific. She went down to the start of the One

Thousand looking a million dollars, and she finished tenth. *Tenth,* I ask you!"

"George must have had them all *checked,*" I said mildly.

"Of course he did. Damn vets crawling all round the place for weeks on end. Dope tests. Everything. All negative. Three brilliant horses all gone useless. And no damned explanation. Nothing!"

I sighed slightly. It sounded to me more like the story of most trainer's lives, not a matter for melodramatic visits in false wigs.

"And now," she said, casually dropping the bomb, "there is Tri-Nitro."

I let out an involuntarily audible breath, halfway to a grunt. Tri-Nitro filled columns just then on every racing page, hailed as the best colt for a decade. His two-year-old career the previous autumn had eclipsed all competitors, and his supremacy in the approaching summer was mostly taken for granted. I had seen him win the Middle Park at Newmarket in September at a record-breaking pace, and had a vivid memory of the slashing stride that covered the turf at almost incredible speed.

"The Guineas is only a fortnight away," Rosemary said. "Two weeks today, in fact. Suppose something happens . . . suppose it's just as bad? What if he fails, like the others . . . ?"

She was trembling again, but when I opened my mouth to speak, she rushed on at a higher pitch. "Tonight was the only chance . . . the only night I could come here . . . and George would be livid. He says nothing can happen to the horse, no one can get at him, the security's too good. But he's scared, I know he is. Strung up. Screwed up tight. I suggested he call you in to guard the horse and he nearly went berserk. I don't know why. I've never seen him in such a fury."

"Rosemary," I began, shaking my head.

"Listen," she interrupted. "I want you to make sure nothing happens to Tri-Nitro before the Guineas. That's all."

"All . . ."

"It's no good wishing afterwards . . . if somebody tries something . . . that I'd asked you. I couldn't stand that. So I had to come. I had to. So say you'll do it. Say how much you want, and I'll pay it."

"It's not money," I said. "Look . . . There's no way I can guard Tri-Nitro without George knowing and approving. It's impossible."

"You can do it. I'm sure you can. You've done things before that people said couldn't be done. I had to come. I can't face it . . . George can't face it. Not three years in a row. Tri-Nitro has got to win. You've got to make sure nothing happens. You've got to."

She was suddenly shaking worse than ever and looked well down the road to hysteria. More to calm her than from any thought of being able in fact to do what she wanted, I said, "Rosemary . . . all right. I'll try to do something."

"He's got to win," she said.

I said soothingly, "I don't see why he shouldn't."

She picked up unerringly the undertone I hadn't known would creep into my voice: the skepticism, the easy complacent tendency to discount her urgency as the fantasies of an excitable woman. I heard the nuances myself, and saw them uncomfortably through her eyes.

"My God, I've wasted my time coming here, haven't I?" she said bitterly, standing up. "You're like all bloody men. You've got menopause on the brain."

"That's not true. And I said I'd try."

"Yes." The word was a sneer. She was stoking up her own anger, indulging an inner need to explode. She practically threw her empty glass at me instead of handing it. I missed catching it, and it fell against the side of the coffee table and broke.

She looked down at the glittering pieces and stuffed the jagged rage halfway back into its box.

"Sorry," she said shortly.

"It doesn't matter."

"Put it down to strain."

"Yes."

"I'll have to go and see that film. George will ask." She slid into her raincoat and moved jerkily toward the door, her whole body still trembling with tension. "I shouldn't have come here. But I thought . . ."

"Rosemary," I said flatly. "I've said I'll try, and I will."

"Nobody knows what it's like."

I followed her into the hall, feeling her jangling desperation almost as if it were making actual disturbances in the air. She picked the black wig off the small table there and put it back on her head, tucking her own brown hair underneath with fierce unfriendly jabs, hating herself, her disguise, and me; hating the visit, the lies to George, the seedy furtiveness of her actions. She painted on a fresh layer of the dark lipstick with unnecessary force, as if assaulting herself; tied the knot on the scarf with a savage jerk, and fumbled in her handbag for the tinted glasses.

"I changed in the lavatories at the tube station," she said. "It's all revolting. But I'm not having anyone see me leaving here. There are things going on. I know there are. And George is scared. . . ."

She stood by my front door, waiting for me to open it; a thin elegant woman looking determinedly ugly. It came to me that no woman did that to herself without a need that made esteem an irrelevance. I'd done nothing to relieve her distress, and it was no good realizing that it was because of knowing her too long in a different capacity. It was she who was subtly used to being in control, and I, from sixteen, who had respectfully followed her wishes. I thought that if tonight I had made her cry and given her warmth and contact and even a kiss, I could have done her more service; but the block was there, and couldn't be lightly dismantled.

"I shouldn't have come here," she said. "I see that now."

"Do you want me . . . to take any action?"

A spasm twisted her face. "Oh, God . . . Yes, I do. But I was stupid. Fooling myself. You're only a jockey after all."

I opened the door.

"I wish," I said lightly, "that I were."

She looked at me unseeingly, her mind already on her return journey, on her film, on her report of it to George.

"I'm not crazy," she said.

She turned abruptly and walked away without a backward glance. I watched her turn toward the stairs and go unhesitatingly out of sight. With a continuing feeling of having been inadequate, I shut the door and went back into the sitting room; and it seemed that the very air there too was restless from her intensity.

I bent down and picked up the larger pieces of broken glass, but there were too many sharp little splinters for total laziness, so I fetched dustpan and brush from the kitchen.

Holding the dustpan could usefully be done left-handed. If I simply tried to bend backward the real hand that wasn't there, the false fingers opened away from the thumb. If I sent the old message to bend my hand inward, they closed. There was always about two seconds' delay between mental instruction and electrical reaction, and taking that interval into account had been the most difficult thing to learn.

The fingers could not of course feel when their grip was tight enough. The people who had fitted the arm had told me that success was picking up eggs: and I'd broken a dozen or two in practicing, at the beginning. Absentmindedness had since resulted in an exploding light bulb and crushed-flat cigarette packets and explained why I used the marvels of science less than I might.

I emptied the bits of glass into the dustbin and switched on the television again; but the comedy was over, and Rosemary came between me and a cops-and-robbers. With a sigh I switched off, and cooked my steak, and after I'd eaten it, picked up the telephone to talk to Bobby Unwin, who worked for the *Daily Planet*.

"Information will cost you," he said immediately, when he found who was on his line.

"Cost me what?"

"A spot of quid pro quo."

"All right," I said.

"What are you after, then?"

"Um," I said. "You wrote a long piece about George Caspar in your Saturday color supplement a couple of months ago. Pages and pages of it."

"That's right. Special feature. In-depth analysis of success. The *Planet*'s doing a once-a-month series on highfliers, tycoons, pop stars, you name it. Putting them under the cliché microscope and coming up with a big yawn-yawn exposé of bugger all."

"Are you horizontal?" I said.

There was short silence, followed by a stifled girlish giggle.

"You just take your intuitions to Siberia," Bobby said. "What made you think so?"

"Envy, I daresay." But I'd really only been asking if he was alone, without making it sound important. "Will you be at Kempton tomorrow?"

"I reckon."

"Could you bring a copy of that magazine, and I'll buy you a bottle of your choice."

"Oh boy, oh boy. You're on."

His receiver went down without more ado, and I spent the rest of the evening reading the flat-racing form books of recent years, tracing the careers of Bethesda, Gleaner, Zingaloo, and Tri-Nitro, and coming up with nothing at all.

Chapter 2

I had fallen into a recent habit of lunching on Thursdays with my father-in-law. To be accurate, with my *ex*-father-in-law; Admiral (retired) Charles Roland, parent of my worst failure. To his daughter Jenny I had given whatever devotion I was capable of, and had withheld the only thing she eventually said she wanted, which was that I should stop riding in races. We had been married for five years: two in happiness, two in discord, and one in bitterness; and now only the itching half-mended wounds remained. Those, and the friendship of her father, which I had come by with difficulty and now prized as the only treasure saved from the wreck.

We met most weeks at noon in the upstairs bar of the Cavendish Hotel, where a pink gin for him and a whisky and water for me now stood on prim little mats beside a bowl of peanuts.

"Jenny will be at Aynsford this weekend," he said.

Aynsford was his house in Oxfordshire. London on

Thursdays was his business. He made the journey between the two in a Rolls.

"I'd be glad if you would come down," he said.

I looked at the fine distinguished face and listened to the drawling noncommittal voice. A man of subtlety and charm who could blast through you like a laser if he felt the need. A man whose integrity I would trust to the gates of hell, and whose mercy, not an inch.

I said carefully, without rancor, "I am not coming to be sniped at."

"She agreed that I should invite you."

"I don't believe it."

He looked with suspicious concentration at his glass. I knew from long experience that when he wanted me to do something he knew I wouldn't like, he didn't look at me. And there would be a pause, like this, while he found it in him to light the fuse. From the length of the pause, I drew no comfort of any sort. He said finally, "I'm afraid she's in some sort of trouble."

I stared at him, but he wouldn't raise his eyes.

"Charles," I said despairingly, "you *can't* . . . you can't ask me. You know how she speaks to me these days."

"You give as good as you get, as I recall."

"No one in their senses walks into a tiger's cage."

He gave me a brief flashing upward glance, and there was a small twitch to his mouth. And perhaps it was not the best way of referring to a man's beautiful daughter.

"I have known you, Sid," he said, "to walk into tigers' cages more than once."

"A tigress, then," I amended, with a touch of humor.

He pounced on it. "So you'll come?"

"No. Some things, honestly, are too much."

He sighed and sat back in his chair, looking at me over the gin. I didn't care for the blank look in his eyes, because it meant he was still plotting.

"Dover sole?" he suggested smoothly. "Shall I call the waiter? We might eat soon, don't you think?"

He ordered sole for both of us, and off the bone, out of habit. I could eat perfectly well in public now, but there had been a long and embarrassing period when my natural hand had been a wasted, useless deformity, which I'd self-consciously hidden in pockets. At about the time I finally got used to it, it had been smashed up again, and I'd lost it altogether. I guessed life was like that. You gained and you lost, and if you saved anything from the ruins, even if only a shred of self-respect, it was enough to take you through the next bit.

The waiter told us our table would be ready in ten minutes and went quietly away, hugging menus and order pad to his dinner jacket and gray silk tie. Charles glanced at his watch and then gazed expansively round the big, light, quiet room, where other couples, like us, sat in beige armchairs and sorted out the world.

"Are you going to Kempton this afternoon?" he said.

I nodded. "The first race is at two-thirty."

"Are you working on a job?" As an inquiry, it was a shade too bland.

"I'm not coming to Aynsford," I said. "Not while Jenny's there."

After a pause, he said, "I wish you would, Sid."

I merely looked at him. His eyes were following the track of a bar waiter delivering drinks to distant customers; and he was taking a great deal too much time thinking out his next sentence.

He cleared his throat and addressed himself to nowhere in particular. "Jenny has lent some money . . . and her name, I'm afraid . . . to a business enterprise which would appear to be fraudulent."

"She's done *what?*" I said.

His gaze switched back to me with suspicious speed, but I interrupted him as he opened his mouth.

"No," I said. "If she's done that, it's well within your province to sort it out."

"It's your name she's used, of course," Charles said. "Jennifer Halley."

I could feel the trap closing round me. Charles studied my silent face and with a tiny sigh of relief let go of some distinct inner anxiety. He was a great deal too adept, I thought bitterly, at hooking me.

"She was attracted to a man," he said dispassionately. "I didn't especially like him, but then I didn't like you, either, to begin with . . . and I have found that error of judgment inhibiting, as a matter of fact, because I no longer always trust my first instincts."

I ate a peanut. He had disliked me because I was a jockey, which he saw as no sort of husband for his well-bred daughter; and I had disliked him right back as an intellectual and social snob. It was odd to reflect that he was now probably the individual I valued most in the world.

He went on, "This man persuaded her to go in for some sort of mail order business . . . all frightfully up-market and respectable, at least on the surface. A worthy way of raising money for charity . . . you know the sort of thing. Like Christmas cards, only in this case I think it was a sort of wax polish for antique furniture. One was invited to buy expensive wax, knowing that most of the profits would go to a good cause."

He looked at me somberly. I simply waited, without much hope.

"The orders rolled in," he said. "And the money with them, of course. Jenny and a girlfriend were kept busy sending off the wax."

"Which, Jenny," I guessed, "had bought ready, in advance?"

Charles sighed. "You don't need to be told, do you?"

"And Jenny paid for the postage and packing and advertisements and general literature?"

He nodded. "She banked all the receipts into a specially opened account in the name of the charity. Those receipts have all been drawn out, the man has disappeared, and the charity, as such, has been found not to exist."

I regarded him in dismay.

"And Jenny's position?" I said.

"Very bad, I'm afraid. There may be a prosecution. And her name is on everything, and the man's nowhere."

My reaction was beyond blasphemy. Charles observed my blank silence and nodded slowly in sympathy.

"She has been exceedingly foolish," he said.

"Couldn't you have stopped her? Warned her?"

He shook his head regretfully. "I didn't know about it until she came to Aynsford yesterday in a panic. She has done it all from that flat she's taken in Oxford."

We went in to lunch, and I couldn't remember, afterward, the taste of the sole.

"The man's name is Nicholas Ashe," Charles said, over the coffee. "At least that's what he said." He paused briefly. "My solicitor chap thinks it would be a good idea if you could find him."

I drove to Kempton with visual and muscular responses on autopilot and my thoughts uncomfortably on Jenny.

Divorce itself, it seemed, had changed nothing. The recent antiseptic drawing of the line, the impersonal court to which neither of us had gone (no children, no maintenance disputes, no flicker of reconciliation, petition granted, next case please), seemed to have punctuated our lives not with a full stop but with hardly a comma. The legal position had not proved a great liberating open door. The recovery from emotional cataclysm seemed a long, slow process, and the certificate was barely an aspirin.

Where once we had clung together with delight and passion, we now, if we chanced to meet, ripped with claws. I had spent eight years in loving, losing, and mourning Jenny, and although I could wish my feelings were dead, they weren't. The days of indifference still seemed a weary way off.

If I helped her out of the mess she was in, she would give me a rotten time. If I didn't help her, I would give it to myself. *Why,* I thought violently, in impotent irritation, had the silly bitch been so *stupid?*

There was a fair attendance at Kempton for a weekday in April, though as often before, I regretted that in Britain, the nearer a racecourse was to London, the more vulnerable it became to stay-away crowds. City dwellers might be addicted to gambling, but not to fresh air and horses. Birmingham and Manchester, in days gone by, had lost their racecourses to indifference, and Liverpool had survived only through the Grand National. Most times it took a course in the country to burst at the seams and run out of race cards: the thriving plants still growing from the oldest roots.

Outside the weighing room there was the same old bunch of familiar faces carrying on chats that had been basically unchanged for centuries: who was going to ride what, and who was going to win, and there should be a change in the rules, and what so-and-so had said about his horse losing, and wasn't the general outlook grim, and did you know young-fella-me-lad has left his wife? There were the scurrilous stories and the slight exaggerations and the downright lies. The same mingling of honor and corruption, of principle and expediency. People ready to bribe, people with the ready palm. Anguished little hopefuls and arrogant big guns. The failures making brave excuses, and the successful hiding the anxieties behind their eyes. All as it had been, and was, and would be, as long as racing lasted.

I had no real right any longer to wander in the space outside the weighing room, although no one ever turned me out. I belonged in the gray area of ex-jockeys: barred from the weighing room itself but tolerantly given the run of much else. The cozy inner sanctum had gone down the drain the day half a ton of horse landed feet first on my metacarpals. Since then I had come to be glad simply to be still part of the brotherhood, and the ache to be riding was just part of the general regret. Another ex-champion had told me it took him twenty years before he no longer yearned to be out there on the horses, and I'd said thanks very much.

George Caspar was there, talking to his jockey, with three runners scheduled that afternoon; and also Rosemary, who reacted with a violent jerk when she saw me at ten paces, and promptly turned her back. I could imagine the waves of alarm quivering through her, although that day she looked her usual well-groomed elegant self: mink coat for the chilly wind, glossy boots, velvet hat. If she feared I would talk about her visit, she was wrong.

There was a light grasp on my elbow and a pleasant voice saying, "A word in your ear, Sid."

I was smiling before I turned to him, because Lord Friarly, earl, landowner, and frightfully decent fellow, had been one of the people for whom I'd ridden a lot of races. He was of the old school of aristocrats: sixtyish, beautifully mannered, genuinely compassionate, slightly eccentric, and more intelligent then people expected. A slight stammer had nothing to do with speech impediment but all to do with not wanting to seem to throw his rank about in an egalitarian world.

Over the years I had stayed several times in his house in Shropshire, mostly on the way to northern race meetings, and had traveled countless miles with him in a succession of elderly cars. The age of the cars was not an extension of the low profile, but rather a disinclination to waste money on nonessentials. Essentials, in terms of the earl's income, were keeping up Friarly Hall and owning as many race horses as possible.

"Great to see you, sir," I said.

"I've told you to call me Philip."

"Yes . . . sorry."

"Look," he said, "I want you to do something for me. I hear you're damned good at looking into things. Doesn't surprise me, of course; I've always valued your opinion, you know that."

"Of course I'll help if I can," I said.

"I've an uncomfortable feeling I'm being *used,"* he said. "You know that I'm a sucker for seeing my horses run, the more the merrier, and all that. Well, during the past year I have agreed to be one of the registered owners in a syndicate . . . you know, sharing the costs with eight or ten other people, though the horses run in my name, and my colors."

"Yeah," I said, nodding. "I've noticed."

"Well . . . I don't know all the other people, personally. The syndicates were formed by a chap who does just that—gets people together and sells them a horse. You know?"

I nodded. There had been cases of syndicate formers buying horses for a smallish sum and selling them to the members of the syndicate for up to four times as much. A healthy little racket, so far legal.

"Those horses don't run true to form, Sid," he said bluntly. "I've a nasty feeling that somewhere in the syndicates we've got someone fixing the way the horses run. So will you find out for me? Nice and quietly?"

"I'll certainly try," I said.

"Good," he said, with satisfaction. "Thought you would. So I brought the names for you, of the people in the syndicates." He pulled a folded paper out of his inner pocket. "There you are," he said, opening it and pointing. "Four horses. The syndicates are all registered with the Jockey Club, everything aboveboard, audited accounts, and so on. It all looks all right on paper, but frankly, Sid, I'm not *happy.*"

"I'll look into it," I promised, and he thanked me profusely, and also genuinely, and moved away, after a minute or two, to talk to Rosemary and George.

Farther away, Bobby Unwin, notebook and pencil in evidence, was apparently giving a middle-rank trainer a hard time. His voice floated over, sharp with northern aggression and tinged with an inquisitorial tone caught from tele-interviewers. "Can you say, then, that you are perfectly satisfied with the way your horses are running?" The trainer looked around for escape and shifted from foot to foot. It was amazing, I thought, that he put up with it, even though Bobby Unwin's printed barbs tended to be worse if he hadn't had the personal pleasure of intimidating his victim face to face. He wrote well, was avidly read, and among most of the racing fraternity was heartily disliked. Between him and me there had been for many years a sort of sparring truce, which in practice had meant a diminution of words like "blind" and "cretinous" to two per paragraph when he was describing any race I'd lost. Since I'd stopped riding I was no longer a target, and in consequence we had developed a perverse satisfaction in talking to each other, like scratching an itch.

Seeing me out of the corner of his eye, he presently released the miserable trainer and steered his beaky nose in my direction. Tall, forty, and forever making copy out of having been born in a back-to-back terrace in Bradford: a fighter, come up the hard way, and letting no one ever forget it. We ought to have had much in common, since I too was the product of a dingy back street, but temperament had nothing to do with environment. He tended to meet fate with fury and I with silence, which meant that he talked a lot and I listened.

"The color mag's in my briefcase in the press room," he said. "What do you want it for?"

"Just general interest."

"Oh, come off it," he said. "What are you working on?"

"And would you," I said, "give me advance notice of your next scoop?"

"All right," he said. "Point taken. And I'll have a bottle of the best vintage bubbly in the members' bar. After the first race. O.K.?"

"And for smoked salmon sandwiches extra, would I acquire some background info that never saw the light of print?"

He grinned nastily and said he didn't see why not; and in due course, after the first race, he kept his bargain.

"You can afford it, Sid, lad," he said, munching a pink-filled sandwich and laying a protective hand on the gold-foiled bottle standing beside us on the bar counter. "So what do you want to know?"

"You went to Newmarket . . . to George Caspar's yard . . . to do this article?" I indicated the color magazine, which lay, folded lengthwise, beside the bottle.

"Yeah. Sure."

"So tell me what you didn't write."

He stopped in midmunch. "In what area?"

"What do you privately think of George as a person?"

He spoke round bits of brown bread. "I said most of it in that." He looked at the magazine. "He knows more about when a horse is ready to race and what race to run him in than any other trainer on the turf. And he's got as much feeling for people as a block of stone. He knows the name and the breeding back to the flood of every one of the hundred and twenty plus horses in his yard, and he can recognize them walking away from him in a downpour, which is practically impossible, but as for the forty lads he's got there working for him, he calls them all Tommy, because he doesn't know tother from which."

"Lads come and go," I said neutrally.

"So do horses. It's in his mind. He doesn't give a bugger's damn for people."

"Women?" I suggested.

"Uses them, poor sods. I bet when he's at it he's got his mind on his next day's runners."

"And Rosemary . . . what does she think about things?"

I poured a refill into his glass, and sipped at my own. Bobby finished his sandwich with a gulp and licked the crumbs off his fingers.

"Rosemary? She's halfway off her rocker."

"She looked all right yesterday at the races," I said. "And she's here today, as well."

"Yeah, well, she can hold on to the grande dame act in public still, I grant you, but I was in and out of the house for three days, and I'm telling you, mate, the goings on there had to be heard to be believed."

"Such as?"

"Such as Rosemary screaming all over the place that they hadn't enough security and George telling her to belt up. Rosemary's got some screwy idea that some of their horses have been got at in the past, and I daresay she's right, at that, because you don't have a yard that size and that successful that hasn't had its share of villains trying to alter the odds. But anyway"—he drank deep and tipped the bottle generously to replenish his supplies—"she seized me by the coat in their hall one day—and that hall's as big as a fair-sized barn—literally seized me by the coat and said what I should be writing was some stuff about Gleaner and Zingaloo being got at—you remember, those two spanking two-year-olds who never developed—and George came out of his office and said she was neurotic and suffering from the change of life, and right then and there in front of me they had a proper slanging match." He took a breath and a mouthful. "Funny thing is, in a way I'd say they were fond of each other. As much as he could be fond of anybody."

I ran my tongue round my teeth and looked only marginally interested, as if my mind was on something else. "What did George say about her ideas on Gleaner and Zingaloo?" I said.

"He took it for granted I wouldn't take her seriously, but anyway, he said it was just that she had the heebie-jeebies that someone would nobble Tri-Nitro, and she was getting everything out of proportion. Her age, he said. Women always went very odd, he said, at that age. He said the security round Tri-Nitro was already double what he considered really necessary, because of her nagging, and when the new season began he'd have night patrols with dogs, and suchlike. Which is now, of course. He told me that Rosemary was quite wrong, anyway, about Gleaner and Zingaloo being got at, but that she had this obsession on the subject, and he was ready to humor her to some degree to stop her going completely bonkers. It seems that both of them—the horses, that is—proved to have a heart murmur, which of course accounted for their rotten performances as they matured and grew heavier. So that was that. No story." He emptied his glass and refilled it. "Well, Sid, mate, what is it you *really* want to know about George Caspar?"

"Um," I said, "do you think there's anything he is afraid of?"

"George?" he said disbelievingly. "What sort of thing?"

"Anything."

"When I was there, I'd say he was about as frightened as a ton of bricks."

"He didn't seem worried?"

"Not a bit."

"Or edgy?"

He shrugged. "Only with his wife."

"How long ago was it that you went there?"

"Oh . . ." He considered, thinking. "After Christmas. Yes . . . second week in January. We have to do those color mags such a long time in advance."

"You don't think, then," I said slowly, sounding disappointed, "that he'd be wanting any extra protection for Tri-Nitro?"

"Is that what you're after?" He gave the leering grin. "No dice, then, Sid, mate. Try someone smaller. George has got his whole ruddy yard sewn up tight. For a start, see, it's one of those old ones enclosed inside a high wall, like a fortress. Then there's ten-foot-high double gates across the entrance, with spikes on top."

I nodded. "Yes . . . I've seen them."

"Well, then." He shrugged, as if that settled things.

There were closed-circuit televisions in all the bars at Kempton to keep serious drinkers abreast of the races going on outside, and on the nearest of these sets Bobby Unwin and I watched the second race. The horse that won by six lengths was the one trained by

George Caspar, and while Bobby was still thoughtfully eyeing the two inches of fizz still left in the bottle, George himself came into the bar. Behind him, in a camel-colored overcoat, came a substantial man bearing all the stigmata of a satisfied winning owner. Cat-with-the-cream smile, big gestures, have this one on me.

"Finish the bottle, Bobby," I said.

"Don't you want any?"

"It's yours."

He made no objections. Poured, drank, and comfortably belched. "Better go," he said. "Got to write up these effing colts in the third. Don't you go telling my editor I watched the second in the bar. I'd get the sack." He didn't mean it. He saw many a race in the bar. "See you, Sid. Thanks for the drink."

He turned with a nod and made a sure passage to the door, showing not a sign of having dispatched seven eighths of a bottle of champagne within half an hour. Merely laying the foundations, no doubt. His capacity was phenomenal.

I tucked his magazine inside my jacket and made my own way slowly in his wake, thinking about what he'd said. Passing George Caspar, I said, "Well done," in the customary politeness of such occasions, and he nodded briefly and said "Sid," and, transaction completed, I continued toward the door.

"Sid . . ." he called after me, his voice rising.

I turned. He beckoned. I went back.

"Want you to meet Trevor Deansgate," he said.

I shook the hand offered: snow-white cuff, gold links, smooth pale skin, faintly moist; well-tended nails, onyx-and-gold signet ring on little finger.

"Your winner?" I said. "Congratulations."

"Do you know who I am?"

"Trevor Deansgate?"

"Apart from that."

It was the first time I'd seen him at close quarters. There was often, in powerful men, a giveaway droop of the eyelids which proclaimed an inner sense of superiority, and he had it. Also dark gray eyes, black controlled hair, and the tight mouth which goes with well-exercised decision-making muscles.

"Go on, Sid," George said into my tiny hesitation. "If you know, say. I told Trevor you knew everything."

I glanced at George, but all that was to be read on his tough, weathered countenance was a sort of teasing expectancy. For many people, I knew, my new profession was a kind of game. There seemed to be no harm, on this occasion, of jumping obligingly through his offered hoop.

"Bookmaker?" I said tentatively; and to Trevor Deansgate directly, added, "Billy Bones?"

"There you are," said George, pleased. "I told you so."

Trevor Deansgate took it philosophically. I didn't try for a further reaction, which might not have been so friendly. His name at birth was reputed to be Shummuck. Trevor Shummuck from Manchester, who'd been born with a razor mind in a slum and changed his name, accent, and chosen company on the way up. As Bobby Unwin might have said, hadn't we all, and why not?

Trevor Deansgate's climb to the big league had been all but completed by buying out the old but ailing firm of "Billy Bones," in itself a blanket pseudonym for some brothers called Rubenstein and their uncle Solly. In the past few years "Billy Bones" had become big business. One could scarcely open a sports paper or go to the races without seeing the blinding fluorescent pink advertising, and slogans like "Make no Bones about it,

Billy's best" tended to assault one's peace on Sundays. If the business was as vigorous as its sales campaign, Trevor Deansgate was doing all right.

We civilly discussed his winner until it was time to adjourn outside to watch the colts.

"How's Tri-Nitro?" I said to George, as we moved toward the door.

"Great," he said. "In great heart."

"No problems?"

"None at all."

We parted outside, and I spent the rest of the afternoon in the usual desultory way, watching the races, talking to people, and thinking unimportant thoughts. I didn't see Rosemary again, and calculated she was avoiding me, and after the fifth race I decided to go.

A racecourse official at the exit gate stopped me with an air of relief, as if he'd been waiting for me a shade too long.

"Note for you, Mr. Hallcy."

"Oh? Thanks."

He gave me an unobtrusive brown envelope. I put it in my pocket and walked on, out to my car. Climbed in. Took out, opened, and read the letter.

> Sid, I've been busy all afternoon but I want to see you. Please can you meet me in the tearoom? After the last?
>
> Lucas Wainwright

Cursing slightly, I walked back across the car park, through the gate, and along to the restaurant, where lunch had given place to sandwiches and cake. The last race being just finished, the tea customers were trickling in in small thirsty bunches, but there was no sign of

Commander Lucas Wainwright, Director of Security to the Jockey Club.

I hung around, and he came in the end, hurrying, anxious, apologizing, and harassed.

"Do you want some tea?" He was out of breath.

"Not much."

"Never mind. Have some. We can sit here without being interrupted, and there are always too many people in the bar." He led the way to a table and gestured to me to sit down.

"Look, Sid. How do you feel about doing a job for us?" No waster of time, Commander Wainwright.

"Does 'us' mean the Security Service?"

"Yes."

"Official?" I said, surprised. The racecourse security people knew in moderate detail what I'd recently been doing and had raised no objection, but I hadn't imagined they actually approved. In some respects, I'd been working in their territory, and stepping on their toes.

Lucas drummed his fingers on the tablecloth.

"Unofficial," he said. "My own private show."

As Lucas Wainwright was himself the top brass of the Security Service, the investigative, policing arm of the Jockey Club, even unofficial requests from him could be considered to be respectably well-founded. Or at least until proved otherwise.

"What sort of job?" I said.

The thought of what sort of job slowed him up for the first time. He hummed and hahed and drummed his fingers some more, but finally shaped up to what proved to be a brute of a problem.

"Look, Sid, this is in strictest confidence."

"Yes."

"I've no higher authority for approaching you like this."

"Well," I said, "never mind. Go on."

"As I've no authority, I can't promise you any pay."

I sighed.

"All I could offer is . . . well . . . help if you should ever need it. And if it was within my power to give it, of course."

"That could be worth more than pay," I said.

He looked relieved. "Good. Now . . . this is very awkward. Very delicate." He still hesitated, but at last, with a sigh like a groan, he said, "I'm asking you to make . . . er . . . discreet inquiries into the . . . er . . . background of one of our people."

There was an instant's silence. Then I said, "Do you mean one of *you?* One of the Security Service?"

"I'm afraid that's right."

"Inquiries into exactly what?" I said.

He looked unhappy. "Bribery. Backhanders. That sort of thing."

"Um," I said. "Have I got this straight? You believe one of your chaps may be collecting payoffs from villains, and you want me to find out?"

"That's it," he said. "Exactly."

I thought it over. "Why don't you do the investigating yourselves? Just detail another of your chaps."

"Ah. Yes." He cleared his throat. "But there are difficulties. If I am wrong, I cannot afford to have it known that I was suspicious. It would cause a great, a very great, deal of trouble. And if I am right, which I fear I am, we—that is, the Jockey Club—would want to be able to deal with things quietly. A public scandal involving the Security Service would be very damaging to racing."

I thought he was perhaps putting it a bit high, but he wasn't.

"The man in question," he said miserably, "is Eddy Keith."

There was another countable silence. In the hierarchy of the Security Service then existing, there was Lucas Wainwright at the top, with two equal deputies one step down. Both of the deputies were retired senior-rank policemen. One of them was ex-Superintendent Eddison Keith.

I had a clear mental picture of him, as I had talked with him often. A big bluff breezy man with a heavy hand for clapping one on the shoulder. More than a trace of Suffolk accent in a naturally loud voice. A large flourishing straw-colored mustache, fluffy light brown hair through which one could see the pink scalp shining, and fleshy-lidded eyes which seemed always to be twinkling with good humor, and often weren't.

I had glimpsed there occasionally a glint as cold and unmerciful as a crevasse. Very much a matter of sun on ice: pretty but full of traps. One for applying the handcuffs with a cheery smile; that was Eddy Keith.

But crooked . . . ? I would never have thought so.

"What are the indications?" I said at last.

Lucas Wainwright chewed his lower lip for a while and then said, "Four of his inquiries over the past year have come up with incorrect results."

I blinked. "That's not very conclusive."

"No. Precisely. If I were sure, I wouldn't be here talking to you."

"I guess not." I thought a bit. "What sort of inquiries were they?"

"They were all syndicates. Inquiries into the suitability of people wanting to form syndicates to own horses. Making sure there weren't any undesirables sneaking into racing through the back door. Eddy gave all-clear reports on four proposed syndicates which do in fact all contain one or more people who would not be allowed through the gates."

"How do you know?" I said. "How did you find out?"

He made a face. "I was interviewing someone last week in connection with a dope charge. He was loaded with spite against a group of people he said had let him down, and he crowed over me that those people all owned horses under false names. He told me the names, and I checked, and the four syndicates which contain them were all passed by Eddy."

"I suppose," I said slowly, "they couldn't possibly be syndicates headed by Lord Friarly?"

He looked depressed. "Yes, I'm afraid so. Lord Friarly mentioned to me earlier this afternoon that he'd asked you to take a look-see. Told me out of politeness. It just reinforced the idea I'd already had of asking you myself. But I want it kept quiet."

"So does he," I said reassuringly. "Can you let me have Eddy's reports? Or copies of them? And the false and true names of the undesirables?"

He nodded. "I'll see you get them." He looked at his watch and stood up, the briskness returning to his manner like an accustomed coat. "I don't need to tell you . . . but do be discreet."

I joined him on his quick march to the door, where he left me at an even faster pace, sketching the merest wave of farewell. His back view vanished uprightly through the weighing room door, and I took myself out again to my car, reflecting that if I went on collecting jobs at the present rate, I would need to call up the troops.

Chapter 3

I telephoned the North London Comprehensive School and asked to speak to Chico Barnes.

"He's teaching judo," a voice said repressively.

"His class usually ends about now."

"Wait a minute."

I waited, driving toward London with my right hand on the wheel and my left round the receiver and a spatter of rain on the windshield. The car had been adapted for one-handed steering by the addition of a knob on the front face of the wheel's rim: very simple, very effective, and no objections from the police.

"Hullo?"

Chico's voice, cheerful, full even in one single word of his general irreverent view of the world.

"Want a job?" I said.

"Yeah." His grin traveled distinctly down the line. "It's been too dead quiet this past week."

"Can you go to the flat? I'll meet you there."

"I've got an extra class. They lumbered me. Some

other guy's evening class of stout ladies. He's ill. I don't blame him. Where are you phoning from?"

"The car. From Kempton to London. I'm calling in at Roehampton, at the limb center, as it's on the way, but I could be outside your school in, say, an hour and a half. I'll pick you up. O.K.?"

"Sure," he said. "What are you going to the limb center for?"

"To see Alan Stephenson."

"He'll have gone home."

"He said he'd be there, working late."

"Your arm hurting again?"

"No. Matter of screws and such."

"Yeah," he said. "O.K. See you."

I put the phone down with the feeling of satisfaction that Chico nearly always engendered. There was no doubt that as a working companion I found him great: funny, inventive, persistent, and deceptively strong. Many a rogue had discovered too late that young slender Chico with his boyish grin could throw a two-hundred-fifty-pound man over his shoulder with the greatest ease.

When I first got to know him he was working, as I was, in the Radnor Detective Agency, where I had learned my new trade. At one point there had been a chance that I would become first a partner and eventually the owner of that agency, but although Radnor and I had come to an agreement, and had even changed the agency's name to Radnor-Halley, life had delivered an earthquake upheaval and decided things otherwise. It must have been only a day before the partnership agreements were ready to be signed, with finances arranged and the champagne approaching the ice, that Radnor himself sat down for a quiet snooze in his armchair at home and never woke up.

Back from Canada, as if on stretched elastic, had immediately snapped an unsuspected nephew, brandishing a will in his favor and demanding his rights. He did not, he said forthrightly, want to sell half his inheritance to a one-handed ex-jockey, especially at the price agreed. He himself would be taking over and breathing new life into the whole works. He himself would be setting it all up in new modern offices, not the old crummy bomb-damaged joint in the Cromwell Road, and anyone who didn't like the transfer could vote with his feet.

Most of the old bunch had stayed on into the new order, but Chico had had a blazing row with the nephew and opted for the dole. Without much trouble he had then found the part-time job teaching judo, and the first time I'd asked for his help he joined up with enthusiasm. Since then I myself seemed to have become the most regularly employed investigator working in racing, and if Radnor's nephew didn't like it (and he was reputed to be furious), it was just too bad.

Chico bounced out through the glass swinging doors of the school, the lights behind him making a halo round his curly hair. Any resemblance to sainthood stopped precisely there, since the person under the curls was in no way long-suffering, God-fearing, or chaste.

He slid into the car, gave me a wide grin, and said, "There's a pub round the corner with a great set of bristols."

Resignedly I pulled into the pub's car park and followed him into the bar. The girl dispensing drinks was, as he'd said, nicely endowed, and moreover, she greeted Chico with telling warmth. I listened to the flirting chitchat and paid for the drinks.

We sat on a bench by the wall, and Chico approached

his pint with the thirst brought on by too much healthy exercise.

"Ah," he said, putting down the tankard temporarily. "That's better." Eyed my glass. "Is that straight orange juice?"

I nodded. "Been drinking on and off all day."

"Don't know how you bear it, all that high life and luxury."

"Easily."

"Yeah." He finished the pint, went back for a refill and another close encounter with the girl, and finally retracked to the bench. "Where do I go then, Sid? And what do I do?"

"Newmarket. Spot of pub crawling."

"Can't be bad."

"You're looking for a head lad called Paddy Young. He's George Caspar's head lad. Find out where he drinks, and sort of drift into conversation."

"Right."

"We want to know the present whereabouts of three horses which used to be in his yard."

"We do?"

"He shouldn't have any reason for not telling you, or at least I don't think so."

Chico eyed me. "Why don't you ask George Caspar right out? Be simpler, wouldn't it?"

"At the moment we don't want George Caspar to know we're asking questions about his horses."

"Like that, is it?"

"I don't know, really." I sighed. "Anyway, the three horses are Bethesda, Gleaner, and Zingaloo."

"O.K. I'll go up there tomorrow. Shouldn't be too difficult. You want me to ring you?"

"Soon as you can."

He glanced at me sideways. "What did the limb man say?"

"Hello, Sid, nice to see you."

He made a resigned noise with his mouth. "Might as well ask questions of a brick wall."

"He said the ship wasn't leaking and the voyage could go on."

"Better than nothing."

"As you say."

I went to Aynsford, as Charles had known I would, driving down on Saturday afternoon and feeling the apprehensive gloom deepen with every mile. For distraction I concentrated on Chico's news from Newmarket, telephoned through at lunchtime.

"I found him," he said. "He's a much-married man who has to take his pay packet home like a good boy on Friday evenings, but he sneaked out for a quick jar just now. The pub's nearly next door to the yard; very handy. Anyway, if you can understand what he says, and he's so Irish it's like talking to a foreigner, what it boils down to is that all three of those horses have gone to stud."

"Did he know where?"

"Sure. Bethesda went to someplace called Garvey's in Gloucestershire, and the other two are at a place just outside Newmarket, which Paddy Young called Traces, or at least I think that's what he said, although as I told you, he chews his words up something horrible."

"Thrace," I said. "Henry Thrace."

"Yeah? Well, maybe you can make sense of some other things he said, which were that Gleaner had a tritus and Zingaloo had the virus and Bruttersmit gave them both the tums down as quick as Concorde.

"Gleaner had a what?"

"Tritus."

I tried turning "Gleaner had a tritus" into an Irish accent in my head and came up with Gleaner had arthritis, which sounded a lot more likely. I said to

Chico, ". . . and Brothersmith gave them the thumbs down . . ."

"Yeah," he said. "You got it."

"Where are you phoning from?"

"Box in the street."

"There's a bit of boozing time left," I said. "Would you see if you can find out if this Brothersmith is George Caspar's vet, and if so, look him up in the phone book and bring back his address and number."

"O.K. Anything else?"

"No." I paused. "Chico, did Paddy Young give you any impression that there was anything odd in these three horses going wrong?"

"Can't say he did. He didn't seem to care much, one way or the other. I just asked him casual like where they'd gone, and he told me, and threw in the rest for good measure. Philosophical, you could say he was."

"Right, then," I said. "Thanks."

We disconnected, but he rang again an hour later to tell me that Brothersmith was indeed George Caspar's vet, and to give me his address.

"If that's all then, Sid, there's a train leaving in half an hour, and I've a nice little dolly waiting for me round Wembley way who'll have her Saturday night ruined if I don't get back."

The more I thought about Chico's report and Bobby Unwin's comments, the less I believed in Rosemary's suspicions; but I'd promised her I would try, and try I still would, for a little while longer. For as long as it took me, anyway, to check up on Bethesda, Zingaloo, and Gleaner, and talk to Brothersmith the vet.

Aynsford still looked its mellow stone self, but the daffodil-studded tranquillity applied to the exterior only. I stopped the car gently in front of the house and sat there wishing I didn't have to go in.

Charles, as if sensing that even then I might back off and drive away, came purposefully out of his front door and strode across the gravel. Watching for me, I thought. Waiting. Wanting me to come.

"Sid," he said, opening my door and stooping down to smile. "I knew you would."

"You hoped," I said.

I climbed out onto my feet.

"All right." The smile stayed in his eyes. "Hoped. But I know you."

I looked up at the front of the house, seeing only blank windows reflecting the grayish sky.

"Is she here?" I said.

He nodded. I turned away, went round to the back of the car, and lugged out my suitcase.

"Come on, then," I said. "Let's get it over."

"She's upset," he said, walking beside me. "She needs your understanding."

I glanced at him and said, "Mm." We finished the short journey in silence, and went through the door.

Jenny was standing there, in the hall.

I had never got used to the pang of seeing her on the rare occasions we had met since she left. I saw her as I had when I first loved her, a girl not of great classical beauty, but very pretty, with brown curling hair and a neat figure, and a way of holding her head high, like a bird on the alert. The old curving smile and the warmth in her eyes were gone, but I tended to expect them, with hopeless nostalgia.

"So you came," she said. "I said you wouldn't."

I put down the suitcase and took the usual deep breath. "Charles wanted me to," I said. I walked the steps toward her, and as always, we gave each other a brief kiss on the cheek. We had maintained the habit as the outward and public mark of a civilized divorce; but privately, I often thought, it was more like the ritual salute before a duel.

Charles shook his head impatiently at the lack of real affection, and walked ahead of us into the drawing room. He had tried in the past to keep us together, but the glue for any marriage had to come from the inside, and ours had dried to dust.

Jenny said, "I don't want any lectures from you, Sid, about this beastly affair."

"No."

"You're not perfect yourself, even though you like to think so."

"Give it a rest, Jenny," I said.

She walked abruptly away into the drawing room, and I more slowly followed. She would use me, I thought, and discard me again, and because of Charles I would let her. I was surprised that I felt no tremendous desire to offer comfort. It seemed that irritation was still well in the ascendancy over compassion.

She and Charles were not alone. When I went in she had crossed the room to stand at the side of a tall blond man whom I'd met before; and beside Charles stood a stranger, a stocky young-old man whose austere eyes were disconcertingly surrounded by a rosy country face.

Charles said in his most ultracivilized voice, "You know Toby, don't you, Sid?" and Jenny's shield and supporter and I nodded to each other and gave the faint smiles of acquaintanceship we would each have been happier without. "And this, Sid, is my solicitor, Oliver Quayle. Gave up his golf to be here. Very good of him."

"So you're Sid Halley," the young-old man said, shaking hands. There was nothing in his voice either way, but his gaze slid down and sideways, seeking to see the half-hidden hand that he wouldn't have looked at if he hadn't known. It often happened that way. He brought his gaze back to my face and saw that I knew what he'd been doing. There was the smallest flicker in his lower eyelids, but no other remark. Judgment suspended, I thought, on either side.

Charles's mouth twitched, and he said smoothly, "I warned you, Oliver. If you don't want him to read your thoughts, you mustn't move your eyes."

"Yours don't move," I said to him.

"I learned that lesson years ago."

He made courteous sit-down motions with his hands, and the five of us sank into comfort and pale gold brocade.

"I've told Oliver," Charles said, "that if anyone can find this Nicholas Ashe person, you will."

"Frightfully useful, don't you know," drawled Toby, "having a plumber in the family when the pipes burst."

It was a fraction short of offensiveness. I gave him the benefit of a doubt I didn't have, and asked nobody in particular whether the police wouldn't do the job more quickly.

"The trouble is," Quayle said, "that technically it is Jenny alone who is guilty of obtaining money by false pretenses. The police have listened to her, of course, and the man in charge seems to be remarkably sympathetic, but"—he slowly shrugged the heavy shoulders in a way that skillfully combined sympathy and resignation—"one feels they might choose to settle for the case they have."

"But I say," protested Toby. "It was that Ashe's idea, all of it."

"Can you prove it?" Quayle said.

"Jenny says so," Toby said, as if that were proof enough.

Quayle shook his head. "As I've told Charles, it would appear from all documents she signed that she did know the scheme was fraudulent. And ignorance, even if genuine, is always a poor, if not impossible, defense.

I said, "If there's no evidence against him, what would you do, even if I did find him?"

Quayle looked my way attentively. "I'm hoping that if you find him, you'll find evidence as well."

Jenny sat up exceedingly straight and spoke in a voice sharp with perhaps anxiety but certainly anger.

"This is all rubbish, Sid. Why don't you say straight out that the job's beyond you?"

"I don't know if it is."

"It's pathetic," she said to Quayle, "how he longs to prove he's clever, now he's disabled."

The flicking sneer in her voice shocked Quayle and Charles into visible discomfort, and I thought dejectedly that this was what I'd caused in her, this compulsive need to hurt. I didn't just mind what she'd said; I minded bitterly that because of me she was not showing to Quayle the sunny-tempered person she would still be if I weren't there.

"If I find Nicholas Ashe," I said grimly, "I'll give him to Jenny. Poor fellow."

None of the men liked it. Quayle looked disillusioned, Toby showed he despised me, and Charles sorrowfully shook his head. Jenny alone, behind her anger, looked secretly pleased. She seldom managed nowadays to goad me into a reply to her insults, and counted it a victory that I'd done it and earned such general disapproval. My own silly fault. There was only one way not to let her see when her barbs went in, and that was to smile . . . and the matter in hand was not very funny.

I said, more moderately, "There might be ways . . . if I can find him. At any rate, I'll do my best. If there's anything I can do, I'll do it."

Jenny looked unplacated, and no one else said anything. I sighed internally. "What did he look like?" I asked.

After a pause Charles said, "I saw him once only, for about thirty minutes, four months ago. I have a general impression, but that's all. Young, personable, dark-haired, clean-shaven. Something too ingratiating in his manner to me. I would not have welcomed him as a junior officer aboard my ship."

Jenny compressed her lips and looked away from him, but could not protest against this judgment. I felt the first faint stirrings of sympathy for her and tried to stamp on them: they would only make me more vulnerable, which was something I could do without.

I said to Toby, "Did you meet him?"

"No," he said loftily. "Actually, I didn't."

"Toby has been in Australia," Charles said, explaining.

They all waited. It couldn't be shirked. I said directly to her, neutrally, "Jenny?"

"He was *fun,*" she said vehemently, unexpectedly. "My God, he was fun. And after you . . ." She stopped. Her head swung around my way with bitter eyes. "He was full of life and jokes. He made me laugh. He was terrific. He lit things up. It was like . . . it was like . . ." She suddenly faltered and stopped, and I knew she was thinking, Like us when we first met. Jenny, I thought desperately, don't say it, please don't.

Perhaps it was too much, even for her. How could people, I wondered for the ten thousandth useless time, how could people who had loved so dearly come to such a wilderness; and yet the change in us was irreversible, and neither of us would even search for a way back. It was impossible. The fire was out. Only a few live coals lurked in the ashes, searing unexpectedly at the incautious touch.

I swallowed. "How tall was he?" I said.

"Taller than you."

"Age?"

"Twenty-nine."

The same age as Jenny. Two years younger than I. If he had told the truth, that was. A confidence trickster might lie about absolutely everything as a matter of prudence.

"Where did he stay, while he was . . . er . . . operating?"

Jenny looked unhelpful, and it was Charles who answered. "He told Jenny he was staying with an aunt, but after he had gone, Oliver and I checked up. The aunt, unfortunately, proved to be a landlady who lets rooms to students in north Oxford. And in any case"—he cleared his throat—"it seems that fairly soon he left the lodgings and moved into the flat Jenny is sharing in Oxford with another girl."

"He lived in your flat?" I said to Jenny.

"So what of it?" She was defiant. And something else . . .

"So when he left, did he leave anything behind?"

"No."

"Nothing at all?"

"No."

"Do you want him found?" I said.

To Charles and Quayle and Toby the answer to that question was an automatic yes, but Jenny didn't answer, and the blush that started at her throat rose fast to two bright spots on her cheekbones.

"He's done you great harm," I said.

With stubbornness stiffening her neck, she said, "Oliver says I won't go to prison."

"Jenny!" I was exasperated. "A conviction for fraud will affect your whole life in all sorts of horrible ways. I see that you liked him. Maybe you even loved him. But he's not just a naughty boy who pinched the jam pot for a lark. He has callously arranged for you to be punished in his stead. *That's* the crime for which I'll catch him if I damned well can, even if you don't want me to."

Charles protested vigorously. "Sid, that's ridiculous. Of course she wants to see him punished. She agreed that you should try to find him. She wants you to, of course she does."

I sighed and shrugged. "She agreed, to please you. And because she doesn't think I'll succeed; and she's very likely right. But even *talk* of my succeeding is putting her in a turmoil and making her angry . . . and it's by no means unknown for women to go on loving scoundrels who've ruined them."

Jenny rose to her feet, stared at me blindly, and walked out of the room. Toby took a step after her and Charles too got to his feet, but I said with some force, "Mr. Quayle, please will you go after her and tell her the consequences if she's convicted. Tell her brutally, make her understand, make it shock."

He had taken the decision and was on his way after her before I'd finished.

"It's hardly kind," Charles said. "We've been trying to spare her."

"You can't expect Halley to show her any sympathy," Toby said waspishly.

I eyed him. Not the brightest of men, but Jenny's choice of undemanding escort, the calm sea after the hurricane. A few months earlier she had been thinking of marrying him, but whether she would do it post-Ashe was to my mind doubtful. He gave me his usual lofty look of noncomprehension and decided Jenny needed him at once.

Charles watched his departing back and said, with a tired note of despair, "I simply don't understand her. And it took you about ten minutes to see . . . what I wouldn't have seen at all." He looked at me gloomily. "It was pointless, then, to try to reassure her, as I've been doing?"

"Oh, Charles, what a bloody muddle . . . It won't have done any harm. It's just given her a way of excusing him—Ashe—and putting off the time when she'll have to admit to herself that she's made a shattering . . . shaming mistake."

The lines in his face had deepened with distress. He said somberly, "It's worse. Worse than I thought."

"Sadder," I said. "Not worse."

"Do you think you can find him?" he said. "How on earth do you start?"

Chapter 4

I started in the morning, having not seen Jenny again, as she'd driven off the previous evening with Toby at high speed to Oxford, leaving Charles and me to dine alone, a relief to us both; and they had returned late and not appeared for breakfast by the time I left.

I went to Jenny's flat in Oxford, following directions from Charles, and rang the doorbell. The lock, I thought, looking at it, would give me no trouble if there was no one in, but in fact, after my second ring, the door opened a few inches, on a chain.

"Louise McInnes?" I said, seeing an eye, some tangled fair hair, a bare foot, and a slice of dark blue dressing gown.

"That's right."

"Would you mind if I talked to you? I'm Jenny's . . . er . . . ex-husband. Her father asked me to see if I could help her."

"You're Sid?" she said, sounding surprised. "Sid Halley?"

"Yes."

"Well . . . wait a minute." The door closed and stayed closed for a good long time. Finally it opened again, this time wide, and the whole girl was revealed. This time she wore jeans, a checked shirt, baggy blue sweater, and slippers. The hair was brushed, and there was lipstick: a gentle pink, unaggressive.

"Come in."

I went in and closed the door behind me. Jenny's flat, as I would have guessed, was not constructed of plasterboard and held together with drawing pins. The general address was a large Victorian house in a prosperous side street, with a semicircular driveway and parking room at the back. Jenny's section, reached by its own enclosed, latterly added staircase, was the whole of the spacious first floor. Bought, Charles had told me, with some of her divorce settlement. It was nice to see that on the whole my money had been well spent.

Switching on lights, the girl led the way into a large bow-fronted sitting room which still had its curtains drawn and the day before's clutter slipping haphazardly off tables and chairs. Newspapers, a coat, some kicked-off boots, coffee cups, an empty yogurt carton in a fruit bowl, with spoon, some dying daffodils, a typewriter with its cover off, some scrunched-up pages that had missed the wastepaper basket.

Louise McInnes drew back the curtains, letting in the gray morning to dilute the electricity.

"I wasn't up," she said unnecessarily.

"I'm sorry."

The mess was the girl's. Jenny was always tidy, clearing up before bed. But the room itself was Jenny's. One or two pieces from Aynsford, and an overall similarity to the sitting room of our own house, the one we'd shared. Love might change, but taste endured. I felt a stranger, and at home.

"Want some coffee?" she said.

"Only if . . ."

"Sure. I'd have some anyway."

"Can I help you?"

"If you like."

She led the way through the hall and into a bare-looking kitchen. There was nothing precisely prickly in her manner, but all the same it was cool. Not surprising, really. What Jenny thought of me, she would say, and there wouldn't be much that was good.

"Like some toast?" She was busy producing a packet of white sliced bread and a jar of powdered coffee.

"Yes, I would."

"Then stick a couple of pieces in the toaster. Over there."

I did as she said, while she ran some water into an electric kettle and dug into a cupboard for butter and marmalade. The butter was a half-used packet still in its torn greaseproof wrapping, the center scooped out and the whole thing messy: exactly like my own butter packet in my own flat. Jenny had put butter into dishes automatically. I wondered if she did when she was alone.

"Milk and sugar?"

"No sugar."

When the toast popped up she spread the slices with butter and marmalade and put them on two plates. Boiling water went onto the brown powder in mugs, and milk followed straight from the bottle.

"You bring the coffee," she said, "and I'll take the toast." She picked up the plates and out of the corner of her eye saw my left hand closing round one of the mugs. "Look out," she said urgently. "That's hot."

I gripped the mug carefully with the fingers that couldn't feel.

She blinked.

"One of the advantages," I said, and picked up the other mug more gingerly by its handle.

She looked at my face, but said nothing; merely turned away and went back to the sitting room.

"I'd forgotten," she said, as I put down the mugs on the space she had cleared for them on the low table in front of the sofa.

"False teeth are more common," I said politely.

She came very near to a laugh, and although it ended up as a doubtful frown, the passing warmth was a glimpse of the true person living behind the slightly brusque façade. She scrunched into the toast and looked thoughtful, and after a chew and a swallow, she said, "What can you do to help Jenny?"

"Try to find Nicholas Ashe."

"Oh . . ." There was another spontaneous flicker of smile, again quickly stifled by subsequent thought.

"You liked him?" I said.

She nodded ruefully. "I'm afraid so. He is . . . was . . . such tremendous fun. Fantastic company. I find it terribly hard to believe he's just gone off and left Jenny in this mess. I mean . . . he lived here, here in this flat . . . and we had so many laughs. What he's done . . . it's incredible."

"Look," I said, "would you mind starting at the beginning and telling me all about it?"

"But hasn't Jenny . . . ?"

"No."

"I suppose," she said slowly, "that she wouldn't like admitting to you that he made such a fool of us."

"How much," I said, "did she love him?"

"Love? What's love? I can't tell you. She was *in* love with him." She licked her fingers. "All fizzy. Bright and bubbly. Up in the clouds."

"Have you been there? Up in the clouds?"

She looked at me straightly. "Do you mean, do I

know what it's like? Yes, I do. If you mean, was I in love with Nicky, then no, I wasn't. He was fun, but he didn't turn me on like he did Jenny. And in any case, it was she who attracted him. Or at least," she finished doubtfully, "it seemed like it." She wagged her licked fingers. "Would you give me that box of tissues that's just behind you?"

I gave her the box and watched her as she wiped off the rest of the stickiness. She had fair eyelashes and English-rose skin, and a face that had left shyness behind. Too soon for life to have printed unmistakable signposts; but there did seem, in her natural expression, to be little in the way of cynicism or intolerance. A practical girl, with sense.

"I don't really know where they met," she said, "except that it was somewhere here in Oxford. I came back one day, and he was *here,* if you see what I mean? They were already . . . well . . . interested in each other."

"Er," I said, "have you always shared this flat with Jenny?"

"More or less. We were at school together . . . didn't you know? Well, we met one day and I told her I was going to be living in Oxford for two years while I wrote a thesis, and she said had I anywhere to stay, because she'd seen this flat, but she'd like some company. . . . So I came. Like a shot. We've got on fine, on the whole."

I looked at the typewriter and the signs of effort. "Do you work here all the time?"

"Here or in the Sheldonian—er, the library, that is—or out doing other research. I pay rent to Jenny for my room . . . and I don't know why I'm telling you all this."

"It's very helpful."

She got to her feet. "It might be as well for you to see

all the stuff. I've put it in his room—Nicky's room—to get it out of sight. It's all too boringly painful, as a matter of fact."

Again I followed her through the hall, and this time to farther down the wide passage, which was recognizably the first-floor landing of the old house.

"That room," she said, pointing at doors, "is Jenny's. That's the bathroom. That's my room. And this one at the end was Nicky's."

"When exactly did he go?" I said, walking behind her.

"Exactly? Who knows? Sometime on Wednesday. Two weeks last Wednesday." She opened the white-painted door and walked into the end room. "He was here at breakfast, same as usual. I went off to the library, and Jenny caught the train to London to go shopping, and when we both got back, he was gone. Just gone. Everything. Jenny was terribly shocked. Wept all over the place. But of course, we didn't know then that he hadn't just left her, he'd cleared out with all the money as well."

"How did you find out?"

"Jenny went to the bank on the Friday to pay in the checks and draw out some cash for postage, and they told her the account was closed."

I looked round the room. It had thick carpet, Georgian dressing chest, big comfort-promising bed, upholstered armchair, pretty, Jenny-like curtains, fresh white paint. Six large brown boxes of thick cardboard stood in a double stack in the biggest available space; and none of it looked as if it had ever been lived in.

I went over to the chest and pulled out a drawer. It was totally empty. I put my fingers inside and drew them along, and they came out without a speck of dust or grit.

Louise nodded. "He had dusted. And vacuumed too.

You could see the marks on the carpet. He cleaned the bathroom, as well. It was all sparkling. Jenny thought it was nice of him . . . until she found out just why he didn't want to leave any trace."

"I should think it was symbolic," I said absently.

"What do you mean?"

"Well . . . not so much that he was afraid of being traced through hair and fingerprints, but just that he wanted to feel that he'd wiped himself out of this place. So that he didn't feel he'd left anything of himself here. I mean . . . if you want to go back to a place, you subconsciously leave things there, you 'forget' them. Well-known phenomenon. So if you subconsciously, as well as consciously, don't want to go back to a place, you may feel impelled to remove even your dust." I stopped. "Sorry. Didn't mean to bore you."

"I'm not bored."

I said matter-of-factly, "Where did they sleep?"

"Here." She looked carefully at my face and judged it safe to proceed. "She used to come along here. Well . . . I couldn't help but know. Most nights. Not always."

"He never went to her?"

"Funny thing, I never ever saw him go into her room, even in the daytime. If he wanted her, he'd stand outside and call."

"It figures."

"More symbolism?" She went to the pile of boxes and opened the topmost. "The stuff in here will tell you the whole story. I'll leave you to read it . . . I can't stand the sight of it. And anyway, I'd better clean the place up a bit, in case Jenny comes back."

"You don't expect her, do you?"

She tilted her head slightly, hearing the faint alarm in my voice. "Are you frightened of her?"

"Should I be?"

"She says you're a worm." A hint of amusement softened the words.

"Yes, she would," I said. "And no, I'm not frightened of her. She just . . . distracts me."

With sudden vehemence she said, "Jenny's a super girl." Genuine friendship, I thought. A statement of loyalties. The merest whiff of challenge. But Jenny, the super girl, was the one I'd married.

I said, "Yes," without inflection, and after a second or two she turned and went out of the room. With a sigh I started on the boxes, shifting them clumsily and being glad neither Jenny nor Louise was watching. They were large, and although one or two were not as heavy as the others, their proportions were all wrong for gripping electrically.

The top one contained two foot-deep stacks of office-size paper, white, good quality, and printed with what looked like a typewritten letter. At the top of each sheet there was an impressive array of headings, including, in the center, an embossed and gilded coat of arms. I lifted out one of the letters, and began to understand how Jenny had fallen for the trick.

"Research into Coronary Disability," it said, and in engraved lettering above the coat of arms, with, beneath it, the words "Registered Charity." To the left of the gold embossing there was a list of patrons, mostly with titles, and to the right a list of the charity's employees, one of whom was listed as Jennifer Halley, Executive Assistant. Below her name, in small capital letters, was the address of the Oxford flat.

The letter bore no date and no salutation. It began about a third of the way down the paper, and said:

> So many families nowadays have had sorrowful firsthand knowledge of the seriousness of coronary artery disease, which even where it does not

kill can leave a man unable to continue with a full, strenuous working life.

Much work has already been done in the field of investigation into the causes and possible prevention of this scourge of modern man, but much more remains still to be done. Research funded by government money being of necessity limited in today's financial climate, it is of the utmost importance that the public should be asked to support directly the essential programs now in hand in privately run facilities.

We do know, however, that many people resent receiving straightforward fund-raising letters, however worthy the cause, so to aid Research into Coronary Disability we ask you to buy something, along the same principle as Christmas cards, the sale of which does so much good work in so many fields. Accordingly the patrons, after much discussion, have decided to offer for sale a supply of exceptionally fine wax polish, which has been especially formulated for the care of antique furniture.

The wax is packed in quarter-kilo tins, and is of the quality used by expert restorers and museum curators. If you should wish to buy, we are offering the wax at five pounds a tin; and you may be sure that at least three quarters of all revenue goes straight to research.

The wax will be good for your furniture, your contribution will be good for the cause, and with your help there may soon be significant advances in the understanding and control of this killing disease.

If you should wish to, please send a donation to the address printed above. (Checks should be made out to Research into Coronary Disability.)

You will receive a supply of wax immediately, and the gratitude of future heart patients everywhere.

Yours sincerely,
Executive Assistant

I said "Phew" to myself, and folded the letter and tucked it into my jacket. Sob stuff; the offer of something tangible in return; and the veiled hint that if you didn't cough up, it could one day happen to you. And, according to Charles, the mixture had worked.

The second big box contained several thousand white envelopes, unaddressed. The third was half full of mostly handwritten letters on every conceivable type of writing paper; orders for wax, all saying, among other things, "Check enclosed."

The fourth contained printed Compliments slips, saying that Research into Coronary Disability acknowledged the contribution with gratitude and had pleasure herewith in sending a supply of wax.

The fifth brown box, half empty, and the sixth, unopened and full, contained numbers of flat white boxes about six inches square by two inches deep. I lifted out a white box and looked inside. Contents, one flat round unprinted tin with a firmly screwed-on lid. The lid put up a fight, but I got it off in the end, and found underneath it a soft midbrown mixture that certainly smelled of polish. I shut it up, returned the tin to its package, and left it out, ready to take.

There seemed to be nothing else. I looked into every cranny in the room and down the sides of the armchair, but there wasn't as much as a pin.

I picked up the square white box and went back slowly and quietly toward the sitting room, opening the closed doors one by one, and looking at what they concealed. There had been two that Louise had not identified: one proved to be a linen cupboard, and the other a small unfurnished room containing suitcases and assorted junk.

Jenny's room was decisively feminine: pink and white, frothy with net and frills. Her scent lay lightly in the air, the violet scent of Mille. No use remembering the first bottle I'd given her, long ago in Paris. Too much time had passed. I shut the door on the fragrance and the memory and went into the bathroom.

A white bathroom. Huge fluffy towels. Green carpet, green plants. Looking glass on two walls, light and bright. No visible toothbrushes: everything in cupboards. Very tidy. Very Jenny. Roger & Gallet soap.

The snooping habit had ousted too many scruples. With hardly a hesitation, I opened Louise's door and put my eyes round, trusting to luck she wouldn't come out into the hall and find me.

Organized mess, I thought. Heaps of papers, and books everywhere. Clothes on chairs. Unmade bed; not surprising, since I'd sprung her out of it.

A washbasin in a corner, no cap on the toothpaste, pair of tights hung to dry. An open box of chocolates. A haphazard scatter on the dressing table. A tall vase with horse chestnut buds bursting. No smell at all. No long-term dirt, just surface clutter. The blue dressing gown on the floor. Basically the room was furnished much like Ashe's: and one could clearly see where Jenny ended and Louise began.

I pulled my head out and closed the door, undetected. Louise, in the sitting room, had been easily sidetracked in her tidying, and was sitting on the floor intently reading a book.

"Oh, hello," she said, looking up vaguely as if she had forgotten I was there. "Have you finished?"

"There must be other papers," I said. "Letters, bills, cash books, that sort of thing."

"The police took them."

I sat on the sofa, facing her. "Who called the police in?" I said. "Was it Jenny?"

She wrinkled her forehead. "No. Someone complained to them that the charity wasn't registered."

"Who?"

"I don't know. Someone who received one of the letters, and checked up. Half those patrons on the letterhead don't exist, and the others didn't know their names were being used."

I thought, and said, "What made Ashe bolt just when he did?"

"We don't know. Maybe someone telephoned here to complain, as well. So he went while he could. He'd been gone for a week when the police turned up."

I put the square white box on the coffee table. "Where did the wax come from?" I said.

"Some firm or other. Jenny wrote to order it, and it was delivered here. Nicky knew where to get it."

"Invoices?"

"The police took them."

"These begging letters . . . who got them printed?"

She sighed. "Jenny, of course. Nicky had some others, just like them, except that they had his name in the space where they put Jenny's. He explained that it was no use sending any more letters with his name and address on, as he'd moved. He was keen, you see, to keep on working for the cause. . . ."

"You bet he was," I said.

She was half irritated. "It's all very well to jeer, but you didn't meet him. You'd have believed him, same as we did."

I left it. Maybe I would have. "These letters," I said. "Who were they sent to?"

"Nicky had lists of names and addresses. Thousands of them."

"Have you got them? The lists?"

She looked resigned. "He took them with him."

"What sort of people were on them?"

"The sort of people who would own antique furniture and cough up a fiver without missing it."

"Did he say where he'd got them from?"

"Yes," she said. "From the charity's headquarters."

"And who addressed the letters and sent them out?"

"Nicky typed the envelopes. Yes—don't ask—on my typewriter. He was very fast. He could do hundreds in a day. Jenny signed her name at the bottom of the letters, and I usually folded them and put them in the envelopes. She used to get writer's cramp doing it and Nicky would often help her."

"Signing her name?"

"That's right. He copied her signature. He did it hundreds of times. You couldn't really tell the difference."

I looked at her in silence.

"I know," she said. "Asking for trouble. But you see, he made all that hard work with the letters seem such fun. Like a game. He was full of jokes. You don't understand. And then, when the checks started rolling in, it was so obviously worth the effort."

"Who sent off the wax?" I said gloomily.

"Nicky typed the addresses on labels. I used to help Jenny stick them on the boxes and seal the boxes with sticky tape, and take them to the post office."

"Ashe never went?"

"Too busy typing. We used to wheel them round to the post office in those shopping bags on wheels."

"And the checks . . . I suppose Jenny herself paid them in?"

"That's right."

"How long did all this go on?" I said.

"A couple of months, once the letters were printed and the wax had arrived."

"How much wax?"

"Oh, we had stacks of it, all over the place. It came in those big brown boxes . . . sixty tins in each, ready packed. They practically filled the flat. Actually, in the end Jenny wanted to order some more, as we were running very low, but Nicky said no, we'd finish what we had and take a breather before starting again."

"He meant to stop, anyway," I said.

Reluctantly, she said, "Yes."

"How much money," I said, "did Jenny bank?"

She looked at me somberly. "In the region of ten thousand pounds. Maybe a bit more. Some people sent much more than a fiver. One or two sent a hundred, and didn't want the wax."

"It's incredible."

"The money just came pouring in. It still does, every day. But it goes direct to the police from the post office. They'll have a hell of a job sending it all back."

"What about that box of letters in Ashe's room, saying 'Check enclosed'?"

"Those," she said, "are people whose money was banked, and who've been sent the wax."

"Didn't the police want those letters?"

She shrugged. "They didn't take them, anyway."

"Do you mind if I do?"

"Help yourself."

After I'd fetched the box of letters and dumped it by the front door, I went back into the sitting room to ask her another question. Deep in the book again, she looked up without enthusiasm.

"How did Ashe get the money out of the bank?"

"He took a typewritten letter signed by Jenny saying she wanted to withdraw the balance so as to be able to give it to the charity in cash at its annual gala dinner, and also a check signed by Jenny for every penny."

"But she didn't . . ."

"No. He did. But I've seen the letter and the check. The bank gave them to the police. You can't tell it isn't Jenny's writing. Even Jenny can't tell the difference."

She got gracefully to her feet, leaving the book on the floor. "Are you going?" she said hopefully. "I've got so much to do. I'm way behind, because of Nicky." She went past me into the hall, but when I followed her she delivered another chunk of dismay.

"The bank clerks can't remember Nicky. They pay out cash in thousands for wages every day, because there's so much industry in Oxford. They were used to Jenny in connection with that account, and it was ten days or more before the police asked questions. No one can remember Nicky there at all."

"He's professional," I said flatly.

"Every pointer to it, I'm afraid." She opened the door while I bent down and awkwardly picked up the brown cardboard box, balancing the small white one on top.

"Thank you," I said, "for your help."

"Let me carry that box downstairs."

"I can do it," I said.

She looked briefly into my eyes. "I'm sure you can. You're too damned proud." She took the box straight out of my arms and walked purposefully away. I followed her, feeling a fool, down the stairs and out onto the tarmac.

"Car?" she said.

"Round the back, but . . ."

As well talk to the tide. I went with her, weakly gestured to the Scimitar, and opened the boot. She dumped the boxes inside, and I shut them in.

"Thank you," I said again. "For everything."

The faintest of smiles came back into her eyes.

"If you think of anything that could help Jenny," I said, "will you let me know?"

"If you give me your address."

I forked a card out of an inner pocket and gave it to her. "It's on there."

"All right." She stood still for a moment with an expression I couldn't read. "I'll tell you one thing," she said. "From what Jenny's said . . . you're not a bit what I expected."

Chapter 5

From Oxford I drove west to Gloucestershire and arrived at Garvey's stud farm at the respectable visiting hour of eleven-thirty, Sunday morning.

Tom Garvey, standing in his stable yard talking to his stud groom, came striding across as I braked to a halt.

"Sid Halley!" he said. "What a surprise. What do you want?"

I grimaced through the open car window. "Does everyone think I want something, when they see me?"

"Of course, lad. Best snooper in the business now, so they say. We hear things, you know, even us dim country bumpkins; we hear things."

Smiling, I climbed out of the car and shook hands with a sixty-year-old near rogue who was about as far from a dim country bumpkin as Cape Horn from Alaska: a big strong bull of a man, with unshakable confidence, a loud domineering voice, and the wily mind of a gypsy. His hand in mine was as hard as his business methods and as dry as his manner. Tough with men, gentle with horses. Year after year he prospered, and if I would have had every foal on the place exhaustively blood-typed before I believed its alleged breeding, I was probably in the minority.

"What are you after, then, Sid?" he said.

"I came to see a mare, Tom. One that you've got here. Just general interest."

"Oh, yes? Which one?"

"Bethesda."

There was an abrupt change in his expression from half amusement to no amusement at all. He narrowed his eyes and said brusquely, "What about her?"

"Well . . . has she foaled, for instance?"

"She's dead."

"Dead?"

"You heard, lad. She's dead. You'd better come in the house."

He turned and scrunched away, and I followed. His house was old and dark and full of stale air. All the life of the place was outside, in fields and foaling boxes and the breeding shed. Inside, a heavy clock ticked loudly into silence, and there was no aroma of Sunday roast.

"In here."

It was a cross between a dining room and an office: heavy old table and chairs at one end, filing cabinets and sagging armchairs at the other. No attempts at cosmetic décor to please the customers. Sales went on outside, on the hoof.

Tom perched against his desk and I on the arm of one of the chairs: not the sort of conversation for relaxing in comfort.

"Now then," he said. "Why are you asking about Bethesda?"

"I just wondered what had become of her."

"Don't fence with me, lad. You don't drive all the way here out of general interest. What do you want to know for?"

"A client wants to know," I said.

"What client?"

"If I was working for you," I said, "and you'd told me to keep quiet about it, would you expect me to tell?"

He considered me with sour concentration.

"No, lad. Guess I wouldn't. And I don't suppose there's much secret about Bethesda. She died foaling. The foal died with her. A colt, it would have been. Small, though."

"I'm sorry," I said.

He shrugged. "It happens sometimes. Not often, mind. Her heart packed up."

"Heart?"

"Aye. The foal was lying wrong, see, and the mare, she'd been straining longer than was good for her. We got the foal turned inside her once we found she was in trouble, but she just packed it in, sudden like. Nothing we could do. Middle of the night, of course, like it nearly always is."

"Did you have a vet to her?"

"Aye, he was there, right enough. I called him when we found she'd started, because there was a chance it would be dicey. First foal, and the heart murmur, and all."

I frowned slightly. "Did she have a heart murmur when she came to you?"

"Of course she did, lad. That's why she stopped racing. You don't know much about her, do you?"

"No," I said. "Tell me."

He shrugged. "She came from George Caspar's yard, of course. Her owner wanted to breed from her on account of her two-year-old form, so we bred her to Timberley, which should have given us a sprinter, but there you are, best-laid plans, and all that."

"When did she die?"

"Month ago, maybe."

"Well, thanks, Tom." I stood up. "Thanks for your time."

He shoved himself off his desk. "Bit of a tame turn-up for you, asking questions, isn't it? I can't square it with the old Sid Halley, all speed and guts over the fences."

"Times change, Tom."

"Aye, I suppose so. I'll bet you miss it, though, that roar from the stands when you'd come to the last and bloody well lift your horse over it." His face echoed remembered excitements. "By God, lad, that was a sight. Not a nerve in your body . . . Don't know how you did it."

I supposed it was generous of him, but I wished he would stop.

"Bit of bad luck, losing your hand. Still, with steeplechasing it's always something. Broken backs and such." We began to walk to the door. "If you go jump racing you've got to accept the risks."

"That's right," I said.

We went outside and across to my car.

"You don't do too badly with that contraption, though, do you lad? Drive a car, and such."

"It's fine."

"Aye, lad." He knew it wasn't. He wanted me to know he was sorry, and he'd done his best. I smiled at him, got into the car, sketched a thank-you salute, and drove away.

At Aynsford they were in the drawing room, drinking sherry before lunch: Charles, Toby, and Jenny.

Charles gave me a glass of fino, Toby looked me up and down as if I'd come straight from a pigsty, and Jenny said she had been talking to Louise on the telephone.

"We thought you had run away. You left the flat two hours ago."

"Sid doesn't run away," Charles said, as if stating a fact.

"Limps, then," Jenny said.

Toby sneered at me over his glass: the male in possession enjoying his small gloat over the dispossessed. I wondered if he really understood the extent of Jenny's attachment to Nicholas Ashe, or, if knowing, he didn't care.

I sipped the sherry: a thin dry taste, suitable to the occasion. Vinegar might have been better.

"Where did you buy all that polish from?" I said.

"I don't remember." She spoke distinctly, spacing out the syllables, willfully obstructive.

"Jenny!" Charles protested.

I sighed. "Charles, the police have the invoices, which will have the name and address of the polish firm on them. Can you ask your friend Oliver Quayle to ask the police for the information, and send it to me?"

"Certainly," he said.

"I cannot see," Jenny said in the same sort of voice, "that knowing who supplied the wax will make the slightest difference one way or the other."

It appeared that Charles privately agreed with her. I didn't explain. There was a good chance, anyway, that they were right.

"Louise said you were prying for ages."

"I liked her," I said mildly.

Jenny's nose, as always, gave away her displeasure. "She's out of your class, Sid," she said.

"In what way?"

"Brains, darling."

Charles said smoothly, "More sherry, anyone?" and, decanter in hand, began refilling glasses. To me, he said, "I believe Louise took a first at Cambridge in mathematics. I have played her at chess. . . . You would beat her with ease."

"A grand master," Jenny said, "can be obsessional and stupid and have a persecution complex."

Lunch came and went in the same sort of atmosphere, and afterward I went upstairs to put my few things into my suitcase. While I was doing it, Jenny came into the room and stood watching me.

"You don't use that hand much," she said.

I didn't answer.

"I don't know why you bother with it."

"Stop it, Jenny."

"If you'd done as I asked, and given up racing, you wouldn't have lost it."

"Probably not."

"You'd have a hand, not half an arm . . . not a stump."

I threw my spongebag with too much force into the suitcase.

"Racing first. Always racing. Dedication and winning and glory. And me nowhere. It serves you right. We'd still have been married . . . you'd still have your hand . . . if you'd have given up your precious racing when I wanted you to. Being champion jockey meant more to you than I did."

"We've said all this a dozen times," I said.

"Now you've got nothing. Nothing at all. I hope you're satisfied."

The battery charger stood on a chest of drawers, with two batteries in it. She pulled the plug out of the main socket and threw the whole thing on the bed. The batteries fell out and lay on the bedspread haphazardly with the charger and its cord.

"It's disgusting," she said, looking at it. "It revolts me."

"I've got used to it." More or less, anyway.

"You don't seem to care."

I said nothing. I cared, all right.

"Do you enjoy being crippled, Sid?"

Enjoy . . . Jesus Christ.

She walked to the door and left me looking down at the charger. I felt more than saw her pause there, and wondered numbly what else there was left that she could say.

Her voice reached me quite clearly across the room.

"Nicky has a knife in his sock."

I turned my head fast. She looked both defiant and expectant. "Is that true?" I asked.

"Sometimes."

"Adolescent," I said.

She was annoyed. "And what's so mature about hurtling around on horses and knowing . . . *knowing* . . . that pain and broken bones are going to happen?"

"You never think they will."

"And you're always wrong."

"I don't do it any more."

"But you would if you could."

There was no answer to that, because we both knew it was true.

"And look at you," Jenny said. "When you have to stop racing, do you look around for a nice quiet job in stockbroking, which you know about, and start to lead a normal life? No, you damned well don't. You go straight into something which lands you up in fights and beatings and hectic scrambles. You can't live without danger, Sid. You're addicted. You may think you aren't, but it's like a drug. If you just imagine yourself working in an office, nine to five, and commuting like any sensible man, you'll see what I mean."

I thought about it, silently.

"Exactly," she said. "In an office, you'd die."

"And what's so safe about a knife in the sock?" I said. "I was a jockey when we met. You knew what it entailed."

"Not from the inside. Not all those terrible bruises, and no food and no drink, and no damned sex half the time."

"Did he show you the knife, or did you just see it?"

"What does it matter?"

"Is he adolescent . . . or truly dangerous?"

"There you are," she said. "You'd prefer him dangerous."

"Not for your sake."

"Well . . . I saw it. In a little sheath, strapped to his leg. And he made a joke about it."

"But you told me," I said. "So was it a warning?"

She seemed suddenly unsure and disconcerted, and after a moment or two simply frowned and walked away down the passage.

If it marked the first crack in her indulgence toward her precious Nicky, so much the better.

I picked Chico up on Tuesday morning and drove north to Newmarket. A windy day, bright, showery, rather cold.

"How did you get on with the wife, then?"

He had met her once and had described her as unforgettable, the overtones in his voice giving the word several meanings.

"She's in trouble," I said.

"Pregnant?"

"There are other forms of trouble, you know."

"Really?"

I told him about the fraud, and about Ashe, and his knife.

"Gone and landed herself in a whoopsy," Chico said.

"Face down."

"And for dusting her off, do we get a fee?"

I looked at him sideways.

"Yeah," he said. "I thought so. Working for nothing again, aren't we? Good job you're well oiled, Sid, mate, when it comes to my wages. What is it this year? You made a fortune in anything since Christmas?"

"Silver, mostly. And cocoa. Bought and sold."

"Cocoa?" He was incredulous.

"Beans," I said. "Chocolate."

"Nutty bars?"

"No, not the nuts. They're risky."

"I don't know how you find the time."

"It takes as long as chatting up barmaids."

"What do you want with all that money, anyway?"

"It's a habit," I said. "Like eating."

Amicably we drew nearer to Newmarket, consulted the map, asked a couple of locals, and finally arrived at the incredibly well kept stud farm of Henry Thrace.

"Sound out the lads," I said, and Chico said, "Sure," and we stepped out of the car onto weedless gravel. I left him to it and went in search of Henry Thrace, who was reported by a cleaning lady at the front door of the house to be "down there on the right, in his office." Down there he was, in an armchair, fast asleep.

My arrival woke him, and he came alive with the instant awareness of people used to broken nights. A youngish man, very smooth, a world away from rough, tough, wily Tom Garvey. With Thrace, according to predigested opinion, breeding was strictly big business; handling the mares could be left to lower mortals. His first words, however, didn't match the image.

"Sorry. Been up half the night. . . . Er . . . who are you, exactly? Do we have an appointment?"

"No." I shook my head. "I just hoped to see you. My name's Sid Halley."

"Is it? Any relation to . . . Good Lord. You're him."

"I'm him."

"What can I do for you? Want some coffee?" He rubbed his eyes. "Mrs. Evans will get us some."

"Don't bother, unless . . ."

"No. Fire away." He looked at his watch. "Ten minutes do? I've got a meeting in Newmarket."

"It's very vague, really," I said. "I just came to inquire into the general health and so on of two of the stallions you've got here."

"Oh. Which two?"

"Gleaner," I said. "And Zingaloo."

We went through the business of why did I want to know, and why should he tell me, but finally, like Tom Garvey, he shrugged and said I might as well know.

"I suppose I shouldn't say it, but you wouldn't want to advise a client to buy shares in either of them," he said, taking for granted this was really the purpose of my visit. "They might have difficulty in covering their full quota of mares, both of them, although they're only four."

"Why's that?"

"They've both got bad hearts. They get exhausted with too much exercise."

"Both?"

"That's right. That's what stopped them racing as three-year-olds. And I reckon they've got worse since then."

"Somebody mentioned Gleaner was lame," I said.

Henry Thrace looked resigned. "He's developed arthritis recently. You can't keep a damn thing to yourself in this town." An alarm clock made a clamor on his desk. He reached over and switched it off. "Time to go, I'm afraid." He yawned. "I hardly take my clothes off at this time of the year." He took a battery razor out of his desk drawer, and attacked his beard. "Is that everything then, Sid?"

"Yes," I said. "Thanks."

Chico pulled the car door shut, and we drove away toward the town.

"Bad hearts," he said.

"Bad hearts."

"Proper epidemic, isn't it?"

"Let's ask Brothersmith the vet."

Chico read out the address, in Middleton Road.

"Yes, I know it. It was old Follett's place. He was our old vet, still alive when I was here."

Chico grinned. "Funny somehow to think of you being a snotty little apprentice with the head lad chasing you."

"And chilblains."

"Makes you seem almost human."

I had spent five years in Newmarket, from sixteen to twenty-one. Learning to ride, learning to race, learning to live. My old guvnor had been a good one, and because every day I saw his wife, his life style, and his administrative ability, I'd slowly changed from a boy from the back streets into something more cosmopolitan. He had shown me how to manage the money I'd begun earning in large quantities, and how not to be corrupted by it; and when he turned me loose I found he'd given me the status that went with having been taught in his stable. I'd been lucky in my guvnor, and lucky to be for a long time at the top of the career I loved; and if one day the luck had run out, it was too damned bad.

"Takes you back, does it?" Chico said.

"Yeah."

We drove across the wide heath and past the

racecourse toward the town. There weren't many horses about: a late morning string, in the distance, going home. I swung the car round familiar corners and pulled up outside the vet's.

Mr. Brothersmith was out.

If it was urgent, Mr. Brothersmith could be found seeing to a horse in a stable along Bury Road. Otherwise he would be home to his lunch, probably, in half an hour. We said thank you, and sat in the car, and waited.

"We've got another job," I said. "Checking on syndicates."

"I thought the Jockey Club always did it themselves."

"Yes, they do. The job we've got is to check on the man from the Jockey Club who checks on the syndicates."

Chico digested it. "Tricky, that."

"Without him knowing."

"Oh, yes?"

I nodded. "Ex-Superintendent Eddy Keith."

Chico's mouth fell open. "You're joking."

"No."

"But he's the fuzz. The Jockey Club fuzz."

I passed on Lucas Wainwright's doubts, and Chico said Lucas Wainwright must have got it wrong. The job, I pointed out mildly, was to find out whether he had or not.

"And how do we do that?"

"I don't know. What do you think?"

"It's you that's supposed to be the brains of this outfit."

A muddy Range-Rover came along Middleton Road and turned into Brothersmith's entrance. As one, Chico and I removed ourselves from the Scimitar and went toward the tweed-jacketed man jumping down from his buggy.

"Mr. Brothersmith?"

"Yes? What's the trouble?"

He was young and harassed, and kept looking over his shoulder, as if something was chasing him. Time, perhaps, I thought. Or lack of it.

"Could you spare us a few minutes?" I said. "This is Chico Barnes, and I'm Sid Halley. It's just a few questions. . . ."

His brain took in the name and his gaze switched immediately toward my hands, fastening finally on the left.

"Aren't you the man with the myoelectric prosthesis?"

"Er . . . yes," I said.

"Come in, then. Can I look at it?"

He turned away and strode purposefully toward the side door of the house. I stood still and wished we were anywhere else.

"Come on, Sid," Chico said, following him. He looked back and stopped. "Give the man what he wants, Sid, and maybe he'll do the same for us."

Payment in kind, I thought; and I didn't like the price. Unwillingly, I followed Chico into what turned out to be Brothersmith's surgery.

He asked a lot of questions in a fairly clinical manner, and I answered him in impersonal tones learned from the limb center.

"Can you rotate the wrist?" he said at length.

"Yes, a little." I showed him. "There's a sort of cup inside there which fits over the end of my arm, with another electrode to pick up the impulses for turning."

I knew he wanted me to take the hand off and show him properly, but I wouldn't have done it, and perhaps he saw there was no point in asking.

"It fits very tightly over your elbow," he said, delicately feeling round the gripping edges.

"So as not to fall off."

He nodded intently. "Is it easy to put on and remove?"

"Talcum powder," I said economically.

Chico's mouth opened, and shut again as he caught my don't-say-it stare, and he didn't tell Brothersmith that removal was often a distinct bore.

"Thinking of fitting one to a horse?" Chico said.

Brothersmith raised his still-harassed face and answered him seriously. "Technically it looks perfectly possible, but it's doubtful if one could train a horse to activate the electrodes, and it would be difficult to justify the expense."

"It was only a joke," Chico said faintly.

"Oh? Oh, I see. But it isn't unknown, you know, for a horse to have a false foot fitted. I was reading the other day about a successful prosthesis fitted to the forelimb of a valuable broodmare. She was subsequently covered, and produced a live foal."

"Ah," Chico said. "Now, that's what we've come about. A broodmare. Only this one died."

Brothersmith detached his attention reluctantly from false limbs and transferred it to horses with bad hearts.

"Bethesda," I said, rolling down my sleeve and buttoning the cuff.

"Bethesda?" He wrinkled his forehead and turned the harassed look into one of anxiety. "I'm sorry. I can't recall . . ."

"She was a filly with George Caspar," I said. "Beat everything as a two-year-old, and couldn't run at three because of a heart murmur. She was sent to stud, but her heart packed up when she was foaling."

"Oh, dear," he said, adding sorrow to the anxiety. "What a pity. But I say, I'm so sorry: I treat so many horses, and I often don't know their names. Is there a question of insurance in this, or negligence, even? Because I assure you . . ."

"No," I said amiably. "Nothing like that. Can you remember, then, treating Gleaner and Zingaloo?"

"Yes, of course. Those two. Wretched shame for George Caspar. So disappointing."

"Tell us about them."

"Nothing much to tell, really. Nothing out of the ordinary, except that they were both so good as two-year-olds. Probably that was the cause of their troubles, if the truth were told."

"How do you mean?" I said.

His nervous tensions escaped in small jerks of his head as he brought forth some unflattering opinions. "Well, one hesitates to say so, of course, to top trainers like Caspar, but it is all too easy to strain a two-year-old's heart, and if they are good two-year-olds they run in top races, and the pressure to win may be terrific, because of stud values and everything, and a jockey, riding strictly to orders, mind you, may press a game youngster so hard that although it wins it is also more or less ruined for the future."

"Gleaner won the Doncaster Futurity in the mud," I said thoughtfully. "I saw it. It was a very hard race."

"That's right," Brothersmith said. "I checked him thoroughly afterwards, though. The trouble didn't start at once. In fact, it didn't show at all, until he ran in the Guineas. He came in from that in a state of complete exhaustion. First of all we thought it was the virus, but then after a few days we got this very irregular heartbeat, and then it was obvious what was the matter."

"What virus?" I said.

"Let's see. . . . The evening of the Guineas he had a very slight fever, as if he were in for equine flu, or some such. But it didn't develop. So it wasn't that. It was his heart, all right. But we couldn't have foreseen it."

"What percentage of horses develop bad hearts?" I said.

Some of the chronic anxiety state diminished as he moved confidently onto neutral ground.

"Perhaps ten percent have irregular heartbeats. It doesn't always mean anything. Owners don't like to buy horses that have them, but look at Night Nurse, which won the Champion Hurdle, and had a heart murmur."

"But how often do you get horses having to stop racing because of bad hearts?"

He shrugged. "Perhaps two or three in a hundred."

George Caspar, I reflected, trained upward of a hundred and thirty horses, year after year.

"On average," I said, "are George Caspar's horses more prone to bad hearts than other trainers'?"

The anxiety state returned in full force. "I don't know if I should answer that."

"If it's 'no,'" I said, "what's the hassle?"

"But your purpose in asking . . ."

"A client," I said, lying with regrettable ease, "wants to know if he should send George Caspar a sparkling yearling. He asked me to check on Gleaner and Zingaloo."

"Oh, I see. Well, no, I don't suppose he has more. Nothing significant. Caspar's an excellent trainer, of course. If your client isn't too greedy when his horse is two, there shouldn't be any risk at all."

"Thanks, then." I stood up and shook hands with him. "I suppose there's no heart trouble with Tri-Nitro?"

"None at all. Sound, through and through. His heart bangs away like a gong, loud and clear."

Chapter 6

"That's that, then," Chico said over a pint and pie in the White Hart Hotel. "End of case. Mrs. Caspar's off her tiny rocker, and no one's been getting at George Caspar's youngsters except George Caspar himself."

"She won't be pleased to hear it," I said.

"Will you tell her?"

"Straight away. If she's convinced, she might calm down."

So I telephoned to George Caspar's house and asked for Rosemary, saying I was a Mr. Barnes. She came on the line and said hello in the questioning voice one uses to unknown callers.

"Mr. . . . Barnes?"

"It's Sid Halley."

The alarm came instantly. "I can't talk to you."

"Can you meet me, then?"

"Of course not. I've no reason for going to London."

"I'm just down the road, in the town," I said. "I've things to tell you. And I don't honestly think there's any need for disguises and so on."

"I'm not being seen with you in Newmarket."

She agreed, however, to drive out in her car, pick up Chico, and go where he directed; and Chico and I worked out a place on the map which looked a tranquilizing spot for paranoiacs. The churchyard at Barton Mills, eight miles toward Norwich.

We parked the cars side by side at the gate, and Rosemary walked with me among the graves. She was wearing again the fawn raincoat and a scarf, but not this time the false curls. The wind blew wisps of her own chestnut hair across her eyes, and she pulled them away impatiently: not with quite as much tension as when she had come to my flat, but still with more force than was needed.

I told her I had been to see Tom Garvey and Henry Thrace at their stud farms. I told her I had talked to Brothersmith; and I told her what they'd all said. She listened, and shook her head.

"The horses were nobbled," she said obstinately. "I'm sure they were."

"How?"

"I don't know how." Her voice rose sharply, the agitation showing in spasms of the muscles round her mouth. "But I told you. I told you, they'll get at Tri-Nitro. A week tomorrow, it's the Guineas. You've got to keep him safe for a week."

We walked along the path beside the quiet mounds and the gray weather-beaten headstones. The grass was mown, but there were no flowers, and no mourners. The dead there were long gone, long forgotten. Raw grief and tears now in the municipal plot outside the town; brown heaps of earth and brilliant wreaths and desolation in tidy rows.

"George has doubled the security on Tri-Nitro," I said.

"I know that. Don't be stupid."

I said reluctantly, "In the normal course of events he'll be giving Tri-Nitro some strong work before the Guineas. Probably on Saturday morning."

"I suppose so. What do you mean? Why do you ask?"

"Well . . ." I paused, wondering if indeed it would be sensible to suggest a way-out theory without testing it, and thinking that there was no way of testing it, anyway.

"Go on," she said sharply. "What do you mean?"

"You could . . . er . . . make sure he takes all sorts of precautions when he gives Tri-Nitro that last gallop." I paused. "Inspect the saddle. . . . That sort of thing."

Rosemary said fiercely, "What are you saying? Spell it out, for God's sake. Don't pussyfoot round it."

"Lots of races have been lost because of too hard training gallops too soon beforehand."

"Of course," she said impatiently. "Everyone knows that. But George would never do it."

"What if the saddle was packed with lead? What if a three-year-old was given a strong gallop carrying fifty pounds dead weight? And then ran under severe pressure a few days later in the Guineas? And strained his heart?"

"My God," she said. "My God."

"I'm not saying that it did happen to Zingaloo and Gleaner, or anything like it. Only that it's a distant possibility. And if it's something like that . . . it must involve someone inside the stable."

She had begun trembling again.

"You must go on," she said. "Please go on trying. I brought some money for you." She plunged a hand into her raincoat pocket and brought out a smallish brown envelope. "It's cash. I can't give you a check."

"I haven't earned it," I said.

"Yes, yes. Take it." She was insistent, and finally I put it in my pocket, unopened.

"Let me consult George," I said.

"No. He'd be furious. I'll do it . . . I mean, I'll warn him about the gallops. He thinks I'm crazy, but if I go on about it long enough he'll take notice." She looked at her watch and her agitation increased. "I'll have to go back now. I said I was going for a walk on the heath. I never do that. I'll have to get back, or they'll be wondering."

"Who'll be wondering?"

"George, of course."

"Does he know where you are every minute of the day?"

We were retracing our steps with some speed toward the churchyard gates. Rosemary looked as if she would soon be running.

"We always talk. He asks where I've been. He's not suspicious . . . it's just a habit. We're always together. Well, you know what it's like in a racing household. Owners come at odd times. George likes me to be there."

We reached the cars. She said goodbye uncertainly, and drove off homeward in a great hurry. Chico, waiting in the Scimitar, said, "Quiet here, isn't it? Even the ghosts must find it boring."

I got into the car and tossed Rosemary's envelope onto his lap. "Count that," I said, starting the engine. "See how we're doing."

He tore it open, pulled out a neat wad of expensive-colored bank notes, and licked his fingers.

"Phew," he said, coming to the end. "She's bonkers."

"She wants us to go on."

"Then you know what this is, Sid," he said, flicking

the stack. "Guilt money. To spur you on when you want to stop."

"Well, it works."

We spent some of Rosemary's incentive in staying overnight in Newmarket and going round the bars, Chico where the lads hung out and me with the trainers. It was Tuesday evening and very quiet everywhere. I heard nothing of any interest and drank more than enough whisky, and Chico came back with hiccups and not much else.

"Ever heard of Inky Poole?" he said.

"Is that a song?"

"No, it's a work jockey. What's a work jockey? Chico, my son, a work jockey is a lad who rides work on the gallops."

"You're drunk," I said.

"Certainly not. What's a work jockey?"

"What you just said. Not much good in races but can gallop the best at home."

"Inky Poole," he said, "is George Caspar's work jockey. Inky Poole rides Tri-Nitro his strong work at home on the gallops. Did you ask me to find out who rides Tri-Nitro's gallops?"

"Yes, I did," I said. "And you're drunk."

"Inky Poole, Inky Poole," he said.

"Did you talk to him?"

"Never met him. Bunch of the lads, they told me. George Caspar's work jockey. Inky Poole."

Armed with race glasses on a strap round my neck, I walked along to Warren Hill at seven-thirty in the morning to watch the strings out at morning exercise. A long time, it seemed, since I'd been one of the tucked-up figures in sweaters and skullcap, with three horses to muck out and care for, and a bed in a hostel with rain-soaked breeches forever drying on an airer in the kitchen. Frozen fingers and not enough baths, ears full of four-letter words and no chance of being alone.

I had enjoyed it all well enough when I was sixteen, on account of the horses. Beautiful, marvelous creatures whose responses and instincts worked on a plane as different from humans' as water and oil, not mingling even where they touched. Insight into their senses and consciousness had been like an opening door, a foreign language glimpsed and half learned, full comprehension maddeningly balked by not having the right sort of hearing or sense of smell, nor sufficient skill in telepathy.

The feeling of oneness with horses I'd sometimes had in the heat of a race had been their gift to an inferior being; and maybe my passion for winning had been my gift to them. The urge to get to the front was born in them; all they needed was to be shown where and when to go. It could fairly be said that like most jump jockeys, I had aided and abetted horses beyond the bounds of common sense.

The smell and sight of them on the Heath was like a sea breeze to a sailor. I filled my lungs and eyes, and felt content.

Each exercise string was accompanied and shepherded by its watchful trainer, some of them arriving in cars, some on horseback, some on foot. I collected a lot of "Good morning, Sid"s. Several smiling faces seemed genuinely pleased to see me; and some that weren't in a hurry stopped to talk.

"Sid!" exclaimed one I'd ridden on the flat for in the years before my weight caught up with my height. "Sid, we don't see you up here much these days."

"My loss," I said, smiling.

"Why don't you come and ride out for me? Next time you're here, give me a ring, and we'll fix it."

"Do you mean it?"

"Of course I mean it. If you'd like to, that is."

"I'd love it."

"Right. That's great. Don't forget, now." He wheeled away, waving, to shout to a lad earning his disfavor by slopping in the saddle like a disorganized jellyfish. "How the bloody hell d'you expect your horse to pay attention if you don't?" The boy sat decently for all of twenty seconds. He'd go far, I thought, starting from Newmarket station.

Wednesday being a morning for full training gallops, there was the usual scattering of interested watchers: owners, pressmen, and assorted bookmakers' touts. Binoculars sprouted like an extra growth of eyes, and notes went down in private shorthand. Though the morning was cold, the new season was warming up. There was a feeling overall of purpose, and the bustle of things happening. An industry flexing its muscles. Money, profit, and tax revenue making their proper circle under the wide Suffolk sky. I was still a part of it, even if not in the old way. And Jenny was right: I'd die in an office.

"Morning, Sid."

I looked around. George Caspar, on a horse, his eyes on a distant string walking down the side of the Heath from his stable in Bury Road.

"Morning, George."

"You staying up here?"

"Just for a night or two."

"You should've let us know. We've always a bed. Give Rosemary a ring." His eyes were on his string; the invitation a politeness, not meant to be accepted. Rosemary, I thought, would have fainted if she'd heard.

"Is Tri-Nitro in that lot?" I said.

"Yes, he is. Sixth from the front." He glanced at the interested spectators. "Have you seen Trevor Deansgate anywhere? He said he was coming up here this morning from London. Setting off early."

"Haven't seen him." I shook my head.

"He's got two in the string. He was coming to see them work." He shrugged. "He'll miss them if he isn't here soon."

I smiled to myself. Some trainers might delay working the horses until the owner did arrive, but not George. Owners queued up for his favors and treasured his comments, and Trevor Deansgate for all his power was just one of a crowd. I lifted my race glasses and watched while the string, forty strong, approached and began circling, waiting for their turn on the uphill gallop. The stable before George's had nearly finished, and George would be next.

The lad on Tri-Nitro wore a red scarf in the neck of his olive-green Husky jacket. I lowered the glasses and kept my eye on him as he circled, and looked at his mount with the same curiosity as everyone else. A good-looking bay colt, well grown, with strong shoulders and a lot of heart room; but nothing about him to shout from the housetops that here was the wildly backed winter favorite for the Guineas and the Derby. If you hadn't known, you wouldn't have known, as they say.

"Do you mind photographs, George?" I said.

"Help yourself, Sid."

"Thanks."

I seldom went anywhere these days without a camera in my pocket. Sixteen-millimeter, automatic light meter, all the expense in its lens. I brought it out and showed it to him, and he nodded. "Take what you like."

He shook up his patient hack and went away, across to his string, to begin the morning's business. The lad who rode a horse down from the stables wasn't necessarily the same one who rode it in fast work, and as usual there was a good deal of swapping around, to put the best lads up where it mattered. The boy with the red scarf dismounted from Tri-Nitro and held him, and presently a much older lad swung up onto his back.

I walked across to be close to the string, and took three or four photographs of the wonder horse and a couple of closer shots of his rider.

"Inky Poole?" I said to him at one point, as he rode by six feet away.

"That's right," he said. "Mind your back. You're in the way."

A right touch of surliness. If he hadn't seen me talking to George first, he would have objected to my being there at all. I wondered if his grudging against-the-world manner was the cause or the result of his not getting on as a jockey, and felt sympathy for him, on the whole.

George began detailing his lads into the small bunches that would go up the gallops together, and I walked back to the fringes of things, to watch.

A car arrived very fast and pulled up with a jerk, alarming some horses alongside and sending them skittering, with the lads' voices rising high in alarm and protest.

Trevor Deansgate climbed out of his Jaguar and for good measure slammed the door. He was dressed in a city suit, in contrast to everyone else there, and looked ready for the board room. Black hair rigorously brushed, chin smoothly shaven, shoes polished like glass. Not the sort of man I would have sought as a friend, because I didn't on the whole like to sit at the feet of power, picking up crumbs of patronage with nervous laughter; but a force to be reckoned with on the racing scene.

Big-scale bookmakers could be and often were a positive influence for good, a stance, I thought sardonically, that they had been pushed into, to survive the lobby that knew a Tote monopoly (and a less greedy tax climate) would put back into racing what bookmakers took out. Trevor Deansgate personified the new breed: urbane, a man of the world, seeking top company, becoming a name in the City, the sycophant of earls.

"Hello," he said, seeing me. "I met you at Kempton. . . . Do you know where George's horses are?"

"Right there," I said, pointing. "You're just in time."

"Bloody traffic."

He strode across the grass toward George, race glasses swinging from his hand, and George said hello briefly and apparently told him to watch the gallops with me, because he came straight back, heavy and confident, and stopped at my side.

"George says my two both go in the first bunch. He said you'd tell me how they're doing, insolent bugger. Got eyes, haven't I? He's going on up the hill."

I nodded. Trainers often went up halfway and watched from there, the better to see their horses' action as they galloped past.

Four horses were wheeling into position at the starting point. Trevor Deansgate applied his binoculars, twisting them to focus. Navy suiting with faint red pin stripes. The well-kept hands, gold cuff links, onyx ring, as before.

"Which are yours?" I said.

"The two chestnuts. That one with the white socks is Pinafore. The other's nothing much."

The nothing much had short cannon bones and a rounded rump. Might make a 'chaser one day, I thought. I liked the look of him better than the whippet-shaped Pinafore. They set off together up the gallop at George's signal, and the sprinting blood showed all the way to the top. Pinafore romped it and the nothing much lived up to his owner's assessment. Trevor Deansgate lowered his binoculars with a sigh.

"That's that, then. Are you coming to George's for breakfast?"

"No. Not today."

He raised the glasses again and focused them on the much nearer target of the circling string, and, from the angle, he was looking at the riders, not the horses. The search came to an end on Inky Poole: he lowered the glasses and followed Tri-Nitro with the naked eye.

"A week today," I said.

"Looks a picture."

I supposed that he, like all bookmakers, would be happy to see the hot favorite lose the Guineas, but there was nothing in his voice except admiration for a great horse. Tri-Nitro lined up in his turn and at a signal from George set off with two companions at a deceptively fast pace. Inky Poole, I was interested to see, sat as quiet as patience and rode with a skill worth ten times what he would be paid. Good work jockeys were undervalued. Bad ones could ruin a horse's mouth and temperament and whole career. It figured that for the stableful he had, George Caspar would employ only the best.

Poole was not riding the flat-out searching gallop the horse would be given on the following Saturday morning over a long smooth surface like the Limekilns. Up the incline of Warren Hill a fast canter was testing enough. Tri-Nitro took the whole thing without a hint of effort, and breasted the top as if he could go up there six times more without noticing.

Impressive, I thought. The press, clearly agreeing, were scribbling in their notebooks. Trevor Deansgate looked thoughtful, as well he might, and George Caspar, coming down the hill and reining in near us, looked almost smugly satisfied. The Guineas, one felt, were in the bag.

After they had done their work, the horses walked down the hill to join the still circling string, where the work riders changed onto fresh mounts and set off again up to the top. Tri-Nitro got back his lad with the olive-green Husky and the red scarf, and eventually the whole lot of them set off home.

"That's that, then," George said. "All set, Trevor? Breakfast?"

They nodded farewells to me and set off, one in the car, one on the horse. I had eyes mostly, however, for Inky Poole, who had been four times up the hill and was walking off a shade morosely to a parked car.

"Inky," I said, coming up behind him. "The gallop on Tri-Nitro . . . that was great."

He looked at me sourly. "I've got nothing to say."

"I'm not from the press."

"I know who you are. Saw you racing. Who hasn't?" Unfriendly: almost a sneer. "What do you want?"

"How does Tri-Nitro compare with Gleaner, this time last year?"

He fished the car keys out of a zipper pocket in his parka, and fitted one into the lock. What I could see of his face looked obstinately unhelpful.

"Did Gleaner, a week before the Guineas, give you the same sort of feel?" I said.

"I'm not talking to you."

"How about Zingaloo?" I said. "Or Bethesda?"

He opened his car door and slid down into the driving seat, taking out time to give me a hostile glare.

"Piss off," he said. Slammed the door. Stabbed the ignition key into the dashboard and forcefully drove away.

Chico had arisen to breakfast but was sitting in the pub's dining room, holding his head.

"Don't look so healthy," he said when I joined him.

"Bacon and eggs," I said. "That's what I'll have. Or kippers, perhaps. And strawberry jam."

He groaned.

"I'm going back to London," I said. "But would you mind staying here?" I pulled the camera from my pocket. "Take the film out of that and get it developed. Overnight if possible. There's some pictures of Tri-Nitro and Inky Poole on there. We might find them helpful; you never know."

"O.K., then," he said. "But you'll have to ring up the Comprehensive and tell them that my black belt's at the cleaners."

I laughed. "There were some girls riding in George Caspar's string this morning," I said. "See what you can do."

"That's beyond the call of duty." But his eyes seemed suddenly brighter. "What am I asking?"

"Things like who saddles Tri-Nitro for exercise gallops, and what's the routine from now until next Wednesday, and whether anything nasty is stirring in the jungle."

"What about you, then?"

"I'll be back Friday night," I said. "In time for the gallops on Saturday. They're bound to gallop Tri-Nitro on Saturday. A strong workout, to bring him to a peak."

"Do you really think anything dodgy's going on?" Chico asked.

"A tossup. I just don't know. I'd better ring Rosemary."

I went through the Mr. Barnes routine again and Rosemary came on the line sounding as agitated as ever.

"I can't talk. We've people here for breakfast."

"Just listen, then," I said. "Try to persuade George to vary his routine when he gallops Tri-Nitro on Saturday. Put up a different jockey, for instance. Not Inky Poole."

"You don't think . . ." Her voice was high, and broke off.

"I don't know at all," I said. "But if George changed everything about, there'd be less chance of skulduggery. Routine is the robber's best friend."

"What? Oh, yes. All right. I'll try. What about you?"

"I'll be out watching the gallop. After that I'll stick around, until after the Guineas is safely over. But I wish you'd let me talk to George."

"No. He'd be livid. I'll have to go now." The receiver went down with a rattle which spoke of still unsteady hands, and I feared that George might be right about his wife's being neurotic.

Charles and I met as usual at the Cavendish the following day, and sat in the upstairs bar's armchairs.

"You look happier," he said, "than I've seen you since . . ." He gestured to my arm with his glass. "Released in spirit. Not your usual stoical self."

"I've been in Newmarket," I said. "Watched the gallops yesterday morning."

"I would have thought . . ." He stopped.

"That I'd be eaten by jealousy?" I said. "So would I. But I enjoyed it."

"Good."

"I'm going up again tomorrow night and staying until after the Guineas next Wednesday."

"And lunch next Thursday?"

I smiled and bought him a large pink gin. "I'll be back for that."

In due course we ate scallops in a wine and cheese sauce, and he gave me the news of Jenny.

"Oliver Quayle sent the address you asked for, for the polish." He took a paper from his breast pocket and handed it over. "Oliver is worried. He says the police are actively pursuing their inquiries, and Jenny is almost certain to be charged."

"When?"

"I don't know. Oliver doesn't know. Sometimes these things take weeks, but not always. And when they charge her, Oliver says, she will have to appear in a magistrates' court, and they are certain to refer the case to the Crown Court, as so much money is involved. They'll give her bail, of course."

"Bail!"

"Oliver says she is unfortunately very likely to be convicted, but that if it is stressed that she acted as she did under the influence of Nicholas Ashe, she'll probably get some sympathy from the judge and a conditional discharge."

"Even if he isn't found?"

"Yes. But of course if he *is* found, and charged, and found guilty, Jenny would with luck escape a conviction altogether."

I took a deep breath that was half a sigh.

"Have to find him then, won't we?" I said.

"How?"

"Well . . . I spent a lot of Monday, and all of this morning, looking through a box of letters. They came from the people who sent money, and ordered wax. Eighteen hundred of them, or thereabouts."

"How do they help?"

"I've started sorting them into alphabetical order, and making a list." He frowned skeptically, but I went on. "The interesting thing is that all the surnames start with the letters *L, M, N,* and *O*. None from *A* to *K*, and none from *P* to *Z*."

"I don't see . . ."

"They might be part of a mailing list," I said. "Like for a catalogue. Or even for a charity. There must be thousands of mailing lists, but this one certainly did produce the required results, so it wasn't a mailing list for dog license reminders, for example."

"That seems reasonable," he said dryly.

"I thought I'd get all the names into order and then see if anyone, like Christie's or Sotheby's, say—because of the polish angle—has a mailing list which matches. A long shot, I know, but there's just a chance."

"I could help you," he said.

"It's a boring job."

"She's my daughter."

"All right, then. I'd like it."

I finished the scallops and sat back in my chair, and drank Charles's good cold white wine.

He said he would stay overnight in his club and come to my flat in the morning to help with the sorting, and I gave him a spare key to get in with, in case I should be out for a newspaper or cigarettes when he came. He lit a cigar and watched me through the smoke. "What did Jenny say to you upstairs after lunch on Sunday?"

I looked at him briefly. "Nothing much."

"She was moody all day afterwards. She even snapped at Toby." He smiled. "Toby protested, and

Jenny said, 'At least Sid didn't whine.'" He paused. "I gathered that she'd been giving you a particularly rough mauling and was feeling guilty."

"It wouldn't be guilt. With luck it was misgivings about Ashe."

"And not before time."

From the Cavendish I went to the Portman Square headquarters of the Jockey Club, to keep an appointment made that morning on the telephone by Lucas Wainwright. Unofficial my task for him might be, but official enough for him to ask me to his office. Ex-Superintendent Eddy Keith, it transpired, had gone to Yorkshire to look into a positive doping test, and no one else was going to wonder much at my visit.

"I've got all the files for you," Lucas said. "Eddy's reports on the syndicates, and some notes on the rogues he O.K.'d."

"I'll make a start, then," I said. "Can I take them away, or do you want me to look at them here?"

"Here, if you would," he said. "I don't want to draw my secretary's attention to them by letting them out or getting Xerox copies, as she works for Eddy too, and I know she admires him. She would tell him. You'd better copy down what you need."

"Right," I said.

He gave me a table to one side of his room, and a comfortable chair, and a bright light, and for an hour or so I read and made notes. At his own desk he did some desultory pen-pushing and rustled a few papers, but in the end it was clear that it was only a pretense of being busy. He wasn't so much waiting for me to finish as generally uneasy.

I looked up from my writing. "What's the matter?" I said.

"The . . . matter?"

"Something's troubling you."

He hesitated. "Have you done all you want?" he said, nodding at my work.

"Only about half," I said. "Can you give me another hour?"

"Yes, but . . . Look, I'll have to be fair with you. There's something you'll have to know."

"What sort of thing?"

Lucas, who was normally urbane even when in a hurry, and whose naval habits of thought I understood from long practice with my admiral father-in-law, was showing signs of embarrassment. The things that acutely embarrassed naval officers were collisions between warships and quaysides, ladies visiting the crew's mess deck with the crew present and at ease, and dishonorable conduct among gentlemen. It couldn't be the first two; so where were we with the third?

"I have not perhaps given you all the facts," he said.

"Go on, then."

"I did send someone else to check on two of the syndicates, some time ago. Six months ago." He fiddled with some paper clips, no longer looking in my direction. "Before Eddy checked them."

"With what result?"

"Ah. Yes." He cleared his throat. "The man I sent . . . his name's Mason . . . We never received his report because he was attacked in the street before he could write it."

Attacked in the street . . . "What sort of attack?" I asked. "And who attacked him?"

He shook his head. "Nobody knows who attacked him. He was found on the pavement by some passers-by, who called the police."

"Well . . . have you asked him—Mason?" But I guessed at something of the answer, if not all of it.

"He's . . . er . . . never really recovered," Lucas

said regretfully. "His head, it seemed, had been repeatedly kicked, as well as his body. There was a good deal of brain damage. He's still in an institution. He always will be. He's a vegetable . . . and he's blind."

I bit the end of the pencil with which I'd been making notes. "Was he robbed?" I said.

"His wallet was missing. But not his watch." His face was worried.

"So it might have been a straightforward mugging?"

"Yes . . . except that the police treated it as intended homicide, because of the number and target of the boot marks."

He sat back in his chair as if he'd got rid of an unwelcome burden. Honor among gentlemen . . . Honor satisfied.

"All right," I said. "Which two syndicates was he checking?"

"The first two that you have there."

"And do you think any of the people on them—the undesirables—are the sort to kick their way out of trouble?"

He said unhappily, "They might be."

"And am I," I said carefully, "investigating the possible corruption of Eddy Keith, or Mason's semi-murder?"

After a pause, he said, "Perhaps both."

There was a long silence. Finally I said, "You do realize that by sending me notes at the races and meeting me in the tearoom and bringing me here, you haven't left much doubt that I'm working for you?"

"But it could be at anything."

I said gloomily, "Not when I turn up on the syndicates' doorsteps."

"I'd quite understand," he said, "if, in view of what I've said, you wanted to . . . er . . ."

So would I, I thought. I would understand that I didn't want my head kicked in. But then what I'd told Jenny was true: one never thought it would happen. And you're always wrong, she'd said.

I sighed. "You'd better tell me about Mason. Where he went and who he saw. Anything you can think of."

"It's practically nothing. He went off in the ordinary way and the next we heard was he'd been attacked. The police couldn't trace where he'd been, and all the syndicate people swore they'd never seen him. The case isn't closed, of course, but after six months it's got no sort of priority."

We talked it over for a while, and I spent another hour after that writing notes. I left the Jockey Club premises at a quarter to six, to go back to the flat; and I didn't get there.

Chapter 7

I went home in a taxi and paid it off outside the entrance to the flats, yet not exactly outside, because a dark car was squarely parked there on the double yellow lines, which was a towaway zone.

I scarcely looked at the car, which was my mistake, because as I reached it and turned away toward the entrance, its curbside doors opened and spilled out the worst sort of trouble.

Two men in dark clothes grabbed me. One hit me dizzyingly on the head with something hard and the other flung what I later found was a kind of lasso of thick rope over my arms and chest and pulled it tight. They both bundled me into the back of the car, where one of them for good measure tied a dark piece of cloth over my dazed half-shut eyes.

"Keys," a voice said. "Quick. No one saw us."

I felt them fumbling in my pockets. There was a clink as they found what they were looking for. I began to come back into focus, so to speak, and to struggle, which was a reflex action but all the same another mistake.

The cloth over my eyes was reinforced by a sickly-smelling wad over my nose and mouth. Anesthetic fumes made a nonsense of consciousness, and the last thing I thought was that if I was going the way of Mason, they hadn't wasted any time.

I was aware, first of all, that I was lying on straw.

Straw, as in stable. Rustling when I tried to move. Hearing, as always, had returned first.

I had been concussed a few times over the years, in racing falls. I thought for a while that I must have come off a horse, though I couldn't remember which, or where I'd been riding.

Funny.

The unwelcome news came back with a rush. I had not been racing. I had one hand. I had been abducted in daylight from a London street. I was lying on my back on some straw, blindfolded, with a rope tied tight round my chest, above the elbows, fastening my upper arms against my body. I was lying on the knot. I didn't know why I was there . . . and had no great faith in the future.

Damn, damn, *damn.*

My feet were tethered to some immovable object. It was black dark, even round the edges of the blindfold. I sat up and tried to get some part of me disentangled: a lot of effort and no results.

Ages later there was a tramp of footsteps outside on a gritty surface, and the creak of a wooden door, and sudden light on the sides of my nose.

"Stop trying, Mr. Halley," a voice said. "You won't undo those knots with one hand."

I stopped trying. There was no point in going on.

"A spot of overkill," he said, enjoying himself. "Ropes *and* anesthetic *and* blackjack *and* blindfold. Well, I did tell them, of course, to be careful, and not to get within hitting distance of that tin arm. A villain I know has very nasty things to say about you hitting him with what he didn't expect."

I knew the voice. Undertones of Manchester, overtones of all the way up the social ladder. The confidence of power.

Trevor Deansgate.

Last seen on the gallops at Newmarket, looking for Tri-Nitro in the string, and identifying him because he knew the work jockey, which most people didn't. Deansgate, going to George Caspar's for breakfast. Bookmaker Trevor Deansgate had been a question mark, a possibility, someone to be assessed, looked into. Something I would have done, and hadn't done yet.

"Take the blindfold off," he said. "I want him to see me."

Fingers took their time over untying the tight piece of cloth. When it fell away, the light was temporarily dazzling; but the first thing I saw was the double barrel of a shotgun pointing my way.

"Guns too," I said sourly.

It was a storage barn, not a stable. There was a stack of several tons of straw bales to my left, and on the right, a few yards away, a tractor. My feet were fastened to the trailer bar of a farm roller. The barn had a high roof, with beams; and one meager electric light, which shone on Trevor Deansgate.

"You're too bloody clever for your own good," he said. "You know what they say? If Halley's after you, watch out. He'll sneak up on you when you think he doesn't know you exist, and they'll be slamming the cell doors on you before you've worked it out."

I didn't say anything. What could one say? Especially sitting trussed up like a fool at the wrong end of a shotgun.

"Well, I'm not waiting for you, do you see?" he said. "I know how bloody close you are to getting me nicked. Just laying your snares, weren't you? Just waiting for me to fall into your hands, like you've caught so many others." He stopped and reconsidered what he'd said. "Into your hand," he said, "and that fancy hook."

He had a way of speaking to me that acknowledged mutual origins, that we'd both come a long way from where we'd started. It was not a matter of accent, but of manner. There was no need for social pretense. The message was raw, and between equals, and would be understood.

He was dressed, as before, in a city suit. Navy; chalk pin stripe this time; Gucci tie. The well-manicured hands held the shotgun with the expertise of many a weekend on country estates. What did it matter, I thought, if the finger that pulled the trigger was clean and cared for? What did it matter if his shoes were polished? . . . I looked at the silly details because I didn't want to think about death.

He stood for a while without speaking: simply watching. I sat without moving, as best I could, and thought about a nice safe job in a stockbroker's office.

"No bloody nerves, have you?" he said. "None at all."

I didn't answer.

The other two men were behind me to the right, out of my sight. I could hear their feet as they occasionally shuffled on the straw. Far too far away for me to reach.

I was wearing what I had put on for lunch with Charles. Gray trousers, socks, dark brown shoes; rope extra. Shirt, tie, and a recently bought blazer, quite expensive. What did that matter? If he killed me, Jenny would get the rest. I hadn't changed my will.

Trevor Deansgate switched his attention to the man behind me.

"Now listen," he said, "and don't snarl it up. Get these two pieces of rope and tie one to his left arm, and one to the right. And watch out for any tricks."

He lifted the gun a fraction until I could see down the barrels. If he shot from there, I thought, he would hit his chums. It didn't after all look like straight execution. The chums were busy tying bits of rope to both my wrists.

"Not the left wrist, you stupid bugger," Trevor Deansgate said. "That one comes right off. Use your bloody head. Tie it high, above his elbow."

The chum in question did as he said and pulled the knots tight, and almost casually picked up a stout metal bar, like a crowbar, and stood there gripping it as if he thought that somehow I could liberate myself like Superman and still attack him.

Crowbar . . . Nasty shivers of apprehension suddenly crawled all over my scalp. There had been another villain, before, who had known where to hurt me most, the one who had hit my already useless left hand with a poker, and turned it from a ruin into a total loss. I had had regrets enough since, and all sorts of private agonies, but I hadn't realized, until that sickening moment, how much I valued what remained. The muscles that worked the electrodes, they at least gave me the semblance of a working hand. If they were injured again I wouldn't have even that. As for the elbow itself . . . If he wanted to put me out of effective action for a long time, he had only to use that crowbar.

"You don't like that, do you, Mr. Halley?" Trevor Deansgate said.

I turned my head back to him. His voice and face

were suddenly full of a mixture of triumph and satisfaction, and what seemed like relief.

I said nothing.

"You're sweating," he said.

He had another order for the chums. "Untie that rope round his chest. And do it carefully. Hold on to the ropes on his arms."

They untied the knot, and pulled the constricting rope away from my chest. It didn't make much difference to my chances of escape. They were wildly exaggerating my ability in a fight.

"Lie down," he said to me; and when I didn't at once comply, he said, "Push him down," to the chums. One way or another, I ended on my back.

"I don't want to kill you," he said. "I could dump your body somewhere, but there would be too many questions. I can't risk it. But if I don't kill you, I've got to shut you up. Once and for all. Permanently."

Short of killing me, I didn't see how he could do it; and I was stupid.

"Pull his arm sideways, away from his body," he said.

The pull on my left arm had a man's weight behind it and was stronger than I was. I rolled my head that way and tried not to beg, not to weep.

"Not that one, you bloody fool," Trevor Deansgate said. "The other one. The right one. Pull it out, to this side."

The chum on my right used all his strength on the rope and hauled so that my arm finished straight out sideways, at right angles to my body, palm upward.

Trevor Deansgate stepped toward me and lowered the gun until the black holes of the barrel were pointing straight at my stretched right wrist. Then he carefully lowered the barrel another inch, making direct contact on my skin, pressing down against the straw-covered floor. I could feel the metal rims hard across the bones and nerves and sinews. Across the bridge to a healthy hand.

I heard the click as he cocked the firing mechanism. One blast from a twelve-bore would take off most of the arm.

A dizzy wave of faintness drenched all my limbs with sweat.

Whatever anyone said, I intimately knew about fear. Not fear of any horse, or of racing or falling, or of ordinary physical pain. But of humiliation and rejection and helplessness and failure . . . all of those.

All the fear I'd ever felt in all my life was as nothing compared with the liquefying, mind-shattering disintegration of that appalling minute. It broke me in pieces. Swamped me. Brought me down to a morass of terror, to a whimper in the soul. And instinctively, hopelessly, I tried not to let it show.

He watched motionlessly through uncountable intensifying silent seconds. Making me wait. Making it worse.

At length he took a deep breath and said, "As you see, I could shoot off your hand. Nothing easier. But I'm probably not going to. Not today." He paused. "Are you listening?"

I nodded the merest fraction. My eyes were full of gun.

His voice came quietly, seriously, giving weight to every sentence. "You can give me your assurance that you'll back off. You'll do nothing more which is directed against me, in any way, ever. You'll go to France tomorrow morning, and you'll stay there until after the Two Thousand Guineas. After that, you can do what you like. But if you break your assurance . . . well, you're easy to find. I'll find you, and I'll blow your right hand off. I mean it, and you'd better believe it.

Sometime or other. You'd never escape it. Do you understand?"

I nodded, as before. I could feel the gun as if it were hot. Don't let him, I thought. Dear God, don't let him.

"Give me your assurance. Say it."

I swallowed painfully. Dredged up a voice. Low and hoarse. "I give it."

"You'll back off."

"Yes."

"You'll not come after me again, ever."

"No."

"You'll go to France and stay there until after the Guineas."

"Yes."

Another silence lengthened for what seemed a hundred years, while I stared beyond my undamaged wrist to the dark side of the moon.

He took the gun away in the end. Broke it open. Removed the cartridges. I felt physically, almost uncontrollably, sick.

He knelt on his pin-striped knees beside me and looked closely at whatever defense I could put into an unmoving face and expressionless eyes. I could feel the treacherous sweat trickling down my cheek. He nodded, with grim satisfaction.

"I knew you couldn't face that. Not the other one as well. No one could. There's no need to kill you."

He stood up again and stretched his body, as if relaxing a wound-up inner tension. Then he put his hands into various pockets, and produced things.

"Here are your keys. Your passport. Your checkbook. Credit cards." He put them on a straw bale. To the chums, he said, "Untie him, and drive him to the airport. To Heathrow."

Chapter 8

I flew to Paris and stayed right there where I landed, in an airport hotel, with no impetus or heart to go farther. I stayed for six days, not leaving my room, spending most of the time by the window, watching the airplanes come and go.

I felt stunned. I felt ill. Disoriented and overthrown and severed from my own roots. Crushed into an abject state of mental misery, knowing that this time I really had run away.

It was easy to convince myself that logically I had had no choice but to give Deansgate his assurance when he asked for it. If I hadn't, he would have killed me. I could tell myself, as I continually did, that sticking to his instructions had been merely common sense; but the fact remained that when the chums decanted me at Heathrow they had driven off at once, and it had been of my own free will that I'd bought my ticket, waited in the departure lounge, and walked to the aircraft.

There had been no one there with guns to make me

do it. Only the fact that as Deansgate had truly said, I couldn't face losing the other hand. I couldn't face even the risk of it. The thought of it, like a conditioned response, brought out the sweat.

As the days passed, the feeling I had had of disintegration seemed not to fade but to deepen.

The automatic part of me still went on working: walking, talking, ordering coffee, going to the bathroom. In the part that mattered there was turmoil and anguish and a feeling that my whole self had been literally smashed in those few cataclysmic minutes on the straw.

Part of the trouble was that I knew my own weaknesses too well. Knew that if I hadn't had so much pride, it wouldn't have destroyed me so much to have lost it.

To have been forced to realize that my basic view of myself had been an illusion was proving a psychic upheaval like an earthquake, and perhaps it wasn't surprising that I felt I had, I really had, come to pieces.

I didn't know that I could face that, either.

I wished I could sleep properly, and get some peace.

When Wednesday came I thought of Newmarket and of all the brave hopes for the Guineas.

Thought of George Caspar, taking Tri-Nitro to the test, producing him proudly in peak condition and swearing to himself that this time nothing could go wrong. Thought of Rosemary, jangling with nerves, willing the horse to win and knowing it wouldn't. Thought of Trevor Deansgate, unsuspected, moving like a mole to vandalize, somehow, the best colt in the kingdom.

I could have stopped him, if I'd tried.

Wednesday for me was the worst day of all, the day I learned about despair and desolation and guilt.

On the sixth day, Thursday morning, I went down to the lobby and bought an English newspaper.

They had run the Two Thousand Guineas, as scheduled.

Tri-Nitro had started as a hot favorite at even money; and he had finished last.

I paid my bill and went to the airport. There were airplanes to everywhere, to escape in. The urge to escape was very strong. But wherever one went, one took oneself along. From oneself there was no escape. Wherever I went, in the end I would have to go back.

If I went back in my split-apart state I'd have to live all the time on two levels. I'd have to behave in the old way, which everyone would expect. Have to think and drive and talk and get on with life. Going back meant all that. It also meant doing all that, and proving to myself that I could do it, when I wasn't the same inside.

I thought that what I had lost might be worse than a hand. For a hand there were substitutes which could grip and look passable. But if the core of oneself had crumbled, how could one manage at all?

If I went back, I would have to try.

If I couldn't try, why go back?

It took me a long lonely time to buy a ticket to Heathrow.

I landed at midday, made a brief telephone call to the Cavendish, to ask them to apologize to the Admiral because I couldn't keep our date, and took a taxi home.

Everything in the lobby, on the stairs, and along the landing looked the same, and yet completely different.

It was I who was different. I put the key in the lock and turned it, and went into the flat.

I had expected it to be empty, but before I'd even shut the door I heard a rustle in the sitting room, and then Chico's voice. "Is that you, Admiral?"

I simply didn't answer. In a brief moment his head appeared, questioning, and after that, his whole self.

"About time too," he said. He looked, on the whole, relieved to see me.

"I sent you a telegram."

"Oh, sure. I've got it here, propped on the shelf. 'Leave Newmarket, and go home, shall be away for a few days, will telephone.' What sort of telegram's that? Sent from Heathrow, early Friday. You been on holiday?"

"Yeah."

I walked past him, into the sitting room. In there, it didn't look at all the same. There were files and papers everywhere, on every surface, with coffee-marked cups and saucers holding them down.

"You went away without the charger," Chico said. "You never do that, even overnight. The spare batteries are all here. You haven't been able to move that hand for six days."

"Let's have some coffee."

"You didn't take any clothes, or your razor."

"I stayed in a hotel. They had throwaway razors, if you asked. What's all this mess?"

"The polish letters."

"What?"

"You know. The polish letters. Your wife's spot of trouble."

"Oh . . ."

I stared at it blankly.

"Look," Chico said. "Cheese on toast? I'm starving."

"That would be nice." It was unreal. It was all unreal.

He went into the kitchen and started banging about. I took the dead battery out of my arm and put in a charged one. The fingers opened and closed, like old times. I had missed them more than I would have imagined.

Chico brought the cheese on toast. He ate his, and I looked at mine. I'd better eat it, I thought, and didn't have the energy. There was the sound of the door of the flat being opened with a key, and after that, my father-in-law's voice from the hall.

"He didn't turn up at the Cavendish, but he did at least leave a message." He came into the room from behind where I sat and saw Chico nodding his head in my direction.

"He's back," Chico said. "The boy himself."

"Hello, Charles," I said.

He took a long slow look. Very controlled, very civilized. "We have, you know, been worried." It was a reproach.

"I'm sorry."

"Where have you been?" he said.

I found I couldn't tell him. If I told him where, I would have to tell him why; and I shrank from why. I just didn't say anything at all.

Chico gave him a cheerful grin. "Sid's got a bad attack of the brick walls." He looked at his watch. "Seeing that you're here, Admiral, I might as well get along and teach the little bleeders at the Comprehensive how to throw their grannies over their shoulders. And, Sid, before I go, there's about fifty messages on the phone pad. There's two new insurance investigations waiting to be done, and a guard job. Lucas Wainwright wants you; he's rung four times. And Rosemary Caspar has been screeching fit to blast the eardrums. It's all there, written down. See you, then. I'll come back here later."

I almost asked him not to, but he'd gone.

"You've lost weight," Charles said.

It wasn't surprising. I looked again at the toasted cheese and decided that coming back also had to include things like eating.

"Want some?" I asked.

He eyed the congealing square. "No, thank you."

Nor did I. I pushed it away. Sat and stared into space.

"What's happened to you?" he asked.

"Nothing."

"Last week you came into the Cavendish like a spring," he said. "Bursting with life. Eyes actually sparkling. And now look at you."

"Well, don't," I said. "Don't look at me. How are you doing with the letters?"

"Sid . . ."

"Admiral." I stood up restlessly, to escape his probing gaze. "Leave me alone."

He paused, considering, then said, "You've been speculating in commodities recently. Have you lost your money, is that it?"

I was surprised almost to the point of amusement.

"No," I said.

He said, "You went dead like this before, when you lost your career and my daughter. So what have you lost this time, if it isn't money? What could be as bad . . . or worse?"

I knew the answer. I'd learned it in Paris, in torment and shame. My whole mind formed the word "courage" with such violent intensity that I was afraid it would leap of its own accord from my brain to his.

He showed no sign of receiving it. He was still waiting for a reply.

I swallowed. "Six days," I said neutrally. "I've lost six days. Let's get on with tracing Nicholas Ashe."

He shook his head in disapproval and frustration, but began to explain what he'd been doing.

"This thick pile is from people with names beginning with *M*. I've put them into strictly alphabetical order, and typed out a list. It seemed to me that we might get results from one letter only . . . Are you paying attention?"

"Yes."

"I took the list to Christie's and Sotheby's, as you suggested, and persuaded them to help. But the *M* section of their catalogue mailing list is not the same as this one. And I found that there may be difficulties with this matching, as so many envelopes are addressed nowadays by computers."

"You've worked hard," I said.

"Chico and I have been sitting here in shifts, answering your telephone and trying to find out where you'd gone. Your car was still here, in the garage, and Chico said you would never have gone anywhere of your own accord without the battery charger for your arm."

"Well . . . I did."

"Sid . . ."

"No," I said. "What we need now is a list of periodicals and magazines dealing with antique furniture. We'll try those first with the *M* people."

"It's an awfully big project," Charles said doubtfully. "And even if we do find it, what then? I mean, as the man at Christie's pointed out, even if we find whose mailing list was being used, where does it get us? The firm or magazine wouldn't be able to tell us which of the many people who had access to the list was Nicholas Ashe, particularly as he is almost certain not to have used that name if he had any dealings with them."

"Mm," I said. "But there's a chance he's started operating again somewhere else, and is still using the same list. He took it with him, when he went. If we can find out whose list it is, we might go and call on some people who are on it, whose names start with *A* to *K*, and *P* to *Z*, and find out if they've received any of those begging letters very recently. Because if they have, the letters will have the address to which the money is to be sent. And there, at that address, we might find Mr. Ashe."

Charles put his mouth into the shape of a whistle, but what came out was more like a sigh.

"You've come back with your brains intact, anyway," he said.

Oh, God, I thought, I'm making myself think to shut out the abyss. I'm in splinters. . . . I'm never going to be right again. The analytical reasoning part of my mind might be marching straight on, but what had to be called the soul was sick and dying.

"And there's the polish," I said. I still had in my pocket the paper he'd given me the week before. I took it out and put it on the table. "If the idea of special polish is closely geared to the mailing list, then to get maximum results the polish is necessary. There can't be many private individuals ordering so much wax in unprinted tins packed in little white boxes. We could ask the polish firm to let us know if another lot is ordered. It's just faintly possible that Ashe will use the same firm again, even if not at once. He ought to see the danger . . . but he might be a fool."

I turned away wearily. Thought about whisky. Went over and poured myself a large one.

"Drinking heavily, are you?" Charles said from behind me, in his most offensive drawl.

I shut my teeth hard, and said, "No." Apart from coffee and water, it was my first drink for a week.

"Your first alcoholic blackout, was it, these last few days?"

I left the glass untouched on the drinks tray and turned round. His eyes were at their coldest, as unkind as in the days when we'd first met.

"Don't be so bloody stupid," I said.

He lifted his chin a fraction. "A spark," he said sarcastically. "Still got your pride, I see."

I compressed my lips and turned my back on him, and drank a lot of the Scotch. After a bit, I deliberately loosened a few tensed-up muscles, and said, "You won't find out that way. I know you too well. You use insults as a lever, to sting people into opening up. You've done it to me in the past. But not this time."

"If I find the right sting," he said, "I'll use it."

"Do you want a drink?" I said.

"Since you ask, yes."

We sat opposite each other in armchairs in unchanged companionship, and I thought vaguely of this and that and shied away from the crucifying bits.

"You know," I said. "We don't have to go trailing that mailing list around to see whose it is. All we do is ask the people themselves. Those . . ." I nodded toward the *M* stack. "We just ask some of them what mailing lists they themselves are on. We'd only need to ask a few. . . . The common denominator would be certain to turn up."

When Charles had gone home to Aynsford I wandered aimlessly round the flat, tie off and in shirtsleeves, trying to be sensible. I told myself that nothing much had happened, only that Trevor Deansgate had used a lot of horrible threats to get me to stop doing something that I hadn't yet started. But I couldn't dodge the guilt. Once he'd revealed himself, once I knew he would do *something,* I could have stopped him, and I hadn't.

If he hadn't got me so effectively out of Newmarket, I would very likely have still been prodding unproductively away, unsure even if there was anything to discover, right up to the moment in the Guineas when Tri-Nitro tottered in last. But I would also be up there now, I thought, certain and inquisitive; and because of his threat, I wasn't.

I could call my absence prudence, common sense, the only possible course in the circumstances. I could rationalize and excuse. I could say I wouldn't have been doing anything that wasn't already being done by the Jockey Club. I returned, all the time, to the swinging truth, that I wasn't there now because I was afraid to be.

Chico came back from his judo class and set to again to find out where I'd been; and for the same reasons I didn't tell him, even though I knew he wouldn't despise me as I despised myself.

"All right," he said finally. "You just keep it all bottled up and see where it gets you. Wherever you've been, it was bad. You've only got to look at you. It's not going to do you any good to shut it all up inside."

Shutting it all up inside, however, was a lifelong habit, a defense learned in childhood, a wall against the world, impossible to change.

I raised at least half a smile. "You setting up in Harley Street?"

"That's better," he said. "You missed all the fun, did you know? Tri-Nitro got stuffed after all in the Guineas yesterday, and they're turning George Caspar's yard inside out. It's all here, somewhere, in the *Sporting Life.* The Admiral brought it. Have you read it."

I shook my head.

"Our Rosemary, she wasn't bonkers after all, was she? How do you think they managed it?"

"They?" I said.

"Whoever did it."

"I don't know."

"I went along to see the gallop on Saturday morning," he said. "Yeah, yeah, I know you sent the telegram about leaving, but I'd got a real little dolly lined up for a bit of the other on Friday night, so I stayed. One more night wasn't going to make any difference, and besides, she was George Caspar's typist."

"She was . . ."

"Does the typing. Rides the horses sometimes. Into everything, she is, and talkative with it."

The new scared Sid Halley didn't even want to listen.

"There was a right old rumpus all day Wednesday in George Caspar's house," Chico said. "It started at breakfast when that Inky Poole turned up and said Sid Halley had been asking questions that he, Inky Poole, didn't like."

He paused for effect. I simply stared.

"Are you listening?" he said.

"Yes."

"You got your stone face act on again."

"Sorry."

"Then Brothersmith the vet turned up and heard Inky Poole letting off, and he said funny, Sid Halley had been around him asking questions too. About bad hearts, he said. Same horses as Inky Poole was talking about. Bethesda, Gleaner, and Zingaloo. And how was Tri-Nitro's heart, for good measure. My little dolly typist said you could've heard George Caspar blowing up all the way to Cambridge. He's real touchy about those horses."

Trevor Deansgate, I thought coldly, had been at

George Caspar's for breakfast, and had heard every word.

"Of course," Chico said, "sometime later they checked the studs, Garvey's and Thrace's, and found you'd been there too. My dolly says your name is mud."

I rubbed my hand over my face. "Does your dolly know you were working with me?"

"Do us a favor. Of course not."

"Did she say anything else?" What the hell am I asking for? I thought.

"Yeah. Well, she said Rosemary got on to George Caspar to change all the routine for the Saturday morning gallop, nagged him all day Thursday and all day Friday, and George Caspar was climbing the walls. And at the yard they had so much security they were tripping over their own alarm bells." He paused for breath. "After that she didn't say much else on account of three martinis and time for tickle."

I sat on the arm of the sofa and stared at the carpet.

"Next morning," Chico said, "I watched the gallop, like I said. Your photos came in very handy. Hundreds of ruddy horses . . . Someone told me which were Caspar's, and there was Inky Poole, scowling like in the pictures, so I just zeroed in on him and hung about. There was a lot of fuss when it came to Tri-Nitro. They took the saddle off and put a little one on, and Inky Poole rode on that."

"It was Inky Poole, then, who rode Tri-Nitro, same as usual?"

"They looked just like your pictures," Chico said. "Can't swear to it more than that."

I stared some more at the carpet.

"So what do we do next?" he said.

"Nothing . . . We give Rosemary her money back and draw a line."

"But hey," Chico said in protest. "Someone got at the horse. You know they did."

"Not our business any more."

I wished that he, too, would stop looking at me. I felt a distinct need to crawl into a hole and hide.

The doorbell rang with the long peal of a determined thumb. "We're out," I said; but Chico went and answered it.

Rosemary Caspar swept past him, through the hall and into the sitting room, advancing in the old fawn raincoat and a fulminating rage. No scarf, no false curls, and no loving kindness.

"So there you are," she said forcefully. "I knew you'd be here, skulking out of sight. Your friend kept telling me when I telephoned that you weren't here, but I knew he was lying."

"I wasn't here," I said. As well try damming the St. Lawrence with a twig.

"You weren't where I paid you to be, which was up in Newmarket. And I told you from the beginning that George wasn't to find out you were asking questions, and he did, and we've been having one God-awful bloody row ever since, and now Tri-Nitro has disgraced us unbearably and it's all your bloody fault."

Chico raised his eyebrows comically. "Sid didn't ride it . . . or train it."

She glared at him with transferred hatred. "And he didn't keep him safe, either."

"Er . . . no," Chico said. "Granted."

"As for you," she said, swinging back to me. "You're a useless bloody humbug. It's all rubbish, this detecting. Why don't you grow up and stop playing games? All you did was stir up trouble, and I want my money back."

"Will a check do?" I said.

"You're not arguing, then?"

"No," I said.

"Do you mean you admit that you failed?"

After a small pause, I said, "Yes."

"Oh." She sounded as if I had unexpectedly deprived her of a good deal of what she had come to say, but while I wrote out a check for her she went on complaining sharply enough.

"All your ideas about changing the routine, they were useless. I've been on and on at George about security and taking care, and he says he couldn't have done any more, no one could, and he's in absolute despair; and I'd hoped, I'd really hoped—what a laugh—that somehow or other you would work a miracle, and that Tri-Nitro would win, because I was so sure, so sure . . . and I was right."

I finished writing. "Why were you always so sure?" I said.

"I don't know. I just *knew*. I've been afraid of it for weeks . . . otherwise I would not have been so desperate as to try you in the first place. And I might as well not have bothered . . . It's caused so much trouble, and I can't bear it. I can't bear it. Yesterday was terrible. He should have won . . . I knew he wouldn't. I felt ill. I still feel ill."

She was trembling again. The pain in her face was acute. So many hopes, so much work had gone into Tri-Nitro, such anxiety and such care. Winning races was to a trainer like a film to a film-maker. If you got it right, they applauded; wrong, and they booed. And either way you'd poured your soul into it, and your thoughts and your skill and weeks of worry. I understood what the lost race meant to George, and to Rosemary equally, because she cared so much.

"Rosemary . . ." I said, in useless sympathy.

"It's pointless Brothersmith saying he must have had an infection," she said. "He's always saying things like that. He's so wet, I can't stand him; always looking over his shoulder. I've never liked him. And it was his job anyway to check Tri-Nitro and he did, over and over, and there was nothing wrong with him, nothing. He went down to the post looking beautiful, and in the parade ring before that there was nothing wrong, nothing. And then in the race, he just went backwards, and he finished . . . he came back . . . exhausted." There was a glitter of tears for a moment, but she visibly willed them from overwhelming her.

"They've done dope tests, I suppose," Chico said.

It angered her again. "Dope tests! Of course they have. What do you expect? Blood tests, urine tests, saliva tests, dozens of bloody tests. They gave George duplicate samples, and that's why we're down here; he's trying to fix up with some private lab . . . but they won't be positive. It will be like before . . . absolutely nothing."

I tore out the check and gave it to her, and she glanced at it blindly.

"I wish I'd never come here. My God, I wish I hadn't. You're only a jockey. I should have known better. I don't want to talk to you again. Don't talk to me at the races, do you understand?"

I nodded. I did understand. She turned abruptly, to go away. "And for God's sake don't speak to George, either." She went alone out of the room, and out of the flat, and slammed the door.

Chico clicked his tongue, and shrugged. "You can't win them all," he said. "What could you do that her husband couldn't, not to mention a private police force and half a dozen guard dogs?" He was excusing me, and we both knew it.

I didn't answer.

"Sid?"

"I don't know that I'm going on with it," I said. "This sort of job."

"You don't want to take any notice of what she said," he protested. "You can't give it up. You're too good at it. Look at all the awful messes you've put right. Just because of one that's gone wrong . . ."

I stared hollowly at a lot of unseen things.

"You're a big boy now," he said. And he was seven years younger than I, near enough. "You want to cry on Daddy's shoulder?" He paused. "Look, Sid, mate, you've got to snap out of it. Whatever's happened, it can't be as bad as when that horse sliced your hand up; nothing could. This is no time to die inside: we've got about five other jobs lined up. The insurance, and the guard job, and Lucas Wainwright's syndicates . . ."

"No," I said. I felt leaden and useless. "Not now, honestly, Chico."

I got up and went into the bedroom. Shut the door. Went purposelessly to the window and looked out at the scenery of roofs and chimney pots, glistening in the beginnings of rain. The pots were still there, though the chimneys underneath were blocked off and the fires long dead. I felt at one with the chimney pots. When fires went out, one froze.

The door opened.

"Sid," Chico said.

I said resignedly, "Remind me to put a lock on that door."

"You've got another visitor."

"Tell him to go away."

"It's a girl. Louise somebody."

I rubbed my hand over my face and head and down to the back of my neck. Eased the muscles. Turned from the window.

"Louise McInnes?"

"That's right."

"She shares the flat with Jenny," I said.

"Oh, that one. Well, then, Sid, if that's all for today, I'll be off. And . . . er . . . be here tomorrow, won't you?"

"Yeah."

He nodded. We left everything else unsaid. The amusement, mockery, friendship, and stifled anxiety were all there in his face and his voice. . . . Maybe he read the same in mine. At any rate, he gave me a widening grin as he departed, and I went into the sitting room thinking that some debts couldn't be paid.

Louise was standing in the middle of things, looking around her as I had in Jenny's flat. Through her eyes I saw my own room afresh: its irregular shape, high-ceilinged, not modern; and the tan leather sofa, the table with drinks by the window, the shelves with books, the prints framed and hung, and on the floor, leaning against the wall, the big painting of racing horses which I'd somehow never bothered to hang up. There were coffee cups and glasses scattered about, and full ashtrays, and the piles of letters on the coffee table and everywhere else.

Louise herself looked different: the full production, not the Sunday morning tumble out of bed. A brown velvet jacket, a blazing white sweater, a soft mottled brown skirt with a wide leather belt round an untroubled waist. Fair hair washed and shining, rose petal make-up on the English-rose skin. A detachment in the eyes which said that all this honey was not chiefly there for the attracting of bees.

"Mr. Halley."

"You could try Sid," I said. "You know me quite well, by proxy."

Her smile reached halfway. "Sid."

"Louise."

"Jenny says Sid is a plumber's mate's sort of name."

"Very good people, plumbers' mates."

"Did you know," she said, looking away and continuing the visual tour of inspection, "that in Arabic 'Sid' means 'lord'?"

"No, I didn't."

"Well, it does."

"You could tell Jenny," I said.

Her gaze came back fast to my face. "She gets to you, doesn't she?"

I smiled. "Like some coffee? Or a drink?"

"Tea?"

"Sure."

She came into the kitchen with me and watched me make it, and made no funny remarks about bionic hands, which was a nicc change from most new acquaintances, who tended to be fascinated, and to say so, at length. Instead she looked around with inoffensive curiosity, and finally fastened her attention on the calendar which hung from the knob on the pine cupboard door. Photographs of horses, a Christmas handout from a bookmaking firm. She flipped up the pages, looking at the pictures of the future months, and stopped at December, where a horse and jockey jumping the Chair at Aintree was silhouetted spectacularly against the sky.

"That's good," she said, and then, in surprise, reading the caption, "That's *you.*"

"He's a good photographer."

"Did you win that race?"

"Yes," I said mildly. "Do you take sugar?"

"No, thanks." She let the pages fall back. "How odd to find oneself on a calendar."

To me, it wasn't odd. How odd, I thought, to have seen one's picture in print so much that one scarcely noticed.

I carried the tray into the sitting room and put it on top of the letters on the coffee table. "Sit down," I said, and we sat.

"All these," I said, nodding to them, "are the letters which came with the checks for the wax."

She looked doubtful. "Are they of any use?"

"I hope so," I said, and explained about the mailing list.

"Good heavens." She hesitated. "Well, perhaps you won't need what I brought." She picked up her brown leather handbag and opened it. "I didn't come all this way specially," she said. "I've an aunt near here whom I visit. Anyway, I thought you might like to have this, as I was here, near your flat."

She pulled out a paperback book. She could have posted it, I thought, but I was quite glad that she hadn't.

"I was trying to put a bit of order into the chaos in my bedroom," she said. "I've a lot of books. They tend to pile up."

I didn't tell her I'd seen them. "Books do," I said.

"Well, this was among them. It's Nicky's."

She gave me the paperback. I glanced at the cover and put it down, in order to pour out the tea. *Navigation for Beginners.* I handed her the cup and saucer. "Was he interested in navigation?"

"I've no idea. But I was. I borrowed it out of his room. I don't think he even knew I'd borrowed it. He had a box with some things in—like a tuck box that boys take to public school—and one day when I went into his room the things were all on the chest of drawers, as if he was tidying. Anyway, he was out, and I borrowed the book—he wouldn't have minded; he was terribly easygoing—and I suppose I put it down in my room, and put something else on top, and just forgot it."

"Did you read it?" I said.

"No. Never got round to it. It was weeks ago."

I picked up the book and opened it. On the flyleaf someone had written "John Viking" in a firm legible signature in black felt-tip.

"I don't know," Louise said, anticipating my question, "whether that is Nicky's writing or not."

"Does Jenny know?"

"She hasn't seen this. She's staying with Toby in Yorkshire."

Jenny with Toby. Jenny with Ashe. For God's sake, I thought, what do you expect? She's gone, she's not yours, you're divorced. And I hadn't been alone, not entirely.

"You look very tired," Louise said doubtfully.

I was disconcerted. "Of course not." I turned the pages, letting them flick over from under my thumb. It was, as it promised to be, a book about navigation, sea and air, with line drawings and diagrams. Dead reckoning, sextants, magnetism, and drift. Nothing of any note except a single line of letters and figures, written with the same black ink, on the inside of the back cover.

$$\text{Lift} = 22 \cdot 024 \times \text{V} \times \text{P} \times \left(\frac{1}{\text{T1}} - \frac{1}{\text{T2}}\right)$$

I handed it over to Louise.

"Does this mean anything to you? Charles said you've a degree in mathematics."

She frowned at it faintly. "Nicky needed a calculator for two plus two."

He had done all right at two plus ten thousand, I thought.

"Um," she said. "Lift equals 22 · 024 times volume times pressure, times . . . I should think this is something to do with temperature change. Not my subject, really. This is physics."

"Something to do with navigation?" I asked.

She concentrated. I watched the way her face grew taut while she did the internal scan. A fast brain, I thought, under the pretty hair.

"It's funny," she said finally, "but I think it's just possibly something to do with how much you can lift with a gasbag."

"Airship?" I said, thinking.

"It depends what 22 · 024 is," she said. "That's a constant. Which means," she added, "it is special to whatever this equation is all about."

"I'm better at what's likely to win the three-thirty."

She looked at her watch. "You're three hours too late."

"It'll come round again tomorrow."

She relaxed into the armchair, handing back the book. "I don't suppose it will help," she said, "but you seemed to want anything of Nicky's."

"It might help a lot. You never know."

"But how?"

"It's John Viking's book. John Viking might know Nicky Ashe."

"But . . . you don't know John Viking."

"No," I said. "But he knows gasbags. And I know someone who knows gasbags. And I bet gasbags are a small world, like racing."

She looked at the heaps of letters, and then at the book. She said slowly, "I guess you'll find him, one way or another."

I looked away from her, and at nothing in particular.

"Jenny says you never give up."

I smiled faintly. "Her exact words?"

"No." I felt her amusement. "'Obstinate, selfish, and determined to get his own way.'"

"Not far off." I tapped the book. "Can I keep this?"

"Of course."

"Thanks."

We looked at each other as people do, especially if they're youngish and male and female, and sitting in a quiet flat at the end of an April day.

She read my expression and answered the unspoken thought. "Some other time," she said dryly.

"How long will you be staying with Jenny?"

"Would that matter to you?" she asked.

"Mm."

"She says you're as hard as flint. She says steel's a pushover beside you."

I thought of terror and misery and self-loathing. I shook my head.

"What I see," she said slowly, "is a man who looks ill being polite to an unwanted visitor."

"You're wanted," I said. "And I'm fine."

She stood up, however, and I also, after her.

"I hope," I said, "that you're fond of your aunt?"

"Devoted."

She gave me a cool, half-ironic smile in which there was also surprise.

"Goodbye . . . Sid."

"Goodbye, Louise."

When she'd gone I switched on a table light or two against the slow dusk, and poured a whisky, and looked at a pale bunch of sausages in the fridge and didn't cook them.

No one else would come, I thought. They had all in their way held off the shadows, particularly Louise. No one else real would come, but he would be with me, as he'd been in Paris . . . Trevor Deansgate. Inescapable. Reminding me inexorably of what I would rather forget.

After a while I stepped out of trousers and shirt and put on a short blue bathrobe, and took off the arm. It was one of the times when taking it off really hurt. It didn't seem to matter, after the rest.

I went back to the sitting room to do something about the clutter, but there was simply too much to bother with, so I stood looking at it, and held my weaker upper arm with my strong, whole, agile right hand, as I often did, for support, and I wondered which crippled one worse, amputation without or within.

Humiliation and rejection and helplessness and failure . . .

After all these years I would *not*, I thought wretchedly, I would damned well *not* be defeated by fear.

Chapter 9

Lucas Wainwright telephoned the next morning while I was stacking cups in the dishwasher.

"Any progress?" he asked, sounding very commanderish.

"I'm afraid," I said regretfully, "that I've lost all those notes. I'll have to do them again."

"For heaven's sake." He wasn't pleased. I didn't tell him that I'd lost the notes on account of being bashed on the head and dropping in the gutter the large brown envelope that contained them. "Come right away, then. Eddy won't be in until this afternoon."

Slowly, absentmindedly, I finished tidying up, while I thought about Lucas Wainwright, and what he could do for me, if he would. Then I sat at the table and wrote down what I wanted. Then I looked at what I'd written, and at my fingers holding the pen, and shivered. Then I folded the paper and put it in my pocket, and went to Portman Square, deciding not to give it to Lucas after all.

He had the files ready in his office, and I sat at the same table as before and recopied all I needed.

"You won't let it drag on much longer, will you, Sid?"

"Full attention," I said. "Starting tomorrow. I'll go to Kent tomorrow afternoon."

"Good." He stood up as I put the new notes into a fresh envelope and waited for me to go, not through impatience with me particularly, but because he was that sort of man. Brisk. One task finished, get on with the next, don't hang about.

I hesitated cravenly and found myself speaking before I had consciously decided whether to or not. "Commander. Do you remember that you said you might pay me for this job not with money but with help, if I should want it?"

I got a reasonable smile and a postponement of the goodbyes.

"Of course I remember. You haven't done the job yet. What help?"

"Er . . . it's nothing much. Very little." I took the paper out and handed it to him. Waited while he read the brief contents. Felt as if I had planted a land mine and would presently step on it.

"I don't see why not," he said. "If that's what you want. But are you on to something that we should know about?"

I gestured to the paper. "You'll know about it as soon as I do, if you do that." It wasn't a satisfactory answer, but he didn't press it. "The only thing I beg of you, though, is that you won't mention my name at all. Don't say it was my idea, not to *anyone*. I . . . er . . . you might get me killed, Commander, and I'm not being funny."

He looked from me to the paper and back again, and frowned. "This doesn't look like a killing matter, Sid."

"You never know what is until you're dead."

He smiled. "All right. I'll write the letter as from the Jockey Club, and I'll take you seriously about the death risk. Will that do?"

"It will indeed."

We shook hands, and I left his office carrying the brown envelope, and at the Portman Square entrance, going out, I met Eddy Keith coming in. We both paused, as one does. I hoped he couldn't see the dismay in my face at his early return, or guess that I was perhaps carrying the seeds of his downfall.

"Eddy," I said, smiling and feeling a traitor.

"Hello, Sid," he said cheerfully, twinkling at me from above rounded cheeks. "What are you doing here?" A good-natured, normal inquiry. No suspicions. No tremor.

"Looking for crumbs," I said.

He chuckled fatly. "From what I hear, it's us picking up yours. Have us all out of work, you will, soon."

"Not a chance."

"Don't step on our toes, Sid."

The smile was still there, the voice devoid of threat. The fuzzy hair, the big mustache, the big broad fleshy face, still exuded good will; but the arctic had briefly come and gone in his eyes, and I was in no doubt that I'd received a serious warning off.

"Never, Eddy," I said insincerely.

"See you, fella," he said, preparing to go indoors, nodding, smiling widely, and giving me the usual hearty buffet on the shoulder. "Take care."

"You too, Eddy," I said to his departing back; and under my breath, again, in a sort of sorrow, "You too."

I carried the notes safely back to the flat, and thought a bit, and telephoned to my man in gasbags.

He said hello and great to hear from you and how

about a jar sometime, and no, he had never heard of anyone called John Viking. I read out the equation and asked if it meant anything to him, and he laughed and said it sounded like a formula for taking a hot air balloon to the moon.

"Thanks very much," I said sarcastically.

"No, seriously, Sid. It's a calculation for maximum height. Try a balloonist. They're always after records . . . the highest, the farthest, that sort of thing."

I asked if he knew any balloonists, but he said sorry, no, he didn't, he was only into airships, and we disconnected with another vague resolution to meet somewhere, sometime, one of these days. Idly, and certain it was useless, I leafed through the telephone directory, and there, incredibly, the words stood out bold and clear: The Hot Air Balloon Company, offices in London, number provided.

I got through. A pleasant male voice at the other end said that of course he knew John Viking, everyone in ballooning knew John Viking, he was a madman of the first order.

Madman?

John Viking, the voice explained, took risks which no sensible balloonist would dream of. If I wanted to talk to him, the voice said, I would undoubtedly find him at the balloon race on Monday afternoon.

Where was the balloon race on Monday afternoon?

Horse show, balloon race, swings and roundabouts, you name it: all part of the May Day holiday junketings at Highalane Park in Wiltshire. John Viking would be there. Sure to be.

I thanked the voice for his help and rang off, reflecting that I had forgotten about the May Day holiday. National holidays had always been workdays for me, as for everyone in racing: providing the entertainment for the public's leisure. I tended not to notice them come and go.

Chico arrived with fish and chips for two in the sort of hygienic greaseproof wrappings that kept the steam in and made the chips go soggy.

"Did you know it's the May Day holiday on Monday?" I said.

"Running a judo tournament for the little bleeders, aren't I?"

He tipped the lunch onto two plates, and we ate it, mostly with fingers.

"You've come to life again, I see," he said.

"It's temporary."

"We'd better get some work done, then, while you're still with us."

"The syndicates," I said; and told him about the luckless Mason having been sent out on the same errand and having his brains kicked to destruction.

Chico shook salt on his chips. "Have to be careful then, won't we?"

"Start this afternoon?"

"Sure." He paused reflectively, licking his fingers. "We're not getting paid for this, didn't you say?"

"Not directly."

"Why don't we do these insurance inquiries, then? Nice quiet questions with a guaranteed fee."

"I promised Lucas Wainwright I'd do the syndicates first."

He shrugged. "You're the boss. But that makes three in a row, counting your wife and Rosemary getting her cash back, that we've worked on for nothing."

"We'll make up for it later."

"You are going on, then?"

I didn't answer at once. Apart from not knowing whether I wanted to, I didn't know if I could. Over the past months Chico and I had tended to get somewhat battered by bully boys trying to stop us in our tracks. We didn't have the protection of being either in the Racecourse Security Service or the police. No one to defend us but ourselves. We had looked upon the bruises as part of the job, as racing falls had been to me and bad judo falls to Chico. What if Trevor Deansgate had changed all that . . . not just for one terrible week, but for much longer: for always?

"Sid," Chico said sharply. "Come back."

I swallowed. "Well . . . er . . . we'll do the syndicates. Then we'll see." Then I'll know, I thought. I'll know inside me, one way or the other. If I couldn't walk into tigers' cages any more, we were done. One of us wasn't enough: it had to be both.

If I couldn't . . . I'd as soon be dead.

The first syndicate on Lucas's list had been formed by eight people, of whom three were registered owners, headed by Philip Friarly. Registered owners were those acceptable to the racing authorities, owners who paid their dues and kept the rules, were no trouble to anybody, and represented the source and mainspring of the whole industry.

Syndicates were a way of involving more people directly in racing, which was good for the sport, and dividing the training costs into smaller fractions, which was good for the owners. There were syndicates of millionaires, coal miners, groups of rock guitarists, the clientele of pubs. Anyone from Auntie Flo to the undertaker could join a syndicate, and all Eddy Keith should have done was check that all those on the list were who they said they were.

"It's not the registered owners we're looking at," I said. "It's all the others."

We were driving through Kent on our way to Tunbridge Wells. Ultrarespectable place, Tunbridge Wells. Resort of retired colonels and ladies who played bridge. Low on the national crime league. Hometown, all the same, of a certain Peter Rammileese, who was, so Lucas Wainwright's informant had said, in fact the instigating member of all four of the doubtful syndicates, although his own name nowhere appeared.

"Mason," I said, conversationally, "was attacked and left for dead in the streets of Tunbridge Wells."

"Now he tells me."

"Chico," I said, "do you want to turn back?"

"You got a premonition or something?"

After a pause, I said, "No," and drove a shade too fast round a sharpish bend.

"Look, Sid," he said. "We don't have to go to Tunbridge Wells. We're on a hiding to nothing, with this lark."

"What do you think, then?"

He was silent.

"We do have to go," I said.

"Yeah."

"So we have to work out what it was that Mason asked, and not ask it."

"This Rammileese," Chico said. "What's he like?"

"I haven't met him myself, but I've heard of him. He's a farmer who's made a packet out of crooked dealings in horses. The Jockey Club won't have him as a registered owner, and most racecourses don't let him through the gates. He'll try to bribe anyone from the senior steward to the scrubbers, and where he can't bribe, he threatens."

"Oh, jolly."

"Two jockeys and a trainer, not so long ago, lost their licenses for taking his bribes. One of the jockeys got the sack from his stable and he's so broke he's hanging around outside the racecourse gates begging for handouts."

"Is that the one I saw you talking to a while ago?"

"That's right."

"And how much did you give him?"

"Never you mind."

"You're a pushover, Sid."

"A case of 'but for the grace of God,'" I said.

"Oh, sure. I could just see you taking bribes from a crooked horse dealer. Most likely thing on earth."

"Anyway," I said, "what we're trying to find out is not whether Peter Rammileese is manipulating four race horses, which he is, but whether Eddy Keith knows it and is keeping quiet."

"Right." We sped deeper into rural Kent, and then he said, "You know why we've had such good results, on the whole, since we've been together on this job?"

"Why, then?"

"It's because all the villains know you. I mean, they know you by sight, most of them. So when they see you poking around on their patch, they get the heebies and start doing silly things like setting the heavies on us, and then we see them loud and clear, and what they're up to, which we wouldn't have done if they'd sat tight."

I sighed and said, "I guess so," and thought about Trevor Deansgate; thought and tried not to. Without any hands one couldn't drive a car . . . Just don't think about it, I told myself. Just keep your mind off it; it's a one-way trip into jellyfish.

I swung round another corner too fast and collected a sideways look from Chico, but no comment.

"Look at the map," I said. "Do something useful."

We found the house of Peter Rammileese without much trouble, and pulled into the yard of a small farm that looked as if the outskirts of Tunbridge Wells had rolled round it like a sea, leaving it isolated and incongruous. There was a large white farmhouse, three stories high, and a modern wooden stable block, and a long, extra-large barn. Nothing significantly prosperous about the place, but no nettles, either.

No one around. I put the brake on as we rolled to a stop, and we got out of the car.

"Front door?" Chico said.

"Back door, for farms."

We had taken only five or six steps in that direction, however, when a small boy ran into the yard from a doorway in the barn and came over to us breathlessly.

"Did you bring the ambulance?"

His eyes looked past me, to my car, and his face puckered into agitation and disappointment. He was about seven, dressed in jodhpurs and T-shirt, and he had been crying.

"What's the matter?" I said.

"I rang for the ambulance . . . a long time ago."

"We might help," I said.

"It's Mum," he said. "She's lying in there, and she won't wake up."

"Come on; you show us."

He was a sturdy little boy, brown-haired and brown-eyed and very frightened. He ran ahead toward the barn, and we followed without wasting time. Once through the door we could see that it wasn't an ordinary barn, but an indoor riding school, a totally enclosed area of about twenty meters wide by thirty-five long, lit by windows in the roof. The floor, wall to wall, was covered with a thick layer of tan-colored wood chips, springy and quiet for horses to work on.

There were a pony and a horse careering about; and, in danger from their hoofs, a crumpled female figure lying on the ground.

Chico and I went over to her, fast. She was young, on

her side, face half downward; unconscious, but not, I thought, deeply. Her breathing was shallow and her skin had whitened in a mottled fashion under her make-up, but the pulse in her wrist was strong and regular. The crash helmet which hadn't saved her lay several feet away on the floor.

"Go and ring again," I said to Chico.

"Shouldn't we move her?"

"No . . . in case she's broken anything. You can do a lot of damage moving people too much when they're unconscious."

"You should know." He turned away and ran off toward the house.

"Is she all right?" the boy said anxiously. "Bingo started bucking and she fell off, and I think he kicked her head."

"Bingo is the horse?"

"His saddle slipped," he said; and Bingo, with the saddle down under his belly, was still bucking and kicking like a rodeo.

"What's your name?" I said.

"Mark."

"Well, Mark, as far as I can see, your mum is going to be all right, and you're a brave little boy."

"I'm six," he said, as if that wasn't so little.

The worst of the fright had died out of his eyes, now that he had help. I knelt on the ground beside his mother and smoothed the brown hair away from her forehead. She made a small moaning sound, and her eyelids fluttered. She was perceptibly nearer the surface, even in the short time we'd been there.

"I thought she was dying," the boy said. "We had a rabbit a little time ago . . . He panted and shut his eyes, and we couldn't wake him up again, and he died."

"Your mum will wake up again."

"Are you sure?"

"Yes, Mark, I'm sure."

He seemed deeply reassured, and told me readily that the pony was called Sooty, and was his own, and that his dad was away until tomorrow morning, and there was only his mum there, and him, and she'd been schooling Bingo because she was selling him to a girl for show jumping.

Chico came back and said the ambulance was on its way. The boy, cheering up enormously, said we ought to catch the horses because they were cantering about and the reins were all loose, and if the saddles and bridles got broken his dad would be bloody angry.

Both Chico and I laughed at the adult words, seriously spoken. While he and Mark stood guard over the patient, I caught the horses one by one, with the aid of a few horse nuts that Mark produced from his pockets, and tied their reins to tethering rings in the walls. Bingo, once the agitating girths were undone and saddle safely off, stood quietly enough, and Mark darted briefly away from his mother to give his own pony some brisk encouraging slaps and some more horse nuts.

Chico said the emergency service had indeed had a call from a child fifteen minutes earlier, but he'd hung up before they could ask him where he lived.

"Don't tell him," I said.

"You're a softie."

"He's a brave little kid."

"Not bad for a little bleeder. While you were catching the bucking bronco, he told me his dad gets bloody angry pretty often." He looked down at the still unconscious girl. "You really reckon she's O.K., do you?"

"She'll come out of it. It's a matter of waiting."

The ambulance came in due course, but Mark's anxiety reappeared, strongly, when the men loaded his mother into the van and prepared to depart. He wanted to go with her, and the men wouldn't take him on his own. She was stirring and mumbling, and it distressed him.

I said to Chico, "Drive him to the hospital . . . follow the ambulance. He needs to see her wide awake and speaking to him. I'll take a look round in the house. His dad's away until tomorrow."

"Convenient," he said sardonically. He collected Mark into the Scimitar and drove away down the road, and through the rear window I could see their heads talking to each other.

I went through the open back door with the confidence of the invited. Nothing difficult about entering a tiger's cage while the tiger was out.

It was an old house filled with brash new opulent furnishings, which I found overpowering. Lush loud carpets, huge stereo equipment, a lamp standard of a golden nymph, and deep armchairs covered in black and khaki zigzags. Sitting and dining rooms shining and tidy, with no sign that a small boy lived there. Kitchen uncluttered, hygienic surfaces wiped clean. Study . . .

The positively aggressive tidiness of the study made me pause and consider. No horse trader that I'd ever come across had kept his books and papers in such neat rectangular stacks; and the ledgers themselves, when I opened them, contained up-to-the-minute entries.

I looked into drawers and filing cabinets, being extremely careful to leave everything squared up after me, but there was nothing there except the outward show of honesty. Not a single drawer or cupboard was locked. It was almost, I thought with cynicism, as if the whole thing were stage dressing, orchestrated to confound any invasion of tax snoopers. The real records, if he kept any, were probably somewhere outside, in a biscuit tin, in a hole in the ground.

I went upstairs. Mark's room was unmistakable, but all the toys were in boxes, and all the clothes in drawers. There were three unoccupied bedrooms with the outlines of folded blankets showing under covers, and a suite of bedroom, dressing room, and bathroom furnished with the same expense and tidiness as downstairs.

An oval dark red bath with taps like gilt dolphins. A huge bed with a bright brocade cover clashing with wall-to-wall jazz on the floor. No clutter on the curvaceous cream-and-gold dressing table, no brushes on any surface in the dressing room.

Mark's mum's clothes were fur and glitter and breeches and jackets. Mark's dad's clothes, thornproof tweeds, vicuña overcoat, a dozen or more suits, none of them handmade, all seemingly bought because they were expensive. Handfuls of illicit cash, I thought, and nothing much to do with it. Peter Rammileese, it seemed, was crooked by nature and not by necessity.

The same incredible tidiness extended through every drawer and every shelf, and even into the soiled-linen basket, where a pair of pajamas were neatly folded.

I went through the pockets of his suits, but he had left nothing at all in them. There were no pieces of paper of any sort anywhere in the dressing room.

Frustrated, I went up to the third floor, where there were six rooms, one containing a variety of empty suitcases, and the others, nothing at all.

No one, I thought on the way down again, lived so excessively carefully if he had nothing to hide; which was scarcely evidence to offer in court. The present life of the Rammileese family was an expensive vacuum, and of the past there was no sign at all. No souvenirs, no old books, not even any photographs, except a recent one of Mark on his pony, taken outside in the yard.

I was looking round the outbuildings when Chico came back. There were no animals except seven horses in the stable and the two in the covered school. No sign of farming in progress. No rosettes in the tack room, just a lot more tidiness and the smell of saddle soap. I went out to meet Chico and ask what he had done with Mark.

"The nurses are stuffing him with jam butties and trying to ring his dad. Mum is awake and talking. How did you get on? Do you want to drive?"

"No, you drive." I sat beside him. "That house is the most suspicious case of no history I've ever seen."

"Like that, eh?"

"Mm. And not a chance of finding any link with Eddy Keith."

"Wasted journey, then," he said.

"Lucky for Mark."

"Yeah. Good little bleeder, that. Told me he's going to be a furniture moving man when he grows up." Chico looked across at me and grinned. "Seems he's moved house three times that he can remember."

Chapter 10

Chico and I spent most of Saturday separately traipsing around all the London addresses on the *M* list of wax names, and met at six o'clock, footsore and thirsty, at a pub we both knew in Fulham.

"We never ought to have done it on a Saturday, and a holiday weekend at that," Chico said.

"No," I agreed.

Chico watched the beer sliding mouth-wateringly into the glass. "More than half of them were out."

"Mine too. Nearly all."

"And the ones that were in were watching the racing or the wrestling or groping their girlfriends, and didn't want to know."

We carried his beer and my whisky over to a small table, drank deeply, and compared notes. Chico had finally pinned down four people, and I only two, but the results were there, all the same.

All six, whatever other mailing lists they had confessed to, had been in regular happy receipt of *Antiques for All.*

"That's it, then," Chico said. "Conclusive." He leaned back against the wall, luxuriously relaxing. "We can't do any more until Tuesday. Everything's shut."

"Are you busy tomorrow?"

"Have a heart. The girl in Wembley." He looked at his watch and swallowed the rest of the beer. "And so long, Sid, boy, or I'll be late. She doesn't like me sweaty."

He grinned and departed, and I more slowly finished my drink and went home.

Wandered about. Changed the batteries. Ate some cornflakes. Got out the form books and looked up the syndicated horses. Highly variable form: races lost at short odds and won at long. All the signs of steady and expert fixing. I yawned. It went on all the time.

I puttered some more, restlessly, sorely missing the peace that usually filled me in that place when I was alone. Undressed, put on a bathrobe, pulled off the arm. Tried to watch the television; couldn't concentrate. Switched it off.

I usually pulled the arm off after I'd put the bathrobe on, because that way I didn't have to look at the bit of me that remained below the left elbow. I could come to terms with the fact of it but still not really the sight, though it was neat enough and not horrific, as the messed-up hand had been. I daresay it was senseless to be faintly repelled, but I was. I hated anyone except the limb man to see it; even Chico. I was ashamed of it, and that too was illogical. People without handicaps never understood that ashamed feeling, nor had I, until the day soon after the original injury when I'd blushed crimson because I'd had to ask someone to cut up my food. There had been many times after that when I'd gone hungry rather than ask. Not having to ask, ever, since I'd had the electronic hand, had been a psychological release of soul-saving proportions.

The new hand had meant, too, a return to full normal human status. No one treated me as an idiot, or with the pity which in the past had made me cringe. No one made allowances any more, or got themselves tongue-tied with trying not to say the wrong thing. The days of the useless deformity seemed in retrospect an unbearable nightmare. I was often quite grateful to the villain who had set me free.

With one hand, I was a self-sufficient man.

Without any . . .

Oh, God, I thought. Don't think about it. "There is nothing good or bad, but thinking makes it so." Hamlet, however, didn't have the same problems.

I got through the night, and the next morning, and the afternoon, but at around six I gave up and got in the car, and drove to Aynsford.

If Jenny was there, I thought, easing up the back drive and stopping quietly in the yard outside the kitchen, I would just turn right around and go back to London, and at least the driving would have occupied the time. But no one seemed to be about, and I walked into the house from the side door, which had a long passage into the hall.

Charles was in the small sitting room that he called the wardroom, sitting alone, sorting out his much-loved collection of fly hooks for fishing.

He looked up. No surprise. No effusive welcome. No fuss. Yet I'd never gone there before without invitation.

"Hello," he said.

"Hello."

I stood there, and he looked at me, and waited.

"I wanted some company," I said.

He squinted at a dry fly. "Did you bring an overnight bag?"

I nodded.

He pointed to the drinks tray. "Help yourself. And pour me a pink gin, will you? Ice in the kitchen."

I fetched him his drink, and my own, and sat in an armchair.

"Come to tell me?" he said.

"No."

He smiled. "Supper, then? And chess."

We ate, and played two games. He won the first, easily, and told me to pay attention. The second, after an hour and a half, was a draw. "That's better," he said.

The peace I hadn't been able to find on my own came slowly back with Charles, even though I knew it had more to do with the ease I felt with him personally, and the timelessness of his vast old house, than with a real resolution of the destruction within. In any case, for the first time in ten days, I slept soundly for hours.

At breakfast we discussed the day ahead. He himself was going to the steeplechase meeting at Towcester, forty-five minutes northward, to act as a steward, an honorary job that he enjoyed. I told him about John Viking and the balloon race, and also about the visits to the *M* people, and *Antiques for All,* and he smiled with his own familiar mixture of satisfaction and amusement, as if I were some creation of his that was coming up to expectations. It was he who had originally driven me to becoming an investigator. Whenever I got anything right, he took the credit for it to himself.

"Did Mrs. Cross tell you about the telephone call?" he said, buttering toast. Mrs. Cross was his housekeeper, quiet, effective, and kind.

"What telephone call?"

"Someone rang here about seven this morning, asking if you were here. Mrs. Cross said you were asleep and could she take a message, but whoever it was said he would ring later."

"Was it Chico? He might guess I'd come here, if he couldn't get me in the flat."

"Mrs. Cross said he didn't give a name."

I shrugged and reached for the coffeepot. "It can't have been urgent, or he'd have told her to wake me up."

Charles smiled. "Mrs. Cross sleeps in curlers and face cream. She'd never have let you see her at seven o'clock in the morning, short of an earthquake. She thinks you're a lovely young man. She tells me so, every time you come."

"For God's sake."

"Will you be back here tonight?" he said.

"I don't know yet."

He folded his napkin, looking down at it. "I'm glad that you came yesterday."

I looked at him. "Yeah," I said. "Well, you want me to say it, so I'll say it. And I mean it." I paused a fraction, searching for the simplest words that would tell him what I felt for him. Found some. Said them. "This is my home."

He looked up quickly, and I smiled twistedly, mocking myself, mocking him, mocking the whole damned world.

Highalane Park was a stately home uneasily coming to terms with the plastic age. The house itself opened to the public like an agitated virgin only half a dozen times a year, but the parkland was always for rent for game fairs and circuses, and things like the May Day jamboree.

They had made little enough effort on the roadside to attract the passing crowd. No bunting, no razzmatazz, no posters with print large enough to read at ten paces; everything slightly coy and apologetic. Considering all that, the numbers pouring onto the showground were impressive. I paid at the gate in my turn and bumped over some grass to park the car obediently in a row in the roped-off parking area. Other cars followed, neatly alongside.

There were a few people on horses cantering busily about in haphazard directions, but the roundabouts on the fairground to one side were silent and motionless, and there was no sight of any balloons.

I stood up out of the car and locked the door, and thought that one-thirty was probably too early for much in the way of action.

One can be so wrong.

A voice behind me said, "Is this the man?"

I turned and found two people advancing into the small space between my car and the one next to it: a man I didn't know, and a little boy, whom I did.

"Yes," the boy said, pleased. "Hello."

"Hello, Mark," I said. "How's your mum?"

"I told Dad about you coming." He looked up at the man beside him.

"Did you, now." I thought his being at Highalane was only an extraordinary coincidence, but it wasn't.

"He described you," the man said. "That hand, and the way you could handle horses . . . I knew who he meant, right enough." His face and voice were hard and wary, with a quality that I by now recognized on sight: guilty knowledge faced by trouble. "I don't take kindly to you poking your nose around my place."

"You were out," I said mildly.

"Aye, I was out. And this nipper here, he left you there all alone."

He was about forty, a wiry, watchful fox of a man, with evil intentions stamped clearly all over him.

"I knew your car too," Mark said proudly. "Dad says I'm clever."

"Kids are observant," his father said, with nasty relish.

"We waited for you to come out of the big house," Mark said. "And then we followed you all the way here." He beamed, inviting me to enjoy the game. "This is our car, next to yours." He patted the maroon Daimler alongside.

The telephone call, I thought fleetingly. Not Chico. Peter Rammileese, checking around.

"Dad says," Mark chatted on happily, "that he'll take me to see those roundabouts while our friends take you for a ride in our car."

His father looked down at him sharply, not having expected so much repeated truth, but Mark, oblivious, was looking at a point behind my back.

I glanced around. Between the Scimitar and the Daimler stood two more people. Large unsmiling men from a muscular brotherhood. Brass knuckles and toecaps.

"Get into the car," Rammileese said, nodding to his, not to mine. "Rear door."

Oh, sure, I thought. Did he think I was mad? I stooped slightly as if to obey and then instead of opening the door scooped Mark up bodily, with my right arm, and ran.

Rammileese turned with a shout. Mark's face, next to mine, was astonished but laughing. I ran about twenty paces with him, and set him down in the path of his furiously advancing father, and then kept on going, away from the cars and toward the crowds in the center part of the showground.

Bloody hell, I thought. Chico was right. These days we had only to twitch an eyelid for them to wheel out the heavies. It was getting too much.

It had been the sort of ambush that might have

worked if Mark hadn't been there: one kidney punch and into the car before I'd got my breath. But they'd needed Mark, I supposed, to identify me, because although they knew me by name, they hadn't by sight. They weren't going to catch me on the open show-ground, that was for sure, and when I went back to my car it would be with a load of protectors. Maybe, I thought hopefully, they would see it was useless, and just go away.

I reached the outskirts of the show-jumping arena, and looked back from over the head of a small girl licking an ice cream cone. No one had called off the heavies. They were still doggedly in pursuit. I decided not to see what would happen if I simply stood my ground and requested the assorted families round about to save me from being frog-marched to oblivion and waking with my head kicked in in the streets of Tunbridge Wells. The assorted families, with dogs and grannies and prams and picnics, were more likely to dither with their mouths open and wonder, once it was over, what it had all been about.

I went on, deeper in to the show, circling the ring, bumping into children as I looked over my shoulder, and seeing the two men always behind me.

The arena itself was on my left, with show jumping in progress inside, and ringside cars encircling it outside. Behind the cars there was the broad grass walkway along which I was going, and on my right, the outer ring of the stalls one always gets at horse shows. Tented shops selling saddlery, riding clothes, pictures, toys, hot dogs, fruit, more saddles, hardware, tweeds, sheepskin slippers . . . an endless circle of small traders.

Among the tents, the vans: ice cream vans, riding associations, trailers, a display of crafts, a fortuneteller, a charity jumble stall, a mobile cinema showing films of sheep dogs, a dropsided caravan spilling out kitchen equipment in orange and yellow and green. Crowds along the fronts of all of them and no depth of shelter inside.

"Do you know where the balloons are?" I asked someone, and he pointed, and it was to a stall selling small gas balloons of brilliant colors, children buying them and tying them to their wrists.

Not those, I thought. Surely not those. I didn't stop to explain, but asked again, farther on.

"The balloon race? In the next field, I think, but it isn't time yet."

"Thanks," I said. The posters had announced a three o'clock start, but I'd have to talk to John Viking well before that, while he was willing to listen.

What was a balloon race? I wondered. Surely all balloons went at the same speed, the speed of the wind.

My trackers wouldn't give up. They weren't running, nor was I. They just followed me steadily, as if locked onto a target by a radio beam; minds taking literally an order to stick to my heels. I'd have to get lost, I thought, and stay lost until after I'd found John Viking, and maybe then I'd go in search of helpful defenses like show secretaries and first aid ladies, and the single policeman out on the road directing the traffic.

I was on the far side of the arena by that time, crossing the collecting ring area, with children on ponies buzzing around like bees, looking strained as they went in to jump, and tearful or triumphant as they came out.

Past then, past the commentators' box—"Jane Smith had a clear round; the next to jump is Robin Daly on Traddles"—past the little private grandstand for the organizers and bigwigs—rows of empty folding seats—past an open-sided refreshment tent, full, and so back to the stalls.

I did a bit of dodging in and out of those, and round the backs, ducking under guy ropes and round dumps of cardboard boxes. From the inside depths of a stall hung thickly outside with riding jackets I watched the two of them go past, hurrying, looking about them, distinctly anxious.

They weren't like the two Trevor Deansgate had sent, I thought. His had been clumsier, smaller, and less professional. These two looked as if this sort of work was their daily bread; and for all the comparative safety of the showground, where as a last resort I could get into the arena itself and scream for help, there was something daunting about them. Rent-a-thugs usually came at so much per hour. These two looked salaried, if not actually on the board.

I left the riding jackets and dodged into the film about sheep dogs, which I daresay would have been riveting but for the shepherding going on outside, with me as the sheep.

I looked at my watch. After two o'clock. Too much time was passing. I had to try another sortie outside and find my way to the balloons.

I couldn't see them. I slithered among the crowd asking for directions.

"Up at the end, mate," a decisive man told me, pointing. "Past the hot dogs, turn right, there's a gate in the fence. You can't miss it."

I nodded my thanks and turned to go that way, and saw one of my trackers coming toward me, searching the stalls with his eyes and looking worried.

In a second he would see me. . . . I looked around in a hurry and found I was outside the caravan of the fortuneteller. There was a curtain of plastic streamers, black and white, over the open doorway, and behind that a shadowy figure. I took four quick strides, brushed through the plastic strips, and stepped up into the van.

It was quieter inside, and darker, with daylight filtering dimly through lace-hung windows. A Victorian sort of décor: mock oil lamps and chenille tablecloths. Outside, the tracker went past, giving the fortuneteller no more than a flickering glance. His attention lay ahead. He hadn't seen me come in.

The fortuneteller, however, had, and to her I represented business.

"Do you want your whole life, dear, the past and everything or just the future?"

"Er . . ." I said. "I don't really know. How long does it take?"

"A quarter of an hour, dear, for the whole thing."

"Let's just have the future."

I looked out the window. A part of my future was searching among the ringside cars, asking questions and getting a lot of shaken heads.

"Sit on the sofa beside me—here, dear—and give me your left hand."

"It'll have to be the right," I said absently.

"No, dear." Her voice was quite sharp. "Always the left."

Amused, I sat down and gave her the left. She felt it, and looked at it, and raised her eyes to mine. She was short and plump, dark-haired, middle-aged, and in no way remarkable.

"Well, dear," she said after a pause, "it will have to be the right, though I'm not used to it, and we may not get such good results."

"I'll risk it," I said; so we changed places on the sofa, and she held my right hand firmly in her two warm ones, and I watched the tracker move along the row of cars.

"You have suffered," she said.

As she knew about my left hand, I didn't think much of that for a guess, and she seemed to sense it. She coughed apologetically.

"Do you mind if I use a crystal?" she said.

"Go ahead."

I had vague visions of her peering into a large ball on a table, but she took a small one, the size of a tennis ball, and put it on the palm of my hand.

"You are a kind person," she said. "Gentle. People like you. People smile at you wherever you go."

Outside, twenty yards away, the two heavies had met to consult. Not a smile, there, of any sort.

"You are respected by everyone."

Regulation stuff, designed to please the customers.

Chico should hear it, I thought. Gentle, kind, respected . . . He'd laugh his head off.

She said doubtfully, "I see a great many people, cheering and clapping. Shouting loudly, cheering you . . . Does that mean anything to you, dear?"

I slowly turned my head. Her dark eyes watched me calmly.

"That's the past," I said.

"It's recent," she said. "It's still there."

I didn't believe it. I didn't believe in fortunetellers. I wondered if she had seen me before, on a racecourse or talking on television. She must have.

She bent her head again over the crystal, which she held on my hand, moving the glass gently over my skin.

"You have good health. You have vigor. You have great physical stamina. . . . There is much to endure."

Her voice broke off, and she raised her head a little, frowning. I had a strong impression that what she had said had surprised her.

After a pause, she said, "I can't tell you any more."

"Why not?"

"I'm not used to the right hand."

"Tell me what you see," I said.

She shook her head slightly and raised the calm dark eyes.

"You will live a long time."

I glanced out through the plastic curtain. The trackers had moved off out of sight.

"How much do I owe you?" I asked. She told me, and I paid her, and went quietly over to the doorway.

"Take care, dear," she said. "Be careful."

I looked back. Her face was still calm, but her voice had been urgent. I didn't want to believe in the conviction that looked out of her eyes. She might have felt the disturbance of my present problem with the trackers, but no more than that. I pushed the curtain gently aside and stepped from the dim world of hovering horrors into the bright May sunlight, where they might in truth lie in wait.

Chapter 11

There was no longer any need to ask where the balloons were. No one could miss them. They were beginning to rise like gaudy monstrous mushrooms, humped on the ground, spread all over an enormous area of grassland beyond the actual showground. I had thought vaguely that there would be two or three balloons, or at most six, but there must have been twenty.

Among a whole stream of people going the same way, I went down to the gate and through into the far field, and realized that I had absolutely underestimated the task of finding John Viking.

There was a rope, for a start, and marshals telling the crowd to stand behind it. I ducked those obstacles at least, but found myself in a forest of half-inflated balloons, which billowed immensely all around and cut off any length of sight.

The first clump of people I came to were busy with a pink-and-purple monster into whose mouth they were blowing air by means of a large engine-driven fan. The balloon was attached by four fine nylon ropes to a basket, which lay on its side, with a young man in a red crash helmet peering anxiously into its depths.

"Excuse me," I said to a girl on the edge of the group. "Do you know where I can find John Viking?"

"Sorry."

The red crash helmet raised itself to reveal a pair of very blue eyes. "He's here somewhere," he said politely. "Flies a Stormcloud balloon. Now would you mind getting the hell out. We're busy."

I walked along the edge of things, trying to keep out of their way. Balloon races, it seemed, were a serious business and no occasion for light laughter and social chat. The intent faces leaned over ropes and equipment, testing, checking, worriedly frowning. No balloons looked much like stormclouds. I risked another question.

"John Viking? That bloody idiot. Yes, he's here. Flies a Stormcloud." He turned away, busy and anxious.

"What color is it?" I said.

"Yellow and green. Look . . . go away, will you?"

There were balloons advertising whisky and marmalade and towns, and even insurance companies. Balloons in brilliant primary colors and pink-and-white pastels, balloons in the sunshine rising from the green grass in glorious jumbled rainbows. On an ordinary day, a scene of delight, but to me, trying to get round them to ask fruitlessly at the next clump gathered anxiously by its basket, a frustrating silky maze.

I circled a soft billowing black-and-white monster and went deeper into the center. As if at a signal, there arose in a chorus from all around a series of deep-throated roars, caused by flames suddenly spurting from the large burners which were supported on frames above the baskets. The flames roared into the open mouths of the half-inflated balloons, heating and expanding the air already there and driving in more. The gleaming envelopes swelled and surged with quickening life, growing from mushrooms to toadstools, the tops rising slowly and magnificently toward the hazy blue sky.

"John Viking? Somewhere over there." A girl swung her arm vaguely. "But he'll be as busy as we are."

As the balloons filled, they began to heave off the ground and sway in great floating masses, bumping into each other, still billowing, still not full enough to live with the birds. Under each balloon the flames roared, scarlet and lusty, with the little clusters of helpers clinging to the baskets to prevent them from escaping too soon.

With the balloons off the ground, I saw a yellow-and-green one quite easily: yellow and green in segments, like a grapefruit with a wide green band at the bottom. There was one man already in the basket, with about three people holding it down, and he, unlike everyone else in sight, wore not a crash helmet but a blue denim cap.

I ran in his direction, and even as I ran there was the sound of a starter's pistol. All around me the baskets were released, and began dragging and bumping over the ground; and a great cheer went up from the watching crowd.

I reached the bunch of people I was aiming for and put my hand on the basket.

"John Viking?"

No one listened. They were deep in a quarrel. A girl in a crash helmet, ski jacket, jeans, and boots stood on the ground, with the two helpers beside her looking glum and embarrassed.

"I'm not coming. You're a bloody madman."

"Get in, get in, dammit. The race has started."

He was very tall, very thin, very agitated.

"I'm not coming."

"You must." He made a grab at her and held her wrist in a sinewy grip. It looked almost as if he were going to haul her wholesale into the basket, and she certainly believed it. She tugged and panted and screamed at him. "Let go, John. Let go. I'm not coming."

"Are you John Viking?" I said loudly.

He swung his head and kept hold of the girl.

"Yes, I am, what do you want? I'm starting this race as soon as my passenger gets in."

"I'm not *going*," she screamed.

I looked around. The other baskets were mostly airborne, sweeping gently across the area a foot or two above the surface, and rising in a smooth, glorious crowd. Every basket, I saw, carried two people.

"If you want a passenger," I said, "I'll come."

He let go of the girl and looked me up and down.

"How much do you weigh?" And then, impatiently as he saw the other balloons getting a head start, "Oh, all right, get in. Get in."

I gripped hold of a stay, and jumped, and wriggled, and ended standing inside a rather small hamper under a very large cloud of balloon.

"Leave go," commanded the captain of the ship, and the helpers somewhat helplessly obeyed.

The basket momentarily stayed exactly where it was. Then John Viking reached above his head and flipped a lever which operated the burners, and there at close quarters, right above our heads, was the flame and the ear-filling roar.

The girl's face was still on a level with mine. "He's mad," she yelled. "And you're crazy."

The basket moved away, bumped, and rose quite

suddenly to a height of six feet. The girl ran after it and delivered a parting encouragement. "And you haven't got a crash helmet."

What I did have, though, was a marvelous escape route from two purposeful thugs, and a crash helmet at that moment seemed superfluous, particularly as my companion hadn't one, either.

John Viking was staring about him in the remnants of fury, muttering under his breath, and operating the burner almost nonstop. His was the last balloon away. I looked down to where the applauding holiday crowd were watching the mass departure, and a small boy darted suddenly from under the restraining rope and ran into the now empty starting area, shouting and pointing. Pointing at John Viking's balloon, pointing excitedly at me.

My pal Mark, with his bright little eyes and his truthful tongue. My pal Mark, whom I'd have liked to strangle.

John Viking started cursing. I switched my attention from ground to air and saw that the reason for the resounding and imaginative obscenities floating to heaven was a belt of trees lying ahead which might prevent our going in the same direction. One balloon already lay in a tangle on the takeoff side, and another, scarlet and purple, seemed set on a collision course.

John Viking yelled at me over the continuing roar of the burner: "Hold on bloody tight with both hands. If the basket hits the tops of the trees, we don't want to be spilled right out."

The trees looked sixty feet high and a formidable obstacle, but most of the balloons had cleared them easily and were drifting away skyward, great bright pear-shaped fantasies hanging on the wind.

John Viking's basket closed with a rush toward the

treetops, with the burner roaring over our heads like a demented dragon. The lift it should have provided seemed totally lacking.

"Turbulence," John Viking shrieked. "Bloody wind turbulence. Hold on. It's a long way down."

Frightfully jolly, I thought, being tipped out of a hamper sixty feet from the ground without a crash helmet. I grinned at him, and he caught the expression and looked startled.

The basket hit the treetops and tipped on its side, tumbling me from the vertical to the horizontal with no trouble at all. I grabbed right-handed at whatever I could to stop myself from falling right out, and I felt as much as saw that the majestically swelling envelope above us was carrying on with its journey regardless. It tugged the baskct after it, crashing and bumping through the tops of the trees, flinging me about like a rag doll with at times most of my body hanging out in space. My host, made of sterner stuff, had one arm clamped like a vise round one of the metal struts that supported the burner, and the other twined into a black rubber strap. His legs were braced against the side of the basket, which was now the floor, and he changed his footholds as necessary, at one point planting one foot firmly on my stomach.

With a last sickening jolt and wrench, the basket tore itself free, and we swung to and fro under the wobbling balloon like a pendulum. I was by this maneuver wedged into a disorganized heap in the bottom of the basket, but John Viking still stood rather splendidly on his feet.

There really wasn't much room, I thought, disentangling myself and straightening upward. The basket, still swaying and shaking, was only four feet square, and reached no higher than one's waist. Along two opposite sides stood eight gas cylinders, four each side, fastened to the wickerwork with rubber straps. The oblong space left was big enough for two men to stand in, but not overgenerous even for that: about two feet by two feet per person.

John Viking gave the burner a rest at last, and into the sudden silence said forcefully, "Why the hell didn't you hold on like I told you to? Don't you know you damned nearly fell out and got me into trouble?"

"Sorry," I said, amused. "Is it usual to go on burning when you're stuck on a tree?"

"It got us clear, didn't it?" he demanded.

"It sure did."

"Don't complain, then. I didn't ask you to come."

He was of about my own age; perhaps a year or two younger. His face under his blue denim yachting cap was craggy, with a bone structure that might one day give him distinction, and his blue eyes shone with the brilliance of the true fanatic. John Viking the madman, I thought, and warmed to him.

"Check round the outsides, will you?" he said. "See if anything's come adrift."

It seemed he meant the outside of the basket, as he was himself looking outward, over the edge. I discovered that on my side, too, there were bundles on the outside of the basket, either strapped to it tight, or swinging on ropes.

One short rope, attached to the basket, had nothing on the end of it. I pulled it up and showed it to him.

"Damnation," he said explosively. "Lost in the trees, I suppose. Plastic water container. Hope you're not thirsty." He stretched up and gave the burner another long burst, and I listened in my mind to the echo of his Etonian drawl and totally understood why he was as he was.

"Do you have to finish first to win a balloon race?" I said.

He looked surprised. "Not this one. This is a two-and-a-half-hour race. The one who gets farthest in that time is the winner." He frowned. "Haven't you ever been in a balloon before?"

"No."

"My God," he said. "What chance have I got?"

"None at all, if I hadn't come," I said mildly.

"That's true." He looked down from somewhere like six feet four. "What's your name?"

"Sid," I said.

He looked as if Sid wasn't exactly the sort of name his friends had, but faced the fact manfully.

"Why wouldn't your girl come with you?" I said.

"Who? Oh, you mean Popsy. She's not my girl. I don't really know her. She was going to come because my usual passenger broke his leg, silly bugger, when we made a bit of a rough landing last week. Popsy wanted to bring some ruddy big handbag. Wouldn't come without it, wouldn't be parted from it. I ask you! Where is the room for a handbag? And it was heavy, as well. Every pound counts. Carry a pound less, you can go a mile farther."

"Where do you expect to come down?" I said.

"It depends on the wind." He looked up at the sky. "We're going roughly northeast at the moment, but I'm going higher. There's a front forecast from the west, and I guess there'll be some pretty useful activity high up. We might make it to Brighton."

"Brighton." I had thought in terms of perhaps twenty miles, not a hundred. And he must be wrong, I thought; one couldn't go a hundred miles in a balloon in two and a half hours.

"If the wind's more from the northwest, we might

reach the Isle of Wight. Or France. Depends how much gas is left; we don't want to come down in the sea, not in this. Can you swim?"

I nodded. I supposed I still could: hadn't tried it one-handed. "I'd rather not," I said.

He laughed. "Don't worry. The balloon's too darned expensive for me to want to sink it."

Once free of the trees we had risen very fast, and now floated across country at a height from which cars on the roads looked like toys, though still recognizable as to size and color.

Noises came up clearly. One could hear the cars' engines, and dogs barking, and an occasional human shout. People looked up and waved to us as we passed. A world removed, I thought. I was in a child's world, idyllically drifting with the wind, sloughing off the dreary earthbound millstones, free and rising and filled with intense delight.

John Viking flipped the lever and the flame roared, shooting up into the green-and-yellow cavern, a scarlet-and-gold tongue of dragon fire. The burn endured for twenty seconds and we rose perceptibly in the sudden ensuing silence.

"What gas do you use?" I said.

"Propane."

He was looking over the side of the basket and around at the countryside, as if judging his position. "Look, get the map out, will you? It's in a pouch thing on your side. And for God's sake don't let it blow away."

I looked over the side and found what he meant. A satchel-like object strapped on through the wicker-work, its outward-facing flap fastened shut with a buckle. I undid the buckle, looked inside, took a fair grip of the large folded map, and delivered it safely to the captain.

He was looking fixedly at my left hand, which I'd used as a sort of counterweight on the edge of the basket while I leaned over. I let it fall by my side, and his gaze swept upward to my face.

"You're missing a hand," he said incredulously.

"That's right."

He waved his own two arms in a fierce gesture of frustration. "How the *hell* am I going to win this race?"

I laughed.

He glanced at me. "It's not damned funny."

"Oh, yes it is. And I like winning races. . . . You won't lose it because of me."

He frowned disgustedly. "I suppose you can't be much more useless than Popsy," he said. "But at least they say she can read a map." He unfolded the sheet I'd given him, which proved to be a map designed for the navigation of aircraft, its surface covered with a plastic film, for writing on. "Look," he said. "We started from here." He pointed. "We're traveling roughly northeast. You take the map, and find out where we are." He paused. "Do you know the first bloody thing about using your watch as a compass, or about dead reckoning?"

I had a book about dead reckoning, which I hadn't read, in a pocket of the light cotton anarak I was wearing; and also, I thanked God, in another zippered compartment, a spare fully charged battery. "Give me the map," I said. "And let's see."

He handed it over with no confidence and started another burn. I worked out roughly where we should be, and looked over the side, and discovered straight away that the ground didn't look like the map. Where villages and roads were marked clearly on the map, they faded into the brown and green carpet of earth like patches of camouflage, the sunlight mottling them with shadows and dissolving them into ragged edges. The spread-out vistas all around all looked the same, defying me to recognize anything special, proving conclusively I was less use than Popsy.

Dammit, I thought. Start again.

We had set off at three o'clock, give a minute or two. We had been airborne for twelve minutes. On the ground the wind had been gentle and from the south, but we were now traveling slightly faster, and north-east. Say, fifteen knots. Twelve minutes at fifteen knots . . . about three nautical miles. I had been looking too far ahead. There should be, I thought, a river to cross; and in spite of gazing earnestly down I nearly missed it, because it was a firm blue line on the map and in reality a silvery reflecting thread that wound unobtrusively between a meadow and a wood. To the right of it, half hidden by a hill, lay a village, and beyond it, a railway line.

"We're there," I said, pointing to the map.

He squinted at the print and searched the ground beneath us.

"Fair enough," he said. "So we are. Right. You keep the map. We might as well know where we are, all the way."

He flipped the lever and gave it a long burn. The balloons ahead of us were also lower. We were definitely looking down on their tops. During the next patch of silence he consulted two instruments which were strapped onto the outside of the basket at his end, and grunted.

"What are those?" I said, nodding at the dials.

"Altimeter and rate-of-climb meter," he said. "We're at five thousand feet now, and rising at eight hundred feet a minute."

"Rising?"

"Yeah." He gave a sudden wolfish grin in which I read unmistakably the fierce unholy glee of the mischievous child. "That's why Popsy wouldn't come. Someone told her I would go high. She didn't want to."

"How high?" I said.

"I don't mess about," he said. "When I race, I race to win. They all know I'll win. They don't like it. They think you should never take risks. They're all safety conscious these days and getting softer. Ha!" His scorn was absolute. "In the old days, at the beginning of the century, when they had the Gordon Bennett races, they would fly for two days and do a thousand miles or more. But nowadays . . . safety bloody first." He glanced at me. "And if I didn't have to have a passenger, I wouldn't. Passengers always argue and complain."

He pulled a packet of cigarettes out of his pocket and lit one with a flick of a lighter. We were surrounded by cylinders of liquid gas. I thought about all the embargoes against naked flames near any sort of stored fuel, and kept my mouth shut.

The flock of balloons below us seemed to be veering away to the left; but then I realized that it is was we who were going to the right. John Viking watched the changing direction with great satisfaction and started another long burn. We rose perceptibly faster, and the sun, instead of shining full on our backs, appeared on our starboard side.

In spite of the sunshine it was getting pretty cold. A look over the side showed the earth very far beneath, and one could now see a very long way in all directions. I checked with the map, and kept an eye on where we were.

"What are you wearing?" he said.

"What you see, more or less."

"Huh."

During the burns, the flame over one's head was almost too hot, and there was always a certain amount of hot air escaping from the bottom of the balloon. There was no wind factor, as of course the balloon was traveling with the wind, at the wind's speed. It was sheer altitude that was making us cold.

"How high are we now?" I said.

He glanced at his instruments. "Eleven thousand feet."

"And still rising?"

He nodded. The other balloons, far below and to the left, were a cluster of distant bright blobs against the green earth.

"All that lot," he said, "will stay down at five thousand feet, because of staying under the airways." He gave me a sideways look. "You'll see on the map. The airways that the airlines use are marked, and so are the heights at which one is not allowed to fly through them."

"And one is not allowed to fly through an airway at eleven thousand feet in a balloon?"

"Sid," he said, grinning, "you're not bad."

He flicked the lever, and the burner roared, cutting off chat. I checked the ground against the map and nearly lost our position entirely, because we seemed suddenly to have traveled much faster, and quite definitely to the southeast. The other balloons, when I next looked, were out of sight.

In the next silence John Viking told me that the helpers of the other balloons would follow them on the ground, in cars, ready to retrieve them when they came down.

"What about you?" I asked. "Do we have someone following?"

Did we indeed have Peter Rammileese following, complete with thugs, ready to pounce again at the farther end? We were even, I thought fleetingly, doing him a favor with the general direction, taking him southeastward, home to Kent.

John Viking gave his wolfish smile, and said, "No car on earth could keep up with us today."

"Do you mean it?" I exclaimed.

He looked at the altimeter. "Fifteen thousand feet," he said. "We'll stay at that. I got a forecast from the air boys for this trip. Fifty-knot wind from two nine zero at fifteen thousand feet; that's what they said. You hang on, Sid, pal, and we'll get to Brighton."

I thought about the two of us standing in a waist-high four-foot-square wicker basket, supported by Dacron and hot air, fifteen thousand feet above the solid ground, traveling without any feeling of speed at fifty-seven miles an hour. Quite mad, I thought.

From the ground, we would be a black speck. On the ground, no car could keep up. I grinned back at John Viking with a satisfaction as great as his own, and he laughed aloud.

"Would you believe it?" he said. "At last I've got someone up here who's not puking with fright."

He lit another cigarette, and then he changed the supply line to the burner from one cylinder to the next. This involved switching off the empty tank, unscrewing the connecting nut, screwing it into the next cylinder, and switching on the new supply. There were two lines to the double burner, one for each set of four cylinders. He held the cigarette in his mouth throughout, and squinted through the smoke.

I had seen from the map that we were flying straight toward the airway that led in and out of Gatwick, where large airplanes thundered up and down not expecting to meet squashy balloons illegally in their path.

His appetite for taking risks was way out of my class.

He made sitting on a horse over fences on the ground seem rather tame. Except, I thought with a jerk, that I no longer did it; I fooled around instead with men who threatened to shoot hands off . . . and I was safer up here with John Viking the madman, propane and cigarettes, midair collisions, and all.

"Right," he said. "We just stay as we are for an hour and a half and let the wind take us. If you feel odd, it's lack of oxygen." He took a pair of wool gloves from his pocket and put them on. "Are you cold?"

"Yes, a bit."

He grinned. "I've got long johns under my jeans, and two sweaters under my anarak. You'll just have to freeze."

"Thanks very much." I stood on the map and put my real hand deep into the pocket of my cotton anarak and he said at least the false hand couldn't get frost-bite.

He operated the burner and looked at his watch and the ground and the altimeter, and seemed pleased with the way things were. Then he looked at me in slight puzzlement and I knew he was wondering, now that there was time, how I had happened to be where I was.

"I came to Highalane Park to see you," I said. "I mean you, John Viking, particularly."

He looked startled. "Do you read minds?"

"All the time." I pulled my hand out of one pocket and dipped into another, and brought out the paper-back on navigation. "I came to ask you about this. It's got your name on the flyleaf."

He frowned at it, and opened the front cover. "Good Lord. I wondered where this had got to. How did you have it?"

"Did you lend it to anyone?"

"I don't think so."

"Um . . ." I said. "If I describe someone to you, will you say if you know him?"

"Fire away."

"A man of about twenty-eight," I said. "Dark hair, good looks, full of fun and jokes, easygoing, likes girls, great company, has a habit of carrying a knife strapped to his leg under his sock, and is very likely a crook."

"Oh, yes," he said, nodding. "He's my cousin."

Chapter 12

His cousin, Norris Abbott. What had he done this time? he demanded, and I asked, What had he done before?

"A trail of bouncing checks that his mother paid for."

Where did he live? I asked. John Viking didn't know. He saw him only when Norris turned up occasionally on his doorstep, usually broke and looking for free meals.

"A laugh a minute for a day or two. Then he's gone."

"Where does his mother live?"

"She's dead. He's alone now. No parents or brothers or sisters. No relatives except me." He peered at me, frowning. "Why do you ask all this?"

"A girl I know wants to find him." I shrugged. "It's nothing much."

He lost interest at once and flicked the lever for another burn. "We use twice the fuel up here as near the ground," he said afterward. "That's why I brought so much. That's how some Nosy Parker told Popsy I was planning to go so high, and through the airways."

By my reckoning the airway was not that far off.

"Won't you get into trouble?" I said.

The wolf grin came and went. "They've got to see us first. We won't show up on radar. We're too small for the equipment they use. With a bit of luck, we'll sneak across and no one will be any the wiser."

I picked up the map and studied it. At fifteen thousand feet we would be illegal from when we entered controlled air space until we landed, all but the last two hundred feet. The airway over Brighton began at a thousand feet above sea level and the hills to the north were eight hundred feet high. Did John Viking know all that? Yes, he did.

When we had been flying for an hour and fifty minutes, he made a fuel line change from cylinder to cylinder that resulted in a thin jet of liquid gas spurting out from the connection like water out of a badly joined hose. The jet shot across the corner of the basket and hit a patch of wickerwork about six inches below the top rail.

John Viking was smoking at the time.

Liquid propane began trickling down the side of the basket in a stream. John Viking cursed and fiddled with the faulty connection, bending over it; and his glowing cigarette ignited the gas.

There was no ultimate and final explosion. The jet burned as jets do, and directed its flame in an organized manner at the patch of basket it was hitting. John Viking threw his cigarette over the side and snatched off his denim cap, and beat at the burning basket with great flailing motions of his arm, while I managed to stifle the jet at source by turning off the main switch on the cylinder.

When the flames and smoke and cursing died down, we had a hole six inches in diameter right through the basket, but no other damage.

"Baskets don't burn easily," he said calmly, as if

nothing had happened. "Never known one to burn much more than this." He inspected his cap, which was scorched into black-edged lace, and gave me a maniacal four seconds from the bright blue eyes. "You can't put out a fire with a crash helmet," he said.

I laughed quite a lot.

It was the altitude, I thought, that was making me giggle.

"Want some chocolate?" he said.

There were no signposts in the sky to tell us when we crossed the boundary of the airway. We saw an airplane or two some way off, but nothing near us. No one came buzzing around to direct us downward. We simply sailed straight on, blowing across the sky as fast as a train.

At ten past five he said it was time to go down, because if we didn't touch ground by five-thirty exactly he would be disqualified, and he didn't want that; he wanted to win. Winning was what it was all about.

"How would anyone know exactly when we touched down?" I said.

He gave me a pitying look and gently directed his toe at a small box strapped to the floor beside one of the corner cylinders.

"In here is a barograph, all stuck about with pompous red seals. The judges seal it before the start. It shows variations in air pressure. Highly sensitive. All our journey shows up like a row of peaks. When you're on the ground, the trace is flat and steady. It tells the judges just when you took off and when you landed. Right?"

"Right."

"O.K. Down we go, then."

He reached up and untied a red cord which was knotted to the burner frame, and pulled it. "It opens a panel at the top of the balloon," he said. "Lets the hot air out."

His idea of descent was all of a piece. The altimeter unwound like a broken clock and the rate-of-climb meter was pointing to a thousand feet a minute downward. He seemed to be quite unaffected, but it made me queasy and hurt my eardrums. Swallowing made things a bit better, but not much. I concentrated, as an antidote, on checking with the map to see where we were going.

The Channel lay like a broad gray carpet to our right, and it was incredible, but whichever way I looked at it, it seemed that we were on a collision course with Beachy Head.

"Yeah," John Viking casually confirmed. "Guess we'll try not to get blown off those cliffs. Might be better to land on the beach farther on. . . ." He checked his watch. "Ten minutes to go. We're still at six thousand feet. . . . That's all right . . . Might be the edge of the sea."

"Not the sea," I said positively.

"Why not? We might have to."

"Well," I said, "this . . ." I lifted my left arm. "Inside this hand-shaped plastic there's actually a lot of fine engineering. Strong pincers inside the thumb and first two fingers. A lot of fine precision gears, and transistors and printed electrical circuits. Dunking it in the sea would be like dunking a radio. A total ruin. And it would cost me two thousand quid to get a new one."

He was astonished. "You're joking."

"No."

"Better keep you dry, then. And anyway, now we're down here, I don't think we'll get as far south as Beachy Head. Probably farther east." He paused and looked at my left hand doubtfully. "It'll be a rough landing. The fuel's cold from being so high . . . the burner doesn't function well on cold fuel. It takes time to heat enough air to give us a softer touch-down."

A softer touchdown took time . . . too much time.

"Win the race," I said.

His face lit into sheer happiness. "Right," he said decisively. "What's that town just ahead?"

I studied the map. "Eastbourne."

He looked at his watch. "Five minutes." He looked at the altimeter and at Eastbourne, upon which we were rapidly descending. "Two thousand feet. Bit dicey, hitting the roofs. There isn't much wind down here, is there . . . But if I burn, we might not get down in time. No; no burn."

A thousand feet a minute, I reckoned, was eleven or twelve miles an hour. I had been used for years to hitting the ground at more than twice that speed . . . though not in a basket, and not when the ground might turn out to be fully inhabited by brick walls.

We were traveling sideways over the town, with houses below us. Descent was very fast. "Three minutes," he said.

The sea lay ahead again, fringing the far side of the town, and for a moment it looked as if it was there we would have to come down after all. John Viking, however, knew better.

"Hang on," he said. "This is it."

He hauled strongly on the red cord he held, which led upward into the balloon. Somewhere above, the vent for the hot air widened dramatically, the lifting power of the balloon fell away, and the solid edge of Eastbourne came up with a rush.

We scraped the eaves of gray slate roofs, made a

sharp diagonal descent over a road and a patch of grass, and smashed down on a broad concrete walk twenty yards from the waves.

"Don't get out. Don't get out," he yelled. The basket tipped on its side and began to slither along the concrete, dragged by the still half-inflated silken mass. "Without our weight, it could still fly away."

As I was again wedged among the cylinders, it was superfluous advice. The basket rocked and tumbled a few more times and I with it, and John Viking cursed and hauled at his red cord and finally let out enough air for us to be still.

He looked at his watch, and his blue eyes blazed with triumph.

"We've made it. Five twenty-nine. That was a bloody good race. The best ever. What are you doing next Saturday?"

I went back to Aynsford by train, which took forever, with Charles picking me up from Oxford station not far short of midnight.

"You went on the balloon race," he repeated disbelievingly. "Did you enjoy it?"

"Very much."

"And your car's still at Highalane Park?"

"It can stay there until morning." I yawned. "Nicholas Ashe now has a name, by the way. He's someone called Norris Abbott. Same initials, silly man."

"Will you tell the police?"

"See if we can find him first."

He glanced at me sideways. "Jenny came back this evening, after you'd telephoned."

"Oh, no."

"I didn't know she was going to."

I supposed I believed him. I hoped she would have

gone to bed before I arrived, but she hadn't. She was sitting on the gold brocade sofa in the drawing room, looking belligerent.

"I don't like you coming here so much," she said.

A knife to the heart of things from my pretty wife.

Charles said smoothly, "Sid is welcome here always."

"Discarded husbands should have more pride than to fawn on their fathers-in-law, who put up with it because they're sorry for them."

"You're jealous," I said, surprised.

She stood up fast, as angry as I'd ever seen her.

"How dare you!" she said. "He always takes your side. He thinks you're bloody marvelous. He doesn't know you like I do, all your stubborn little ways and your meanness and thinking you're always *right.*"

"I'm going to bed," I said.

"And you're a coward as well," she said furiously. "Running away from a few straight truths."

"Good night, Charles," I said. "Good night, Jenny. Sleep well, my love, and pleasant dreams."

"You . . ." she said. "You . . . I hate you, Sid."

I went out of the drawing room without fuss and upstairs to the bedroom I thought of as mine, the one I always slept in nowadays at Aynsford.

You don't have to hate me, Jenny, I thought miserably: I hate myself.

Charles drove me to Wiltshire in the morning to collect my car, which still stood where I'd left it, though surrounded now by acres of empty grass. There was no Peter Rammileese in sight, and no thugs waiting in ambush. All clear for an uneventful return to London.

"Sid," Charles said, as I unlocked the car door. "Don't pay any attention to Jenny."

"No."

"Come to Aynsford whenever you want."

I nodded.

"I mean it, Sid."

"Yeah."

"Damn Jenny," he said explosively.

"Oh, no. She's unhappy. She . . ." I paused. "I guess she needs comforting. A shoulder to cry on, and all that."

He said austerely, "I don't care for tears."

"No." I sighed and got into the car, waved goodbye, and drove over the bumpy grass to the gate. The help that Jenny needed, she wouldn't take from me; and her father didn't know how to give it. Just another of life's bloody muddles, another irony in the general mess.

I drove into the city and around in a few small circles, and ended up in the publishing offices of *Antiques for All,* which proved to be only one of a number of specialist magazines put out by a newspaper company. To the *Antiques* editor, a fair-haired, earnest young man in heavy-framed specs, I explained both the position and the need.

"Our mailing list?" he said doubtfully. "Mailing lists are strictly private, you know."

I explained all over again, and threw in a lot of pathos. My wife behind bars if I didn't find the con man, that sort of thing.

"Oh, very well," he said. "But it will be stored in a computer. You'll have to wait for a printout."

I waited patiently, and received in the end a stack of paper setting out fifty-three thousand names and addresses, give or take a few dead ones.

"And we want it back," he said severely. "Unmarked and complete."

"How did Norris Abbott get hold of it?" I asked.

He didn't know, and neither the name nor the

description of Abbott/Ashe brought any glimmer of recognition.

"How about a copy of the magazine, for good measure?"

I got that too, and disappeared before he could regret all his generosity. Back in the car, I telephoned to Chico and got him to come to the flat. Meet me outside, I said. Carry my bag upstairs and earn your salary.

He was there when I pulled up at a vacant parking meter and we went upstairs together. The flat was empty, and quiet, and safe.

"A lot of legwork, my son," I said, taking the mailing list out of the package I had transported it in, and putting it on the table. "All your own."

He eyed it unenthusiastically. "And what about you?"

"Chester races," I said. "One of the syndicate horses runs there tomorrow. Meet me back here Thursday morning, ten o'clock. O.K.?"

"Yeah." He thought. "Suppose our Nicky hasn't got himself organized yet, and sends out his begging letters next week, after we've drawn a blank?"

"Mm . . . Better take some sticky labels with this address on, and ask them to send the letter here if they get them."

"We'll be lucky."

"You never know. No one likes being conned."

"May as well get started, then." He picked up the folder containing the magazine and mailing list, and looked ready to leave.

"Chico . . . Stay until I've repacked my bag. I think I'll start northward right now. Stay until I go."

He was puzzled. "If you like, but what for?"

"Er . . . "

"Come on, Sid. Out with it."

"Peter Rammileese and a couple of guys came looking for me yesterday at Aynsford. So I'd just like you around while I'm here."

"What sort of guys?" he said suspiciously.

I nodded. "Those sort. Hard eyes and boots."

"Guys who kick people half to death in Tunbridge Wells?"

"Maybe," I said.

"You dodged them, I see."

"In a balloon." I told him about the race while I put some things in a suitcase. He laughed at the story but afterward came quite seriously back to business.

"Those guys of yours don't sound like your ordinary run-of-the-mill rent-a-thug," he said. "Here, let me fold that jacket; you'll turn up at Chester all creased." He took my packing out of my hands and did it for me, quickly and neatly. "Got all the spare batteries? There's one in the bathroom." I fetched it. "Look, Sid, I don't like these syndicates." He snapped the locks shut and carried the case into the hall. "Let's tell Lucas Wainwright we're not doing them."

"And who tells Peter Rammileese?"

"We do. We ring him up and tell him."

"You do it," I said. "Right now."

We stood and looked at each other. Then he shrugged and picked up the suitcase. "Got everything?" he said. "Raincoat?" We went down to the car and stowed my case in the boot. "Look, Sid, you just take care, will you? I don't like hospital visiting, you know that."

"Don't lose that mailing list," I said. "Or the editor of *Antiques* will be cross."

I booked unmolested into a motel and spent the evening watching television, and the following afternoon arrived without trouble at Chester races.

All the usual crowd were there, standing around, making the usual conversations. It was my first time on a racecourse since the dreary week in Paris, and it seemed to me when I walked in that the change in me must be clearly visible. But no one, of course, noticed the blistering sense of shame I felt at the sight of George Caspar outside the weighing room, or treated me any differently from usual. It was I alone who knew I didn't deserve the smiles and the welcome. I was a fraud. I shrank inside. I hadn't known I would feel so bad.

The trainer from Newmarket who had offered me a ride with his string was there, and repeated his offer.

"Sid, do come. Come this Friday, stay the night with us, and ride work on Saturday morning."

There wasn't much, I reflected, that anyone could give me that I'd rather accept: and besides, Peter Rammileese and his merry men would have a job finding me there.

"Martin . . . Yes, I'd love to."

"Great." He seemed pleased. "Come for evening stables, Friday night."

He went on into the weighing room, and I wondered if he would have asked me if he'd known how I'd spent Guineas day.

Bobby Unwin buttonholed me with inquisitive eyes. "Where have you been?" he said. "I didn't see you at the Guineas."

"I didn't go."

"I thought you'd be bound to, after all your interest in Tri-Nitro."

"No."

"I reckon you had the smell of something going on there, Sid. All that interest in the Caspars, and about

Gleaner and Zingaloo. Come clean, now: what do you know?"

"Nothing, Bobby."

"I don't believe you." He gave me a hard unforgiving stare and steered his beaky nose toward more fruitful copy in the shape of a top trainer enduring a losing streak. I would have trouble persuading him, I thought, if I should ever ask for his help again.

Rosemary Caspar, walking with a woman friend to whom she was chatting, almost bumped into me before either of us was aware of the other's being there. The look in her eyes made Bobby Unwin seem loving.

"Go away," she said violently. "Why are you here?"

The woman friend looked very surprised. I stepped out of the way without saying a word, which surprised her still further. Rosemary impatiently twitched her onward, and I heard her voice rising: "But surely, Rosemary, that was Sid Halley. . . . "

My face felt stiff. It's too bloody much, I thought. I couldn't have made their horse win if I'd stayed. *I couldn't. . . .* But I might have. I would always think I might have, if I'd tried. If I hadn't been scared out of my mind.

"Hello, Sid," a voice said at my side. "Lovely day, isn't it?"

"Oh, lovely."

Philip Friarly smiled and watched Rosemary's retreating back. "She's been snapping at everyone since that disaster last week. Poor Rosemary. Takes things so much to heart."

"You can't blame her," I said. "She said it would happen, and no one believed her."

"Did she tell you?" he said curiously.

I nodded.

"Ah," he said, in understanding. "Galling for you."

I took a deep loosening breath and made myself concentrate on something different.

"That horse of yours today," I said. "Are you just giving it a sharpener, running it here on the flat?"

"Yes," he said briefly. "And if you ask me how it will run, I'll have to tell you that it depends on who's giving the orders, and who's taking them."

"That's cynical."

"Have you found out anything for me?"

"Not very much. It's why I came here." I paused. "Do you know the name and address of the person who formed your syndicates?"

"Not offhand," he said. "I didn't deal with him myself, do you see? The syndicates were already well advanced when I was asked to join. The horses had already been bought, and most of the shares were sold."

"They used you," I said. "Used your name. A respectable front."

He nodded unhappily. "I'm afraid so."

"Do you know Peter Rammileese?"

"Who?" He shook his head. "Never heard of him."

"He buys and sells horses," I said. "Lucas Wainwright thinks it was he who formed your syndicates, and he who is operating them, and he's bad news to the Jockey Club and barred from most racecourses."

"Oh, dear." He sounded distressed. "If Lucas is looking into them . . . What do you think I should do, Sid?"

"From your own point of view," I said, "I think you should sell your shares, or dissolve the syndicates entirely, and get your name out of them as fast as possible."

"All right, I will. And, Sid . . . next time I'm tempted, I'll get you to check on the other people in the syndicate. The Security Service are supposed to have done these, and look at them!"

"Who's riding your horse today?" I said.

"Larry Server."

He waited for an opinion, but I didn't give it. Larry Server was middle ability, middle employed, rode mostly on the flat and sometimes over hurdles, and was to my mind in the market for unlawful bargains.

"Who chooses the jockey?" I said. "Larry Server doesn't ride all that often for your horse's trainer."

"I don't know," he said doubtfully. "I leave all that to the trainer, of course."

I made a small grimace.

"Don't you approve?" he said.

"If you like," I said, "I'll give you a list of jockeys for your jumpers that you can at least trust to be trying to win. Can't guarantee their ability, but you can't have everything."

"Now who's a cynic?" He smiled, and said with patent and piercing regret, "I wish you were still riding them, Sid."

"Yeah." I said it with a smile, but he saw the flicker I hadn't managed to keep out of my eyes.

With a compassion I definitely didn't want, he said, "I'm so sorry."

"It was great while it lasted," I said lightly. "That's all that matters."

He shook his head, annoyed with himself for his clumsiness.

"Look," I said, "if you were *glad* I'm not still riding them, I'd feel a whole lot worse."

"We had some grand times, didn't we? Some exceptional days."

"Yes, we did."

There could be an understanding between an owner and a jockey, I thought, that was intensely intimate. In the small area where their lives touched, where the speed and the winning were all that mattered, there could be a privately shared joy, like a secret, that endured like cement. I hadn't felt it often, nor with many of the people I had ridden for, but with Philip Friarly, nearly always.

A man detached himself from another group near us, and came toward us with a smiling face.

"Philip, Sid. Nice to see you."

We made the polite noises back, but with genuine pleasure, as Sir Thomas Ullaston, the reigning Senior Steward, head of the Jockey Club, head, more or less, of the whole racing industry, was a sensible man and a fair and open-minded administrator. A little severe at times, some thought, but it wasn't a job for a soft man. In the short time since he'd been put in charge of things, there had been some good new rules and a clearing out of injustices, and he was as decisive as his predecessor had been weak.

"How's it going, Sid?" he said. "Caught any good crooks lately?"

"Not lately," I said ruefully.

He smiled to Philip Friarly. "Our Sid's putting the Security Service's nose out of joint, did you know? I had Eddy Keith along in my office on Monday complaining that we give Sid too free a hand, and asking that we shouldn't let him operate on the racecourse."

"Eddy Keith?" I said.

"Don't look so shocked, Sid," Sir Thomas said teasingly. "I told him that racing owed you a great deal, starting with the saving of Seabury racecourse itself and going right on from there, and that in no way would the Jockey Club ever interfere with you, unless you did something absolutely diabolical, which on past form I can't see you doing."

"Thank you," I said faintly.

"And you may take it," he said firmly, "that that is the official Jockey Club view, as well as my own."

"Why," I said slowly, "does Eddy Keith want me stopped?"

He shrugged. "Something about access to the Jockey Club files. Apparently you saw some, and he resented it. I told him he'd have to live with it, because I was certainly not in any way going to put restraints on what I consider a positive force for good in racing."

I felt grindingly undeserving of all that, but he gave me no time to protest.

"Why don't both of you come upstairs for a drink and a sandwich? Come along, Sid, Philip. . . . " He turned, gesturing us to follow, leading the way.

We went up those stairs marked "Private" which on most racecourses lead to the civilized luxuries of the stewards' box, and into a carpeted glass-fronted room looking out to the white-railed track. There were several groups of people there already, and a manservant handing around drinks on a tray.

"I expect you know most people," Sir Thomas said, hospitably making introductions. "Madelaine, my dear"—to his wife—"do you know Lord Friarly, and Sid Halley?" We shook her hand. "And oh, yes, Sid," he said, touching my arm to bring me around face to face with another of his guests. . . .

"Have you met Trevor Deansgate?"

Chapter 13

We stared at each other, probably equally stunned.

I thought of how he had last seen me, on my back in the straw barn, spilling my guts out with fear. He'll see it still in my face, I thought. He knows what he's made of me. I can't just stand here without moving a muscle . . . and yet I must.

My head seemed to be floating somewhere above the rest of my body, and an awful lot of awfulness got condensed into four seconds.

"Do you know each other?" Sir Thomas said, slightly puzzled.

Trevor Deansgate said, "Yes. We've met."

There was at least no sneer in either his eyes or his voice. If it hadn't been impossible, I would have thought that what he looked was *wary*.

"Drink, Sid?" said Sir Thomas; and I found the man with the tray at my elbow. I took a tumbler with whisky-colored contents and tried to stop my fingers from trembling.

Sir Thomas said conversationally, "I've just been telling Sid how much the Jockey Club appreciates his successes, and it seems to have silenced him completely."

Neither Trevor Deansgate nor I said anything. Sir Thomas raised his eyebrows a fraction and tried again. "Well, Sid, tell us a good thing for the big race."

I dragged my scattered wits back into at least a pretense of life going uneventfully on.

"Oh . . . Winetaster, I should think."

My voice sounded strained to me, but Sir Thomas seemed not to notice. Trevor Deansgate looked down to the glass in his own well-manicured hand and swiveled the ice cubes round in the golden liquid. Another of the guests spoke to Sir Thomas, and he turned away, and Trevor Deansgate's gaze came immediately back to my face, filled with naked savage threat. His voice, quick and hard, spoke straight from the primitive underbelly, the world of violence and vengeance and no pity at all.

"If you break your assurance, I'll do what I said."

He held my eyes until he was sure I had received the message, and then he too turned away, and I could see the heavy muscles of his shoulders bunching formidably inside his coat.

"Sid," Philip Friarly said, appearing once more at my side. "Lady Ullaston wants to know . . . I say, are you feeling all right?"

I nodded.

"My dear chap, you look frightfully pale."

"I . . . er . . . " I took a vague grip on things. "What did you say?"

"Lady Ullaston wants to know . . . " He went on at some length, and I listened and answered with a feeling of complete unreality. One could literally be torn apart in spirit while standing with a glass in one's hand making social chitchat to the Senior Steward's lady. I couldn't remember, five minutes later, a word that was said. I couldn't feel my feet on the carpet. I'm a mess, I thought.

The afternoon went on. Winetaster got beaten in the big race by a glossy dark filly called Mrs. Hillman, and in the race after that Larry Server took Philip Friarly's syndicate horse to the back of the field, and stayed there. Nothing improved internally, and after the fifth I decided it was pointless staying any longer, since I couldn't even effectively think.

Outside the gate there was the usual gaggle of chauffeurs leaning against cars, waiting for their employers; and also, with them, one of the jump jockeys whose license had been lost through taking bribes from Rammileese.

I nodded to him as I passed. "Jacksy."

"Sid."

I walked on to the car, and unlocked it, and slung my race glasses onto the back seat. Got in. Started the engine. Paused for a bit, and reversed all the way back to the gate.

"Jacksy?" I said. "Get in. I'm buying."

"Buying what?" He came over and opened the passenger door, and sat in beside me. I fished my wallet out of my rear trouser pocket and tossed it into his lap.

"Take all the money," I said. I drove forward through the car park and out through the distant gate onto the public road.

"But you dropped me quite a lot not long ago," he said.

I gave him a fleeting sideways smile. "Yeah. Well . . . this is for services about to be rendered."

He counted the notes. "All of it?" he said doubtfully.

"I want to know about Peter Rammileese."

"Oh, no." He made as if to open the door, but the car by then was going too fast.

"Jacksy," I said, "no one's listening but me, and I'm

not telling anyone else. Just say how much he paid you and what for, and anything else you can think of."

He was silent for a bit. Then he said, "It's more than my life's worth, Sid. There's a whisper out that he's brought two pros down from Glasgow for a special job and anyone who gets in his way just now is liable to be stamped on."

"Have you seen these pros?" I said, thinking that I had.

"No. It just come through on the grapevine, like."

"Does the grapevine know what the special job is?"

He shook his head.

"Anything to do with syndicates?"

"Be your age, Sid. Everything to do with Rammileese is always to do with syndicates. He runs about twenty. Maybe more."

Twenty, I thought, frowning. I said, "What's his rate for the job of doing a Larry Server, like today?"

"Sid," he protested.

"How does he get someone like Larry Server onto a horse he wouldn't normally ride?"

"He asks the trainer nicely, with a fistful of dollars."

"He bribes the *trainers?*"

"It doesn't take much sometimes." He looked thoughtful for a while. "Don't you quote me, but there were races run last autumn where Rammileese was behind every horse in the field. He just carved them up as he liked."

"It's impossible," I said.

"No. All that dry weather we had, remember? Fields of four, five, or six runners sometimes, because the ground was so hard? I know of three races for sure when all the runners were his. The poor sodding bookies didn't know what had hit them."

Jacksy counted the money again. "Do you know how much you've got here?" he said.

"Just about."

I glanced at him briefly. He was twenty-five, an ex-apprentice grown too heavy for the flat and known to resent it. Jump jockeys on the whole earned less than the flat boys, and there were the bruises besides, and it wasn't everyone who, like me, found steeplechasing double the fun. Jacksy didn't; but he could ride pretty well, and I'd raced alongside him often enough to know he wouldn't put you over the rails for nothing at all. For a consideration, yes, but for nothing, no.

The money was troubling him. For ten or twenty he would have lied to me easily: but we had a host of shared memories of changing rooms and horses and wet days and mud and falls and trudging back over sodden turf in paper-thin racing boots, and it isn't so easy, if you're not a real villain, to rob someone you know as well as that.

"Funny," he said, "you taking to this detecting lark."

"Riotous."

"No, straight up. I mean, you don't come after the lads for little things."

"No," I agreed. Little things like taking bribes. My business, on the whole, was with the people who offered them.

"I kept all the newspapers," he said, "after that trial."

I shook my head resignedly. Too many people in the racing world had kept those papers, and the trial had been a trial for me in more ways than one. Defense counsel had reveled in deeply embarrassing the victim; and the prisoner, charged with causing grievous bodily harm with intent, contrary to Section 18 of the Offenses Against the Person Act 1861 (or in other words, bopping an ex-jockey's left hand with a poker), had been rewarded by four years in the clink. It would be difficult to say who had enjoyed the proceedings less, the one in the witness box or the one in the dock.

Jacksy kept up his disconnected remarks, which I gathered were a form of time filling while he sorted himself out underneath.

"I'll get my license back for next season," he said.

"Great."

"Seabury's a good track. I'll be riding there in August. All the lads think it's fine the course is still going, even if . . ." He glanced at my hand. "Well . . . you couldn't race with it anyway, could you, as it was?"

"Jacksy," I said, exasperated. "Will you or won't you?"

He flipped through the notes again, and folded them, and put them in his pocket.

"Yes. All right. Here's your wallet."

"Put it in the glove box."

He did that, and looked out the window. "Where are we going?" he said.

"Anywhere you like."

"I got a lift to Chester. He'll have gone without me by now. Can you take me south, like, and I'll hitch the rest."

So I drove toward London, and Jacksy talked.

"Rammileese gave me ten times the regular fee, for riding a loser. Now listen, Sid, you swear this won't get back to him?"

"Not through me."

"Yeah. Well, I suppose I do trust you."

"Get on, then."

"He buys quite good horses. Horses that can win. Then he syndicates them. I reckon sometimes he makes five hundred percent profit on them, for a start. He bought one I knew of for six thousand and sold ten shares at three thousand each. He's got two pals who are O.K. registered owners, and he puts one of them in each syndicate, and they swing it so some fancy figurehead takes a share, so the whole thing looks right."

"Who are the two pals?"

He gulped a lot, but told me. One name meant nothing, but the other had appeared on all of Philip Friarly's syndicates.

"Right," I said. "On you go."

"The horses get trained by anyone who can turn them out looking nice for double the usual training fees and no questions asked. Then Rammileese works out what races they're going to run in, and they're all running way below their real class, see, so that when he says go, by Christ you're on a flier." He grinned. "Twenty times the riding fee, for a winner."

It sounded a lot more than it was.

"How often did you ride for him?"

"One or two, most weeks."

"Will you do it again, when you get your license back?"

He turned in his seat until his back was against the car's door and spent a long time studying the half he could see of my face. His silence itself was an answer, but when we had traveled fully three miles he sighed deeply and said, finally, "Yes."

As an act of trust, that was remarkable.

"Tell me about the horses," I said, and he did, at some length. The names of some of them were a great surprise, and the careers of all of them as straightforward as Nicholas Ashe.

"Tell me how you got your license suspended," I said.

He had been riding for one of the amenable trainers, he said, only the trainer hadn't had an amenable wife. "She had a bit of a spite on, so she shopped him with the Jockey Club. Wrote to Thomas Ullaston personally,

I ask you. Of course, the whole bleeding lot of stewards believed her, and suspended the lot of us—me, him, and the other jock who rides for him, poor sod, who never got a penny from Rammileese and wouldn't know a backhander if it smacked him in the face."

"How come," I asked casually, "that no one in the Jockey Club has found out about all these syndicates and done something positive about Rammileese?"

"Good question."

I glanced at him, hearing the doubt in his voice and seeing the frown. "Go on," I said.

"Yeah . . . This is strictly a whisper, see, not even a rumor hardly, just something I heard. . . ." He paused, then he said, "I don't reckon it's true."

"Try me."

"One of the bookies . . . I was waiting about outside the gates at Kempton, see, and these two bookies came out, and one was saying that the bloke in the Security Service would smooth it over if the price was right." He stopped again, and went on. "One of the lads said I'd've never got suspended if that bitch of a trainer's wife had sent her letter to the Security Service and not to the big white chief himself."

"Which of the lads said that?"

"Yeah. Well, I can't remember. And don't look like that, Sid; I really can't. It was months ago. I mean, I didn't even think about it until I heard the bookies at Kempton. I don't reckon there could be anyone that bent in the Security Service, do you? I mean, not in the Jockey Club."

His faith was touching, I thought, considering his present troubles, but in days gone by I would have thought he was right. Once plant the doubt, though, and one could see there were a lot of dirty misdeeds that Eddy Keith might have ignored in return for a tax-free gain. He had passed the four Friarly syndicates, and he might have done all of the twenty or more. He might even have put Rammileese's two pals on the respectable owners' list, knowing they weren't. Somehow or other, I would have to find out.

"Sid," Jacksy said, "don't you get me in bad with the brass. I'm not repeating what I just told you, not to no stewards."

"I won't say you told me," I assured him. "Do you know those two bookies at Kempton?"

"Not a chance. I mean, I don't even know they were bookies. They just looked like them. I mean, I thought 'bookies' when I saw them."

So strong an impression was probably right, but not of much help; and Jacksy, altogether, had run dry. I dropped him where he wanted, at the outskirts of Watford, and the last thing he said was that if I was going after Rammileese, to keep him, Jacksy, strictly out of it, like I'd promised.

I stayed in a hotel in London instead of the flat, and felt overcautious. Chico, however, when I telephoned, said it made sense. Breakfast, I suggested, and he said he'd be there.

He came, but without much hooray. He had trudged around all day visiting the people on the mailing list, but no one had received a begging letter from Ashe within the last month.

"Tell you what, though," he said. "People beginning with *A* and *B* and right down to *K* have had wax in the past, so it'll be the *P*'s and *R*'s that get done next time, which narrows the legwork."

"Great," I said, meaning it.

"I left sticky labels everywhere with your address on, and some of them said they'd let us know if it came. But whether they'll bother . . ."

"It would only take one," I said.

"That's true."

"Feel like a spot of breaking and entering?"

"Don't see why not." He started on a huge order of scrambled eggs and sausages. "Where and what for?"

"Er . . ." I said. "This morning you do a recce. This evening, after office hours but before it gets dark, we drift along to Portman Square."

Chico stopped chewing in midmouthful, and then carefully swallowed before saying, "By Portman Square, do you mean the Jockey Club?"

"That's right."

"Haven't you noticed they let you in the front door?"

"I want a quiet look-see that they don't know about."

He shrugged. "All right, then. Meet you back here after the recce?"

I nodded. "The Admiral's coming here for lunch. He went down to the wax factory yesterday."

"That should put a shine in his eyes."

"Oh, very funny."

While he finished the eggs and attacked the toast, I told him most of what Jacksy had said about the syndicates, and also about the rumors of kickbacks in high places.

"And that's what we're looking for? Turning out Eddy Keith's office to see what he didn't do when he should've?"

"You got it. Sir Thomas Ullaston—Senior Steward—says Eddy was along complaining to him about me seeing the files, and Lucas Wainwright can't let me see them without Eddy's secretary knowing, and she's loyal to Eddy. So if I want to look, it has to be quiet." And would breaking into the Jockey Club, I wondered, be considered "absolutely diabolical" if I was found out?

"O.K.," he said. "I got the judo today, don't forget."

"The little bleeders," I said, "are welcome."

Charles came at twelve, sniffing the air of the unfamiliar surroundings like an unsettled dog.

"I got your message from Mrs. Cross," he said. "But why here? Why not the Cavendish, as usual?"

"There's someone I don't want to meet," I said. "He won't look for me here. Pink gin?"

"A double."

I ordered the drinks. He said, "Is that what it was, for those six days? Evasive action?"

I didn't reply.

He looked at me quizzically. "I see it still hurts you, whatever it was."

"Leave it, Charles."

He sighed and lit a cigar, sucking in smoke and eyeing me through the flame of the match. "So who don't you want to meet?"

"A man called Peter Rammileese. If anyone asks, you don't know where I am."

"I seldom do." He smoked with enjoyment, filling his lungs and inspecting the burning ash as if it were precious. "Going off in balloons. . . ."

I smiled. "I got offered the post of regular copilot to a madman."

"It doesn't surprise me," he said dryly.

"How did you get on with the wax?"

He wouldn't tell me until after the drinks had come, and then he wasted a lot of time asking why I was drinking Perrier water and not whisky.

"To keep a clear head for burglary," I said truthfully, which he half believed and half didn't.

"The wax is made," he said finally, "in a sort of

cottage industry flourishing next to a plant which processes honey."

"Beeswax!" I said incredulously.

He nodded. "Beeswax, paraffin wax, and turpentine, that's what's in that polish." He smoked luxuriously, taking his time. "A charming woman there was most obliging. We spent a long time going back over the order books. People seldom ordered as much at a time as Jenny had done, and very few stipulated that the tins should be packed in white boxes for posting." His eyes gleamed over the cigar. "Three people, all in the last year, to be exact."

"Three . . . Do you think . . . it was Nicholas Ashe three times?"

"Always about the same amount," he said, enjoying himself. "Different names and addresses, of course."

"Which you did bring away with you?"

"Which I did." He pulled a folded paper out of an inner pocket. "There you are."

"Got him," I said, with intense satisfaction. "He's a fool."

"There was a policeman there on the same errand," Charles said. "He came just after I'd written out those names. It seems they really are looking for Ashe themselves."

"Good. Er . . . did you tell them about the mailing list?"

"No, I didn't." He squinted at his glass, holding it up to the light, as if one pink gin were not the same as the next and he wanted to memorize the color. "I would like it to be you who finds him first."

"Hm." I thought about that. "If you think Jenny will be grateful, you'll be disappointed."

"But you'll have got her off the hook."

"She would prefer it to be the police." She might

even be nicer to me, I thought, if she was sure I had failed; and it wasn't the sort of niceness I would want.

Chico telephoned the hotel during the afternoon.

"What are you doing in your bedroom at this time of day?" he demanded.

"Watching Chester races on television."

"Stands to reason," he said resignedly. "Well, look, I've done the recce, and we can get in all right, but you'll have to be through the main doors before four o'clock. I've scubbed the little bleeders. Look, this is what you do. You go in through the front door, right, as if you'd got pukka business. Now, in the hall there's two lifts. One that goes to a couple of businesses that are on the first and second floors, and as far as the third, which is all Jockey Club, as you know."

"Yes," I said.

"When all the little workers and stewards and such have gone home, they leave that lift at the third floor, with its doors open, so no one can use it. There's a night porter, but after he's seen to the lift he doesn't do any rounds, he just stays downstairs. And oh, yes, when he's fixed the lift he goes down your actual stairs, locking a door across the stairway at each landing, which makes three in all. Got it?"

"Yes."

"Right. Now, there's another lift, which goes to the top four floors of the building, and up there there's eight flats, two on each floor, with people living in them. And between those floors and the Jockey Club below, there's only one door locked across the stairway."

"I'm with you," I said.

"Right. Now, I reckon the porter in the hall, or whatever you call him, he might just know you by sight, so he'd think it odd if you came after the offices were closed. So you'd better get there before, and go up in the lift to the flats, go right up to the top, and I'll meet you there. It's O.K., there's a sort of seat by a window; read a book or something."

"I'll see you," I said.

I went in a taxi, armed with a plausible reason for my visit if I should meet anyone I knew in the hall; but in fact I saw no one, and stepped into the lift to the flats without any trouble. At the top, as Chico had said, there was a bench by a window, where I sat and thought unproductively for over an hour. No one came or went from either of the two flats. No one came up in the lift. The first time its doors opened, it brought Chico.

Chico was dressed in white overalls and carried a bag of tools. I gave him a sardonic head-to-foot inspection.

"Well, you got to look the part," he said defensively. "I came here like this earlier, and when I left I told the chap I'd be back with spare parts. He just nodded when I walked in just now. When we go, I'll keep him talking while you gumshoe out."

"If it's the same chap."

"He goes off at eight. We better be finished before then."

"Was the Jockey Club lift still working?" I said.

"Yeah."

"Is the stairway door above the Jockey Club locked?"

"Yeah."

"Let's go down there, then, so we can hear when the porter brings the lift up and leaves it."

He nodded. We went through the door beside the lift, into the stairwell, which was utilitarian, not plushy, and lit by electric lights, and just inside there dumped the clinking bag of tools. Four floors down, we came to the locked door, and stood there, waiting.

The door was flat, made of some filling covered on

the side on which we stood by a sheet of silvery metal. The keyhole proclaimed a mortice lock set into the depth of the door, the sort of barrier which it took Chico about three minutes, usually, to negotiate.

As usual on these excursions, we had brought gloves. I thought back to one of the first times, when Chico had said, "One good thing about that hand of yours, it can't leave any dabs." I wore a glove over it anyway, as being a lot less noticeable if we were ever casually seen where we shouldn't be.

I had never got entirely used to breaking in, not to the point of not feeling my heart beat faster or my breath go shallow. Chico, for all his longer experience at the same game, gave himself away always by smoothing out the laughter lines round his eyes as the skin tautened over his cheekbones. We stood there waiting, the physical signs of stress with us, knowing the risks.

We heard the lift come up and stop. Held our breaths to see if it would go down again, but it didn't. Instead, we were electrified by the noise of someone unlocking the door we were standing behind. I caught a flash of Chico's alarmed eyes as he leaped away from the lock and joined me on the hinge side, our backs pressed hard against the wall.

The door opened until it was touching my chest. The porter coughed and sniffed on the other side of the barrier, looking, I thought, up the stairs, checking that all was as it should be.

The door swung shut again, and the key clicked in the lock. I let a long-held breath out in a slow soundless whistle, and Chico gave me the sort of sick grin that came from semireleased tension.

We felt the faint thud through the fabric of the building as the door on the floor below us was shut and locked. Chico raised his eyebrows and I nodded, and he addressed his bunch of lockpickers to the problem. There was a faint scraping noise as he sorted his way into the mechanism, and then the application of some muscle, and finally his clearing look of satisfaction as the metal tongue retracted into the door.

We went through, taking the keys but leaving the door unlocked, and found ourselves in the familiar headquarters of British racing. Acres of carpet, comfortable chairs, polished wood furniture, and the scent of extinct cigars.

The Security Service had its own corridor of smaller workaday offices, and down there without difficulty we eased into Eddy Keith's.

None of the internal doors seemed to be locked, and I supposed there was in fact little to steal, bar electric typewriters and other such trifles. Eddy Keith's filing cabinets all slid open easily, and so did the drawers in his desk.

In the strong evening sunlight we sat and read the reports on the extra syndicates that Jacksy had told me of. Eleven horses whose names I had written down, when he'd gone, so as not to forget them. Eleven syndicates apparently checked and accepted by Eddy, with Rammileese's two registered-owner pals appearing inexorably on all of them: and as with the previous four, headed by Philip Friarly, there was nothing in the files themselves to prove anything one way or the other. They were carefully, meticulously presented, openly ready for inspection.

There was one odd thing: the four Friarly files were all missing.

We looked through the desk. Eddy kept in it a few personal objects: a battery razor, indigestion tablets, a comb, and about sixteen packs of book matches, all from gambling clubs. Otherwise there was simply stationery, pens, a pocket calculator, and a desk diary.

His engagements, past and future, were merely down as the race meetings he was due to attend.

I looked at my watch. Seven forty-five. Chico nodded and began putting the files back neatly into their drawers. Frustrating, I thought. An absolute blank.

When we were ready to go, I took a quick look into a filing cabinet marked "Personnel," which contained slim factual files about everyone presently employed by the Jockey Club, and everyone receiving its pensions. I looked for a file headed "Mason," but someone had taken that too.

"Coming?" Chico said.

I nodded regretfully. We left Eddy's office as we'd found it and went back to the door to the stairway. Nothing stirred. The headquarters of British racing lay wide open to intruders, who were having to go empty away.

Chapter 14

On Friday afternoon, depressed on many counts, I drove comparatively slowly to Newmarket.

The day itself was hot, the weather reportedly stoking up to the sort of intense heat wave one could get in May, promising a glorious summer that seldom materialized. I drove in shirtsleeves with the window open, and decided to go to Hawaii and lie on the beach for a while, like a thousand years.

Martin England was out in his stable yard when I got there, also in shirtsleeves and wiping his forehead with a handkerchief.

"Sid!" he said, seeming truly pleased. "Great. I'm just starting evening stables. You couldn't have timed it better."

We walked round the boxes together in the usual ritual, the trainer visiting every horse and checking its health, the guest admiring and complimenting and keeping his tongue off the flaws. Martin's horses were middling to good, like himself, like the majority of trainers, the sort that provided the bulk of all racing, and of all jockeys' incomes.

"A long time since you rode for me," he said, catching my thought.

"Ten years or more."

"What do you weigh now, Sid?"

"About ten stone, stripped." Thinner, in fact, than when I'd stopped racing.

"Pretty fit, are you?"

"Same as usual," I said. "I suppose."

He nodded, and we went from the fillies' side of the yard to the colts'. He had a good lot of two-year-olds, it seemed to me, and he was pleased when I said so.

"This is Flotilla," he said, going to the next box. "He's three. He runs in the Dante at York next Wednesday, and if that's O.K. he'll go for the Derby."

"He looks well," I said.

Martin gave a carrot to his hope of glory. There was pride in his kind, fiftyish face, not for himself but for the shining coat and quiet eyes and waiting muscles of the splendid four-legged creature. I ran my hand down the glossy neck, and patted the dark bay shoulder, and felt the slender, rock-hard forelegs.

"He's in grand shape," I said. "Should do you proud."

He nodded with the thoroughly normal hint of anxiety showing under the pride, and we continued down the line, patting and discussing, and feeling content. Perhaps this was what I really needed, I thought: forty horses and hard work and routine. Planning and administering and paper work. Pleasure enough in preparing a winner, sadness enough in seeing one lose. A busy, satisfying, out-of-doors life style, a businessman on the back of a horse.

I thought of what Chico and I had been doing for months. Chasing villains, big and small. Wiping up a few messy bits of the racing industry. Getting knocked about, now and then. Taking our wits into minefields and fooling with people with shotguns.

It would be no public disgrace if I gave it up and decided to train. A much more normal life for an ex-jockey, everyone would think. A sensible, orderly decision, looking forward to middle and old age. I alone—and Trevor Deansgate—would know why I'd done it. I could live for a long time, knowing it.

I didn't want to.

In the morning at seven-thirty I went down to the yard in jodhpurs and boots and a pull-on jersey shirt. Early as it was, the air was warm, and with the sounds and bustle and smell of the stables all around, my spirits rose from bedrock and hovered at somewhere about knee level.

Martin, standing with a list in his hand, shouted good morning, and I went down to join him to see what he'd given me to ride. There was a five-year-old, up to my weight, that he'd think just the job.

Flotilla's lad was leading him out of his box, and I watched him admiringly as I turned toward Martin.

"Go on, then," he said. There was amusement in his face, enjoyment in his eyes.

"What?" I said.

"Ride Flotilla."

I swung toward the horse, totally surprised. His best horse, his Derby horse, and I out of practice and with one hand.

"Don't you want to?" he said. "He'd've been yours ten years ago as of right. And my jockey's gone to Ireland to race at the Curragh. It's either you or one of my lads, and to be honest, I'd rather have you."

I didn't argue. One doesn't turn down a chunk of heaven. I thought he was a bit mad, but if that was what he wanted, so did I. He gave me a leg up, and I pulled the stirrup leathers to my own length, and felt like an exile coming home.

"Do you want a helmet?" he said, looking around vaguely as if expecting one to materialize out of the tarmac.

"Not for this."

He nodded. "You never have." And he himself was wearing his usual checked cloth cap, in spite of the heat. I had always preferred riding bareheaded except in races: something to do with liking the feel of lightness and moving air.

"What about a whip?" he said.

He knew that I'd always carried one automatically, because a jockey's whip was a great aid to keeping a horse balanced and running straight: a tap down the shoulder did the trick, and one pulled the stick through from hand to hand, as required. I looked at the two hands in front of me. I thought that if I took a whip and fumbled it, I might drop it: and I needed above all to be efficient.

I shook my head. "Not today."

"Right, then," he said. "Let's be off."

With me in its midst, the string pulled out of the yard and went right through Newmarket town on the horse walks along the back roads, out to the wide sweeping Limekilns gallops to the north. Martin, himself riding the quiet five-year-old, pulled up there beside me.

"Give him a sharpish warm-up canter for three furlongs, and then take him a mile up the trial ground, upsides with Gulliver. It's Flotilla's last workout before the Dante, so make it a good one. O.K.?"

"Yes," I said.

"Wait until I get up there"—he pointed—"to watch."

"Yep."

He rode away happily toward a vantage point more than half a mile distant, from where he could see the whole gallop. I wound the left-hand rein round my plastic fingers and longed to be able to feel the pull from the horse's mouth. It would be easy to be clumsy, to upset the lie of the bit and the whole balance of the horse, if I got the tension wrong. In my right hand, the reins felt alive, carrying messages, telling Flotilla, and Flotilla telling me, where we were going, and how, and how fast. A private language, shared, understood.

Let me not make a mess of it, I thought. Let me just be able to do what I'd done thousands of times in the past; let the old skill be there, one hand or no. I could lose him the Dante and the Derby and any other race you cared to mention, if I got it really wrong.

The boy on Gulliver circled with me, waiting for the moment, answering my casual remarks in monosyllables and grunts. I wondered if he was the one who would have ridden Flotilla if I hadn't been there, and asked him, and he said, grumpily, yes. Too bad, I thought. Your turn will come.

Up the gallop, Martin waved. The boy on Gulliver kicked his mount into a fast pace at once, not waiting to start evenly together. You little sod, I thought. You do what you damned well like, but I'm going to take Flotilla along at the right speeds for the occasion and distance, and to hell with your tantrums.

It was absolutely great, going up there. It suddenly came right, as natural as if there had been no interval, and no missing limb. I threaded the left rein through bad and good hands alike and felt the vibrations from both sides of the bit, and if it wasn't the most perfect style ever seen on the Heath, it at least got the job done.

Flotilla swept over the turf in a balanced working gallop and came upsides with Gulliver effortlessly. I stayed beside the other horse then for most of the way, but as Flotilla was easily the better, I took him on from six furlongs and finished the mile at a good pace that was still short of strain. He was fit, I thought, pulling him back to a canter. He would do well in the Dante. He'd given me a good feel.

I said so to Martin, when I rejoined him, walking back. He was pleased, and laughed. "You can still ride, can't you? You looked just the same."

I sighed internally. I had been let back for a brief moment into the life I'd lost, but I wasn't just the same. I might have managed one working gallop without making an ass of myself, but it wasn't the Gold Cup at Cheltenham.

"Thanks," I said, "for a terrific morning."

We walked back through the town to his stable, and to breakfast, and afterward I went with him in his Land-Rover to see his second lot work on the racecourse side. When we got back from that we sat in his office and drank coffee and talked for a bit, and with some regret I said it was time I was going.

The telephone rang. Martin answered it, and held out the receiver to me.

"It's for you, Sid."

I thought it would be Chico, but it wasn't. It was, surprisingly, Henry Thrace, calling from his stud farm just outside the town.

"My girl assistant says she saw you riding work on the Heath," he said. "I didn't really believe her, but she was sure. Your head, without a helmet, unmistakable. With Martin England's horses, she said, so I rang on the off chance."

"What can I do for you?" I said.

"Actually it's the other way round," he said. "Or at least, I think so. I had a letter from the Jockey Club earlier this week, all very official and everything, asking me to let them know at once if Gleaner or Zingaloo died, and not to get rid of the carcass. Well, when I got that letter I rang Lucas Wainwright, who signed it, to ask what the hell it was all about, and he said it was really *you* who wanted to know if either of those horses died. He was telling me that in confidence, he said."

My mouth went as dry as vinegar.

"Are you still there?"

"Yes," I said.

"Then I'd better tell you that Gleaner has, in fact, just died."

"When?" I said, feeling stupid. "Er . . . How?" My heart rate had gone up to at least double. Talk about overreacting, I thought, and felt the fear stab through like toothache.

"A mare he was due to cover came into use, so we put him to her," he said, "this morning. An hour ago, maybe. He was sweating a lot, in this heat. It's hot in the breeding shed, with the sun on it. Anyway, he served her, and got down all right, and then he just staggered and fell, and died almost at once."

I unstuck my tongue. "Where is he now?"

"Still in the breeding shed. We're not using it again this morning, so I've left him there. I've tried to ring the Jockey Club, but it's Saturday and Lucas Wainwright isn't there, and anyway, as my girl said that you yourself were actually here in Newmarket . . ."

"Yes," I said. I took a shaky breath. "A post-mortem. You would agree, wouldn't you?"

"Essential, I'd say. Insurance, and all that."

"I'll try and get Ken Armadale," I said. "From the Equine Research Establishment. I know him. . . . Would he do you?"

"Couldn't be better."

"I'll ring you back."

"Right," he said, and disconnected.

I stood with Martin's telephone in my hand and looked into far dark spaces. It's too soon, I thought. Much too soon.

"What's the matter?" Martin said.

"A horse I've been inquiring about has died." Oh, God almighty . . . "Can I use your phone?" I said.

"Help yourself."

Ken Armadale said he was gardening and would much rather cut up a dead horse. I'll pick you up, I said, and he said he'd be waiting. My hand, I saw remotely, was actually shaking.

I rang back to Henry Thrace, to confirm. Thanked Martin for his tremendous hospitality. Put my suitcase and myself in the car, and picked up Ken Armadale from his large modern house on the southern edge of Newmarket.

"What am I looking for?" he said.

"Heart, I think."

He nodded. He was a strong, dark-haired research vet in his middle thirties, a man I'd dealt with on similar jaunts before, to the extent that I felt easy with him and trusted him, and as far as I could tell, he felt the same about me. A professional friendship, extending to a drink in a pub but not to Christmas cards, the sort of relationship that remained unchanged and could be taken up and put down as need arose.

"Anything special?" he said.

"Yes . . . but I don't know what."

"That's cryptic."

"Let's see what you find."

Gleaner, I thought. If there were three horses I should definitely be doing nothing about, they were Gleaner and Zingaloo and Tri-Nitro. I wished I hadn't asked Lucas Wainwright to write those letters, one to

Henry Thrace, the other to George Caspar. If those horses died, let me know . . . but not so soon, so appallingly soon.

I drove into Henry Thrace's stud farm and pulled up with a jerk. He came out of his house to meet us, and we walked across to the breeding shed. As with most such structures, its walls swept up to a height of ten feet, unbroken except for double entrance doors. Above that there was a row of windows, and above those, a roof. Very like Peter Rammileese's covered riding school, I thought, only smaller.

The day, which was hot outside, was very much hotter inside. The dead horse lay where he had fallen on the tan-covered floor, a sad brown hump with milky gray eyes.

"I rang the knackers," Ken said. "They'll be here pretty soon."

Henry Thrace nodded. It was impossible to do the post-mortem where the horse lay, as the smell of blood would linger for days and upset any other horse that came in there. We waited for not very long until the lorry arrived with its winch, and when the horse was loaded, we followed it down to the knackers' yard, where Newmarket's casualties were cut up for dog food. A small hygienic place; very clean.

Ken Armadale opened the bag he had brought and handed me a washable nylon boiler suit, like his own, to cover trousers and shirt. The horse lay in a square room with whitewashed walls and a concrete floor. In the floor, runnels and a drain. Ken turned on a tap so that water ran out of the hose beside the horse, and pulled on a pair of long rubber gloves.

"All set?" he said.

I nodded, and he made the first long incision. The smell, as on past occasions, was what I liked least about the next ten minutes, but Ken seemed not to notice it as he checked methodically through the contents. When the chest cavity had been opened, he removed its whole heart-lung mass and carried it over to the table which stood under the single window.

"This is odd," he said, after a pause.

"What is?"

"Take a look."

I went over beside him and looked where he was pointing, but I hadn't his knowledge behind my eyes, and all I saw was a blood-covered lump of tissue with tough-looking ridges of gristle in it.

"His heart?" I said.

"That's right. Look at these valves. . . . " He turned his head to me, frowning. "He died of something horses don't get." He thought it over. "It's a great pity we couldn't have had a blood sample before he died."

"There's another horse at Henry Thrace's with the same thing," I said. "You can get your blood sample from him."

He straightened up from bending over the heart, and stared at me.

"Sid," he said, "you'd better tell me what's up. And outside, don't you think, in some fresh air."

We went out, and it was a great deal better. He stood listening, with blood all over his gloves and down the front of his coveralls, while I wrestled with the horrors in the back of my mind and spoke with flat lack of emotion from the front.

"There are—or were—four of them," I said. "Four that I know of. They were all top star horses, favorites all winter for the Guineas and the Derby. That class. The very top. They all came from the same stable. They all went out to race in Guineas week looking marvelous. They all started hot favorites, and they all totally flopped. They all suffered from a mild virus infection at about that time, but it didn't develop. They all were subsequently found to have heart murmurs."

Ken frowned heavily. "Go on."

"There was Bethesda, who ran in the One Thousand Guineas two years ago. She went to stud, and she died of heart failure this spring, while she was foaling."

Ken took a deep breath.

"There's this one," I said, pointing. "Gleaner. He was favorite for the Guineas last year. He then got a really bad heart, and also arthritis. The other horse at Henry Thrace's, Zingaloo, he went out fit to a race and afterwards could hardly stand from exhaustion."

Ken nodded. "And which is the fourth one?"

I looked up at the sky. Blue and clear. I'm killing myself, I thought. I looked back at him and said, "Tri-Nitro."

"Sid!" He was shocked. "Only ten days ago."

"So what is it?" I said. "What's the matter with them?"

"I'd have to do some tests to be certain," he said. "But the symptoms you've described are typical, and those heart valves are unmistakable. That horse died from swine erysipelas, which is a disease you get only in pigs."

Ken said, "We need to keep that heart for evidence."

"Yes," I said.

Dear God . . .

"Get one of those bags, will you?" he said. "Hold it open." He put the heart inside. "We'd better go along to the research center later. I've been thinking. . . . I know I've got some reference papers there about erysipelas in horses. We could look them up, if you like."

"Yes," I said.

He peeled off his blood-spattered coveralls. "Heat and exertion," he said. "That's what did for this fellow. A deadly combination, with a heart in that state. He might have lived for years, otherwise."

Ironic, I thought bitterly.

He packed everything away, and we went back to Henry Thrace. A blood sample from Zingaloo? No problem, he said.

Ken took enough blood to float a battleship, it seemed to me, but what was a liter to a horse, which had gallons? We accepted reviving Scotches from Henry with gratitude, and afterward took our trophies to the Equine Research Establishment, along the Bury Road.

Ken's office was a small extension to a large laboratory, where he took the bag containing Gleaner's heart over to the sink and told me he was washing out the remaining blood.

"Now come and look," he said.

This time I could see exactly what he meant. Along all the edges of the valves were small knobbly growths, like baby cauliflowers, creamy white.

"That's vegetation," he said. "It prevents the valves from closing. Makes the heart as efficient as a leaking pump."

"I can see it would."

"I'll put this in the fridge, then we'll look through those veterinary journals for that paper."

I sat on a hard chair in his utilitarian office while he searched for what he wanted. I looked at my fingers. Curled and uncurled them. This can't all be happening, I thought. It's only three days since I saw Trevor Deansgate at Chester. *"If you break your assurance, I'll do what I said."*

"Here it is," Ken exclaimed, flattening a paper open. "Shall I read you the relevant bits?"

I nodded.

" 'Swine erysipelas . . . in 1938 . . . occurred in a horse, with vegetative endocarditis . . . the chronic form of the illness in pigs.' " He looked up. "That's those cauliflower growths. Right?"

"Yes."

He read again from the paper. " 'During 1944 a mutant strain of erysipelas rhusiopathiae appeared suddenly in a laboratory specializing in antisera production and produced acute endocarditis in the serum horses.' "

"Translate," I said.

He smiled. "They used to use horses for producing vaccines. You inject the horse with pig disease, wait until it develops antibodies, draw off blood, and extract the serum. The serum, injected into healthy pigs, prevents them getting the disease. Same process as for all human vaccinations, smallpox and so on. Standard procedure."

"O.K.," I said. "Go on."

"What happened was that instead of growing antibodies as usual, the horses themselves got the disease."

"How could that happen?"

"It doesn't say here. You'd have to ask the pharmaceutical firm concerned, which I see is the Tierson vaccine lab along at Cambridge. They'd tell you, I should think, if you asked. I know someone there, if you want an introduction."

"It's a long time ago," I said.

"My dear fellow, germs don't die. They can live like time bombs, waiting for some fool to take stupid liberties. Some of these labs keep virulent strains around for decades. You'd be surprised."

He looked down again at the paper, and said, "You'd better read these next paragraphs yourself. They look pretty straightforward." He pushed the journal across to me, and I read the page where he pointed.

1. 24–48 hours after intramuscular injection of the pure culture, inflammation of one or more of the heart valves commences. At this time, apart from a slight rise in temperature and occasional palpitations, no other symptoms are seen unless the horse is subjected to severe exertion, when auricular fibrillation or interference with the blood supply to the lungs occurs; both occasion severe distress which only resolves after 2–3 hours rest.

2. Between the second and the sixth day, pyrexia (temperature rise) increases and white cell count of the blood increases and the horse is listless and off food. This could easily be loosely diagnosed as "the virus." However, examination by stethoscope reveals a progressively increasing heart murmur. After about ten days the temperature returns to normal and, unless subjected to more than walk or trot, the horse may appear to have recovered. The murmur is still present and it then becomes necessary to retire the horse from fast work since this induces respiratory distress.

3. Over the next few months vegetations grow on the heart valves, and arthritis in some joints, particularly of the limbs, may or may not appear. The condition is permanent and progressive and death may occur suddenly following exertion or during very hot weather, sometimes years after the original infection.

I looked up. "That's it, exactly, isn't it?" I said. "Bang on the nose."

I said slowly, "Intramuscular injection of the pure culture could absolutely not have occurred accidentally."

"Absolutely not," he agreed.

I said, "George Caspar had his yard sewn up so tight this year with alarm bells and guards and dogs that no one could have got within screaming distance of Tri-Nitro with a syringeful of live germs."

He smiled. "You wouldn't need a syringeful. Come into the lab and I'll show you."

I followed him, and we fetched up beside one of the cupboards with sliding doors that lined the whole of the wall. He opened the cupboard and pulled out a box, which proved to contain a large number of smallish plastic envelopes.

He tore open one of the envelopes and tipped the contents onto his hand: a hypodermic needle attached to a plastic capsule only the size of a pea. The whole thing looked like a tiny dart with a small round balloon at one end, about as long, altogether, as one's little finger.

He picked up the capsule and squeezed it. "Dip that into liquid, you draw up half a teaspoonful. You don't need that much pure culture to produce a disease."

"You could hold that in your hand, out of sight," I said.

He nodded. "Just slap the horse with it. Done in a flash. I use these sometimes for horses that shy away from a syringe." He showed me how, holding the capsule between thumb and index finger, so that the sharp end pointed down from his palm. "Shove the needle in and squeeze," he said.

"Could you spare one of these?"

"Sure," he said, giving me an envelope. "Anything you like."

I put it in my pocket. Dear God in heaven.

Ken said slowly, "You know, we might just be able to do something about Tri-Nitro."

"How do you mean?"

He pondered, looking at the large bottle of Zingaloo's blood, which stood on the draining board beside the sink.

"We might find an antibiotic which would cure the disease."

"Isn't it too late?" I said.

"Too late for Zingaloo. But I don't think those vegetations would start growing at once. If Tri-Nitro was infected, say . . ."

"Say two weeks ago today, after his final working gallop."

He looked at me with amusement. "Say, two weeks ago, then. His heart will be in trouble, but the vegetation won't have started. If he gets the right antibiotic soon, he might make a full recovery."

"Do you mean . . . back to normal?"

"Don't see why not."

"What are you waiting for?" I said.

Chapter 15

I spent most of Sunday beside the sea, driving north-east from Newmarket to the wide deserted coast of Norfolk. Just for somewhere to go, something to do, to pass the time.

Even though the sun shone, the wind off the North Sea was keeping the beaches almost empty: small groups were huddled into the shelter of flimsy canvas screens, and a few intrepid children built castles.

I sat in the sun in a hollow in a sand dune which was covered with coarse tufts of grass, and watched the waves come and go. I walked along the shore, kicking the worm casts. I stood looking out to sea, holding up my left upper arm for support, aware of the weight of the machinery lower down, which was not so very heavy, but always there.

I had often felt released and restored by lonely places, but not on that day. The demons came with me. The cost of pride . . . the price of safety. If you didn't expect so much of yourself, Charles had said once, you'd give yourself an easier time. It hadn't really made sense. One was as one was. Or at least, one was as one was until someone came along and broke you all up.

If you sneezed on the Limekilns, they said in Newmarket, it was heard two miles away on the racecourse. The news of my attendance at Gleaner's post-mortem would be given to George Caspar within a day. Trevor Deansgate would hear of it; he was sure to.

I could still go away, I thought. It wasn't too late. Travel. Wander by other seas, under other skies. I could go away and keep very quiet. I could still escape from the terror he induced in me. I could still . . . run away.

I left the coast and drove numbly to Cambridge. Stayed in the University Arms Hotel and, in the morning, went to Tierson Pharmaceuticals Vaccine Laboratories. I asked for, and got, a Mr. Livingston, who was maybe sixty and grayishly thin. He made small nibbling movements with his mouth when he spoke. He looks a dried-up old cuss, Ken Armadale had said, but he's got a mind like a monkey.

"Mr. Halley, is it?" Livingston said, shaking hands in the entrance hall. "Mr Armadale has been on the phone to me, explaining what you want. I think I can help you, yes, I do indeed. Come along, come along, this way."

He walked in small steps before me, looking back frequently to make sure I was following. It seemed to be a precaution born of losing people, because the place was a labyrinth of glass-walled passages with laboratories and gardens apparently intermixed at random.

"The place just grew," he said, when I remarked on it. "But here we are." He led the way into a large laboratory which looked through glass walls into the passage on one side, and a garden on another, and straight into another lab on the third.

"This is the experimental section," he said, his gesture embracing both rooms. "Most of the laboratories just manufacture the vaccines commercially, but in here we putter about inventing new ones."

"And resurrecting old ones?" I said.

He looked at me sharply. "Certainly not. I believe you came for information, not to accuse us of carelessness."

"Sorry," I said placatingly. "That's quite right."

"Well, then. Ask your question."

"Er . . . Yes. How did the serum horses you were using in the 1940's get swine erysipelas?"

"Ah," he said. "Pertinent. Brief. To the point. We published a paper about it, didn't we? Before my time, of course. But I've heard about it. Yes. Well, it's possible. It happened. But it shouldn't have. Sheer carelessness, do you see? I hate carelessness. Hate it."

Just as well, I thought. In his line of business, carelessness might be fatal.

"Do you know anything about the production of erysipelas antiserum?" he said.

"You could write it on a thumbnail."

"Ah," he said. "Then I'll explain as to a child. Will that do?"

"Nicely," I said.

He gave me another sharp glance, in which there was this time amusement.

"You inject live erysipelas germs into a horse. Are you with me? I am talking about the past now, when they did use horses. We haven't used horses since the early 1950's, nor have Burroughs Wellcome, and Bayer in Germany. The past, do you see?"

"Yes," I said.

"The horse's blood produces antibodies to fight the germ, but the horse does not develop the disease, because it is a disease pigs get and horses don't."

"A child," I assured him, "would understand."

"Very well. Now, sometimes the standard strain of

erysipelas becomes weakened, and in order to make it virulent again we pass it through pigeons."

"Pigeons?" I said, very politely.

He raised his eyebrows. "Customary practice. Pass a weak strain through pigeons to recover virulence."

"Oh, of course," I said.

He pounced on the satire in my voice. "Mr. Halley," he said severely. "Do you want to know all this or don't you?"

"Yes, please," I said meekly.

"Very well, then. The virulent strain was removed from the pigeons and subcultured onto blood agar plates." He broke off, looking at the blankness of my ignorance. "Let me put it this way. The live virulent germs were transferred from the pigeons onto dishes containing blood, where they they multiplied, thus producing a useful quality for injecting into the serum horses."

"That's fine," I said. "I do understand."

"All right." He nodded. "Now, the blood on the dishes was bull's blood. Bovine blood."

"Yes," I said.

"But owing to someone's stupid carelessness, the blood agar plates were prepared one day with horse blood. This produced a mutant strain of the disease." He paused. "Mutants are changes which occur suddenly and for no apparent reason throughout nature."

"Yes," I said again.

"No one realized what had happened," he said. "Until the mutant strain was injected into the serum horses and they all got erysipelas. The mutant strain proved remarkably constant. The incubation period was always twenty-four to forty-eight hours after inoculation, and endocarditis— that is, inflammation of the heart valves—was always the result."

A youngish man in a white coat, unbuttoned down

the front, came into the room next door, and I watched him vaguely as he began puttering about.

"What became of this mutant strain?" I said.

Livingston nibbled a good deal with the lips, but finally said, "We would have kept some, I daresay, as a curiosity. But of course it would be weakened by now, and to restore it to full virulence, one would have to . . ."

"Yeah," I said. "Pass it through pigeons."

He didn't think it was funny. "Quite so," he said.

"And all this passing through pigeons and subculture on agar plates . . . how much skill does this take?"

He blinked. "I could do it, of course."

"I couldn't. Any injections I'd handled had come in neat little ampules, packed in boxes.

The man in the next room was opening cupboards, looking for something.

I said, "Would there be any of this mutant strain anywhere else in the world, besides here? I mean, did this laboratory send any of it out to anywhere else?"

The lips pursed themselves and the eyebrows went up. "I've no idea," he said. He looked through the glass and gestured toward the man in the next room. "You could ask Barry Shummuck. He would know. Mutant strains are his specialty."

He pronounced "Shummuck" to rhyme with "hummock." I know the name, I thought. I . . . *Oh, my God.*

The shock of it fizzed through my brain and left me half breathless. I knew someone too well whose real name was Shummuck.

I swallowed and felt shivery. "Tell me more about your Mr. Shummuck," I said.

Livingston was a natural chatterer and saw no harm in it. He shrugged. "He came up the hard way. Still talks like it. He used to have a terrible chip on his shoulder. The world owed him a living, that sort of thing. Shades of student demos. He's settled down recently. He's good at his job."

"You don't care for him?" I said.

Livingston was startled. "I didn't say that."

He had, plainly, in his face and in his voice. I said only, "What sort of accent?"

"Northern. I don't know exactly. What does it matter?"

Barry Shummuck looked like no one I knew. I said slowly, hesitantly, "Do you know if he has . . . a brother?"

Livingston's face showed surprise. "Yes, he has. Funny thing, he's a bookmaker." He pondered. "Some name like Terry. Not Terry . . . Trevor, that's it. They come here together sometimes, the two of them. . . . Thick as thieves."

Barry Shummuck gave up his search and moved toward the door.

"Would you like to meet him?" Mr. Livingston said.

Speechlessly, I shook my head. The last thing I wanted, in a building full of virulent germs which he knew how to handle and I didn't, was to be introduced to the brother of Trevor Deansgate.

Shummuck went through the door and into the glass-walled corridor, and turned in our direction.

Oh, no, I thought.

He walked purposefully along and pushed open the door of the lab we were in. Head and shoulders leaned forward.

"Morning, Mr. Livingston," he said. "Have you seen my box of transparencies anywhere?"

The basic voice was the same, self-confident and slightly abrasive. Manchester accent, much stronger. I held my left arm out of sight half behind my back and willed him to go away.

"No," said Mr. Livingston, with just a shade of pleasure. "But, Barry, can you spare . . ."

Livingston and I were standing in front of a workbench which held various empty glass jars and a row of clamps. I turned leftward, with my arm still hidden, and clumsily, with my right hand, knocked over a clamp and two glass jars.

More clatter than breakage. Livingston gave a quick nibble of surprised annoyance, and righted the rolling jars. I gripped the clamp, which was metal and heavy, and would have to do.

I turned back toward the door.

The door was shutting. The back view of Barry Shummuck was striding away along the corridor, the front edges of his white coat flapping.

I let a shuddering breath out through my nose and carefully put the clamp back at the end of the row.

"He's gone," Mr. Livingston said. "What a pity."

I drove back to Newmarket, to the Equine Research Establishment and Ken Armadale.

I wondered how long it would take chatty Mr. Livingston to tell Barry Shummuck of the visit of a man called Halley who wanted to know about a pig disease in horses.

I felt faintly, and continuously, sick.

"It's been made resistant to all ordinary antibiotics," Ken said. "A real neat little job."

"How do you mean?"

"If any old antibiotic would kill it, you couldn't be sure the horse wouldn't be given a shot as soon as he had a temperature, and never develop the disease."

I sighed. "So how do they make it resistant?"

"Feed it tiny doses of antibiotic until it becomes immune."

"All this is technically difficult, isn't it?"

"Yes, fairly."

"Have you ever heard of Barry Shummuck?"

He frowned. "No, I don't think so."

The craven inner voice told me urgently to shut up, to escape, to fly to safety . . . to Australia . . . to a desert.

"Do you have a cassette recorder here?" I said.

"Yes. I use it for making notes while I'm operating." He went out and fetched it and set it up for me on his desk, loaded with a new tape. "Just talk," he said. "It has a built-in microphone."

"Stay and listen," I said. "I want . . . a witness."

He regarded me slowly. "You look so strained. . . . It's no gentle game, is it, what you do?"

"Not always."

I switched on the recorder, and for introduction spoke my name, the place, and the date. Then I switched off again and sat looking at the fingers I needed for pressing the buttons.

"What is it, Sid?" Ken said.

I glanced at him and down again. "Nothing."

I had to do it, I thought. I absolutely had to. I was never in any way going to be whole again if I didn't.

If I had to choose, and it seemed to me that I did have to choose, I would have to settle for wholeness of mind, and put up with what it cost. Perhaps I could deal with physical fear. Perhaps I could deal with anything that happened to my body, and even with helplessness. What I could not forever deal with—and I saw it finally with clarity and certainty—was despising myself.

I pressed the "play" and "record" buttons together, irrevocably broke my assurance to Trevor Deansgate.

Chapter 16

I telephoned Chico at lunchtime and told him what I'd found out about Rosemary's horses.

"What it amounts to," I said, "is that those four horses had bad hearts because they'd been given a pig disease. There's a lot of complicated info about how it was done, but that's now the stewards' headache."

"Pig disease?" Chico said disbelievingly.

"Yeah. That big bookmaker Trevor Deansgate has a brother who works in a place that produces vaccines for inoculating people against smallpox and diphtheria and so on, and they cooked up a plan to squirt pig germs into those red-hot favorites."

"Which duly lost," Chico said, "while the bookmaker raked in the lolly."

"Right," I said.

It felt very odd to put Trevor Deansgate's scheme into casual words and to be talking about him as if he were just one of our customary puzzles.

"How did you find out?" Chico said.

"Gleaner died at Henry Thrace's, and the pig disease turned up at the post-mortem. When I went to the vaccine lab I saw a man called Shummuck who deals in odd germs, and I remembered that Shummuck was Trevor Deansgate's real name. And Trevor Deansgate is very thick with George Caspar . . . and all the affected horses, that we know of, have come from George Caspar's stable."

"Circumstantial, isn't it?" Chico said.

"A bit, yes. But the Security Service can take if from there."

"Eddy Keith?" he said skeptically.

"He can't hush this one up; don't you worry."

"Have you told Rosemary?"

"Not yet."

"Bit of a laugh," Chico said.

"Mm."

"Well, Sid, mate," he said, "this is results day all round. We got a fix on Nicky Ashe."

Nicky Ashe, with a knife in his sock. A pushover, compared with . . . compared with . . .

"Hey," Chico's voice said aggrievedly through the receiver. "Aren't you pleased?"

"Yes, of course. What sort of fix?"

"He's been sending out some of those damnfool letters. I went to your place this morning, just to see, like, and there were two envelopes there with our sticky labels on."

"Great," I said.

"I opened them. They'd both been sent to us by people whose names start with *P*. All that legwork paid off."

"So we've got the begging letter?"

"We sure have. It's exactly the same as the ones your wife had, except for the address to send the money to, of course. Got a pencil?"

"Yeah."

He read out the address, which was in Clifton, Bristol. I looked at it thoughtfully. I could either give it straight to the police, or I could check it first myself. Checking it, in one certain way, had persuasive attractions.

"Chico," I said, "ring Jenny's flat in Oxford and ask for Louise McInnes. Ask her to ring me here at the Rutland Hotel in Newmarket."

"Scared of your missus, are you?"

"Will you do it?"

"Oh, sure." He laughed, and rang off. When the bell rang again, however, it was not Louise on the other end, but still Chico.

"She's left the flat," he said. "Your wife gave me her new number." He read it out. "Anything else?"

"Can you bring your cassette player to the Jockey Club, Portman Square, tomorrow afternoon at, say, four o'clock?"

"Like last time?"

"No," I said. "Front door, all the way."

Louise, to my relief, answered her telephone. When I told her what I wanted, she was incredulous.

"You've actually *found* him?"

"Well," I said, "probably. Will you come there and identify him?"

"Yes." No hesitation. "Where and when?"

"Someplace in Bristol." I paused, and said diffidently, "I'm in Newmarket now. I could pick you up in Oxford this afternoon, and we could go straight on. We might spot him this evening . . . or tomorrow morning."

There was a silence at the other end. Then she said, "I've moved out of Jenny's flat."

"Yes."

"Another silence, and then her voice, quiet, and committed.

"All right."

She was waiting for me in Oxford, and she had brought an overnight bag.

"Hello," I said, getting out of the car.

"Hello."

We looked at each other. I kissed her cheek. She smiled with what I had to believe was enjoyment, and slung her case in the boot beside mine.

"You can always retreat," I said.

"So can you."

We sat in the car, however, and I drove to Bristol feeling contented and carefree. Trevor Deansgate wouldn't yet have started looking for me, and Peter Rammileese and his boys hadn't been in sight for a week, and no one except Chico knew where I was going. The shadowy future, I thought, was not going to spoil the satisfactory present. I decided not even to think of it, and for most of the time, I didn't.

We went first to an inn that someone had once told me of, high on the cliffs overlooking the Avon gorge, and geared to rich-American-tourist comfort.

"We'll never get in here," Louise said, eyeing the opulence.

"I telephoned."

"How organized! One room or two?"

"One."

She smiled as if that suited her well, and we were shown into a large wood-paneled room with stretches of carpet, antique polished furniture, and a huge fourposter bed decked with American-style white muslin frills.

"My God," Louise said. "And I expected a motel."

"I didn't know about the fourposter," I said a little weakly.

"Wow," she said, laughing. "This is more *fun.*"

We parked the suitcases and freshened up in the modern bathroom tucked discreetly behind the paneling, and went back to the car; and Louise smiled to herself all the way to the new address of Nicholas Ashe.

It was a prosperous-looking house in a prosperous-looking street. A solid five- or six-bedroom affair, mellowed and white-painted and uninformative in the early evening sun.

I stopped the car on the same side of the road, pretty close, at a place from where we could see both the front door and the gate into the driveway. Nicky, Louise had said on the way down, often used to go out for a walk at about seven o'clock, after a hard day's typing. Maybe he would again, if he was there.

Maybe he wouldn't.

We had the car's windows open because of the warm air. I lit a cigarette, and the smoke floated in a quiet curl through lack of wind. Very peaceful, I thought, waiting there.

"Where do you come from?" Louise said.

I blew a smoke ring. "I'm the posthumous illegitimate son of a twenty-year-old window cleaner who fell off his ladder just before his wedding."

She laughed. "Very elegantly put."

"And you?"

"The legitimate daughter of the manager of a glass factory and a magistrate, both alive and living in Essex."

We consulted about brothers and sisters, of which I had none and she had two, one of each. About education, of which I'd had some and she a lot. About life in general, of which she'd seen a little, and I a bit more.

An hour passed in the quiet street. A few birds sang. Sporadic cars drove by. Men came home from work and turned into the driveways. Distant doors slammed. No one moved in the house we were watching.

"You're patient," Louise said.

"I spend hours doing this sometimes."

"Pretty unexciting."

I looked at her clear intelligent eyes. "Not this evening."

Seven o'clock came and went; and Nicky didn't.

"How long will we stay?"

"Until dark."

"I'm hungry."

Half an hour drifted by. I learned that she liked curry and paella and hated rhubarb. I learned that the thesis she was writing was giving her hell.

"I'm so far behind schedule," she said. "And . . . Oh, my goodness, *there he is.*"

Her eyes had opened very wide. I looked where she looked, and saw Nicholas Ashe.

Coming not from the front door, but from the side of the house. My age, or a bit younger. Taller, but of my own thin build. My coloring. Dark hair, slightly curly. Dark eyes. Narrow jaw. All the same.

He looked sufficiently like me for it to be a shock, but was nevertheless quite different. I took my baby camera out of my trouser pocket and pulled it open with my teeth as usual, and took his picture.

When he reached the gate he paused and looked back, and a woman ran after him, calling, "Ned, Ned, wait for me."

"Ned!" Louise said, sliding down in her seat. "If he comes this way, won't he see me?"

"Not if I kiss you."

"Well, do it," she said.

I took, however, another photograph.

The woman looked older, about forty; slim, pleasant, excited. She tucked her arm into his and looked up at his eyes, her own clearly, even from twenty feet away, full of adoration. He looked down and laughed delightfully, then he kissed her forehead and swung her in a little circle onto the pavement, and put his arm around her waist, and walked toward us with vivid gaiety and a bounce in his step.

I risked one more photograph from the shadows of the car, and leaned across and kissed Louise with enthusiasm.

Their footsteps went past. Abreast of us, they must have seen us, or at least my back, for they both suddenly giggled lightheartedly, lovers sharing their secret with lovers. They almost paused, then went on, their steps growing softer until they had gone.

I sat up reluctantly.

Louise said, "Whew!" but whether it was the result of the kiss, or the proximity of Ashe, I wasn't quite sure.

"He's just the same," she said.

"Casanova himself," I said dryly.

She glanced at me swiftly and I guess she was wondering whether I was jealous of his success with Jenny, but in fact I was wondering whether Jenny had been attracted to him because he resembled me, or whether she had been attracted to me in the first place, and also to him, because we matched some internal picture she had of a sexually interesting male. I was more disturbed than I liked by the physical appearance of Nicholas Ashe.

"Well," I said, "that's that. Let's find some dinner."

I drove back to the hotel, and we went upstairs before we ate, Louise saying she wanted to change out of the blouse and skirt she had worn all day.

I took the battery charger out of my suitcase and

plugged it in; took a spent battery from my pocket, and rolled up my shirtsleeve and snapped out the one from my arm, and put them both in the charger. Then I took a charged battery from my suitcase and inserted it in the empty socket in the arm. And Louise watched.

I said, "Are you . . . revolted?"

"No, of course not."

I pulled my sleeve down and buttoned the cuff.

"How long does a battery last?" she said.

"Six hours, if I use it a lot. About eight, usually."

She merely nodded, as if people with electric arms were as normal as people with blue eyes. We went down to dinner and ate sole and afterward strawberries, and if they'd tasted of seaweed I wouldn't have cared. It wasn't only because of Louise, but also because since that morning I had stopped tearing myself apart, and had slowly been growing back toward peace. I could feel it happening, and it was marvelous.

We sat side by side on a sofa in the hotel lounge, drinking small cups of coffee.

"Of course," she said, "now that we have seen Nicky, we don't really need to stay until tomorrow."

"Are you thinking of leaving?" I said.

"About as much as you are."

"Who is seducing whom?" I said.

"Mm," she said, smiling. "This whole thing is so unexpected."

She looked calmly at my left hand, which rested on the sofa between us. I couldn't tell what she was thinking, but I said on impulse, "Touch it."

She looked up at me quickly. "What?"

"Touch it. Feel it."

She tentatively moved her right hand until her fingers were touching the tough, lifeless, plastic skin. There was no drawing back, no flicker of revulsion in her face.

"It's metal, inside there," I said. "Gears and levers and electric circuits. Press harder, and you'll feel them."

She did as I said, and I saw her surprise as she discovered the shape of the inner realities.

"There's a switch inside there too," I said. "You can't see it from the outside, but it's just below the thumb. One can switch the hand off, if one wants."

"Why would you want to?"

"Very useful for carrying things, like a briefcase. You shut the fingers round the handle, and switch the current off, and the hand just stays shut without you having to do it all yourself."

I put my right hand over and pushed the switch off and on, to show her.

"It's like the push-through switch on a table lamp," I said. "Feel it. Push it."

She fumbled a bit because it wasn't all that easy to find if one didn't know, but in the end pushed it both ways, off and on. Nothing in her expression but concentration.

She felt some sort of tension relax in me, and looked up, accusingly.

"You were testing me," she said.

I smiled. "I suppose so."

"You're a pig."

I felt an unaccustomed uprush of mischief. "As a matter of fact," I said, holding my left hand in my right, "if I unscrew it firmly round this way several times, the whole hand will come right off at the wrist."

"Don't do it," she said, horrified.

I laughed with absolute enjoyment. I wouldn't have thought I would ever feel that way about that hand.

"Why does it come right off?" she said.

"Oh . . . servicing. Stuff like that."

"You look so different," she said.

I nodded. She was right. I said, "Let's go to bed."

"What a world of surprises," she said, a good while later. "Almost the last thing I would have expected you to be as a lover is gentle."

"Too gentle?"

"No. I liked it."

We lay in the dark, drowsily. She herself had been warmly receptive and generous, and had made it for me an intense sunburst of pleasure. It was a shame, I thought hazily, that the act of sex had got so cluttered up with taboos and techniques and therapists and sin and voyeurs and the whole commercial ballyhoo. Two people fitting together in the old design should be a private matter, and if you didn't expect too much, you'd get on better. One was as one was. Even if a girl wanted it, I could never have put on a pretense of being a rough, aggressive bull of a lover, because, I thought sardonically, I would have laughed at myself in the middle. And it had been all right, I thought, as it was.

"Louise," I said.

No reply.

I shifted a little for deeper comfort, and drifted, like her, to sleep.

A while later, awake early as usual, I watched the daylight strengthen on her sleeping face. The fair hair lay tangled round her head in the way I had seen it first, and her skin looked soft and fresh. When she woke, even before she opened her eyes, she was smiling.

"Good morning," I said.

"Morning."

She moved toward me in the big bed, the white muslin frills on the canopy overhead surrounding us like a frame.

"Like sleeping in clouds," she said.

She came up against the hard shell of my left arm, and blinked from the awareness of it.

"You don't sleep in this when you're alone, do you?" she said.

"No."

"Take it off, then."

I said with a smile, "No."

She gave me a long considering inspection.

"Jenny's right about you being like flint," she said.

"Well, I'm not."

"She told me that at the exact moment some chap was smashing up your arm you were calmly working out how to defeat him."

I made a face.

"Is it true?" she said.

"In a way."

"Jenny said . . ."

"To be honest," I said, "I'd rather talk about you."

"I'm not interesting."

"That's a right come-on, that is," I said.

"What are you waiting for, then?"

"I do so like your retreating maidenly blushes."

I touched her lightly on her breast and it seemed to do for her what it did for me. Instant arousal, mutually pleasing.

"Clouds," she said contentedly. "What do you think of when you're doing it?"

"Sex?"

She nodded.

"I feel. It isn't thought."

"Sometimes I see roses . . . on trellises . . . scarlet and pink and gold. Sometimes spiky stars. This time it will be white frilly muslin clouds."

I asked her, after.

"No. All bright sunlight. Quite blinding."

The sunlight, in truth, had flooded into the room,

making the whole white canopy translucent and shimmering.

"Why didn't you want the curtains drawn last night?" she asked. "Don't you like the dark?"

"I don't like sleeping when my enemies are up and about."

I said it without thinking. The actual truth of it followed after, like a freezing shower.

"Like an animal," she said, and then, "What's the matter?"

Remember me, I thought, as I am. And I asked, "Like some breakfast?"

We went back to Oxford. I took the film to be developed, and we had lunch at Les Quat' Saisons, where the delectable pâté de turbot and the superb quenelle de brochet soufflée kept the shadows at bay a while longer. With the coffee, though, came the unavoidable minute.

"I have to be in London at four o'clock," I said.

Louise said, "When are you going to the police about Nicky?"

"I'll come back here on Thursday, day after tomorrow, to pick up the photos. I'll do it then." I reflected. "Give that lady in Bristol two more happy days."

"Poor thing."

"Will I see you Thursday?" I said.

"Unless you're blind."

Chico was propping up the Portman Square building with a look of resignation, as if he'd been there for hours. He shifted his shoulder off the stonework at my on-foot approach and said, "Took your time, didn't you?"

"The car park was full."

From one hand he dangled the black cassette recorder

we used occasionally, and he was otherwise wearing jeans and a sports shirt and no jacket. The hot weather, far from vanishing, had settled in on an almost stationary high pressure system, and I was also in shirtsleeves, though with a tie on, and a jacket over my arm. On the third floor all the windows were open, the street noises coming up sharply, and Sir Thomas Ullaston, sitting behing his big desk, had dealt with the day in pale blue shirting with white stripes.

"Come in, Sid," he said, seeing me appear in his open doorway. "I've been waiting for you."

"I'm sorry I'm late," I said, shaking hands. "This is Chico Barnes, who works with me."

He shook Chico's hand. "Right," he said. "Now you're here, we'll get Lucas Wainwright and the others along." He pressed an intercom button and spoke to his secretary. "And bring some more chairs, would you?"

The office slowly filled up with more people than I'd expected, but all of whom I knew at least to talk to. The top administrative brass in full force, about six of them, all urbane worldly men, the people who really ran racing. Chico looked at them slightly nervously, as if at an alien breed, and seemed to be relieved when a table was provided for him to put the recorder on. He sat with the table between himself and the room, like a barrier. I fished into my jacket for the cassette I'd brought, and gave it to him.

Lucas Wainwright came with Eddy Keith on his heels, Eddy looking coldly out of the genial face; big, bluff Eddy, whose warmth for me was slowly dying.

"Well, Sid," Sir Thomas said, "here we all are. Now, on the telephone yesterday you told me you had discovered how Tri-Nitro had been nobbled for the Guineas, and—as you see—we are all very interested." He smiled. "So fire away."

I made my own manner match theirs: calm and

dispassionate, as if Trevor Deansgate's threat wasn't anywhere in my mind, instead of continually flashing through it like stabs.

"I've . . . er . . . put it all onto tape," I said. "You'll hear two voices. The other is Ken Armadale, from Equine Research. I asked him to clarify the veterinary details, which are his province, not mine."

The well-brushed heads nodded. Eddy Keith merely stared. I glanced at Chico, who pressed the start button, and my own voice, disembodied, spoke loudly into a wholly attentive silence.

"This is Sid Halley, at the Equine Research Establishment, on Monday, May fourteenth. . . ."

I listened to the flat sentences, spelling it out. The identical symptoms in four horses, the lost races, the bad hearts. My request, via Lucas Wainwright, to be informed if any of the three still alive should die. The post-mortem on Gleaner, with Ken Armadale repeating in greater detail my own simpler account. His voice explaining, again after me, how horses had come to be infected by a disease of pigs. His voice saying, "I found active live germs in the lesions on Gleaner's heart valves, and also in the blood taken from Zingaloo . . ." and my voice continuing, "A mutant strain of the disease was produced at the Tierson Vaccine Laboratories at Cambridge in the following manner. . . ."

It wasn't the easiest of procedures to understand, but I watched the faces and saw that they did, particularly by the time Ken Armadale had gone through it all again, confirming what I'd said.

"As to motive and opportunity," my voice said, "we come to a man called Trevor Deansgate. . . ."

Sir Thomas's head snapped back from its forward, listening posture, and he stared at me bleakly from across the room. Remembering, no doubt, that he had entertained Trevor Deansgate in the stewards' box at

Chester. Remembering, perhaps, that he had brought me and Trevor Deansgate there face to face.

Among the other listeners the name had created an almost equal stir. All of them either knew him or knew of him: the big up-and-coming influence among bookmakers, the powerful man shouldering his way into top-rank social acceptance. They knew Trevor Deansgate, and their faces were shocked.

"The real name of Trevor Deansgate is Trevor Shummuck," my voice said. "There is a research worker at the vaccine laboratory called Barry Shummuck, who is his brother. The two brothers, on friendly terms, have been seen together at the laboratories on several occasions. . . ."

Oh, God, I thought. My voice went on, and I listened in snatches. I've really done it. There's no going back.

"This is the laboratory where the mutant strain originally arose . . . unlikely after all this time for there to be any of it anywhere else. . . .

"Trevor Deansgate owns a horse which George Caspar trains. Trevor Deansgate is on good terms with Caspar . . . watches the morning gallops and goes to breakfast. Trevor Deansgate stood to make a fortune if he knew in advance that the over-winter favorites for the Guineas and the Derby couldn't win. Trevor Deansgate had the means—the disease; the motive—money; and the opportunity—entry into Caspar's well-guarded stable. It would seem, therefore, that there are grounds for investigating his activities further."

My voice stopped, and a few seconds later Chico switched off the recorder. Looking slightly dazed himself, he ejected the cassette and laid it carefully on the table.

"It's incredible," Sir Thomas said, but not as if he didn't believe it. "What do you think, Lucas?"

Lucas Wainwright cleared his throat. "I think we

should congratulate Sid on an exceptional piece of work."

Except for Eddy Keith, they agreed with him and did so, to my embarrassment, and I thought it generous of him to have said it at all, considering the Security Service themselves had done negative dope tests and left it at that. But then the Security Service, I reflected, hadn't had Rosemary Caspar visiting them in false curls and hysteria; and they hadn't had the benefit of Trevor Deansgate's revealing himself to them as a villain before they even positively suspected him, threatening vile things if they didn't leave him alone.

As Chico had said, our successes had stirred up the enemy to the point where they were likely to clobber us before we knew why.

Eddy Keith sat with his head held very still, watching me. I looked back at him, probably with much the same deceptively blank outer expression. Whatever he was thinking, I couldn't read. What I thought about was breaking into his office, and if he could read that, he was clairvoyant.

Sir Thomas and the administrators, consulting among themselves, raised their heads to listen when Lucas Wainwright asked a question.

"Do you really think, Sid, that Deansgate infected those horses himself?" He seemed to think it unlikely. "Surely he couldn't produce a syringe anywhere near any of those horses, let alone all four."

"I did think," I said, "that it might have been someone else . . . like a work jockey, or even a vet." Inky Poole and Brothersmith, I thought, would have had me for slander if they could have heard. "But there's a way almost anyone could do it."

I dipped again into my jacket and produced the pocket containing the needle attached to the pea-sized bladder. I gave the packet to Sir Thomas, who opened it, tipping the contents onto his desk.

They all looked. Understood. Were convinced.

"He'd be more likely to do it himself if he could," I said. "He wouldn't want to risk anyone else knowing, and perhaps having a hold over him."

"It amazes me," Sir Thomas said, with apparent genuineness, "how you work these things out, Sid."

"But I . . ."

"Yes," he said, smiling. "We all know what you're going to say. At heart you're still a jockey."

There seemed to be a long pause. Then I said, "Sir, you're wrong. This"—I pointed to the cassette—"is what I am now. And from now on."

His face sobered into a long frowning look in which it seemed that he was reassessing his whole view of me, as so many others had recently done. It was to him, as to Rosemary, that I still appeared as a jockey, but to myself, no longer. When he spoke again his voice was an octave lower, and thoughtful.

"We've taken you too lightly." He paused. "I did mean what I said to you at Chester about being a positive force for good in racing, but I also see that I thought of it as something of an unexpected joke." He shook his head slowly. "I'm sorry."

Lucas Wainwright said briskly, "It's been increasingly clear what Sid has become." He was tired of the subject and waiting as usual to spur on to the next thing. "Do you have any plans, Sid, as to what to do next?"

"Talk to the Caspars," I said. "I thought I might drive up there tomorrow."

"Good idea," Lucas said. "You won't mind if I come? It's a matter for the Security Service now, of course."

"And for the police, in due course," said Sir Thomas, with a touch of gloom. He saw all public prosecutions for racing-based crimes as sources of disgrace to the whole industry, and was inclined to let people get away with things, if prosecuting them would involve a damaging scandal. I tended to agree with him, to the point of doing the same myself, but only if privately one could fix it so that the offense wouldn't be repeated.

"If you're coming, Commander," I said to Lucas Wainwright, "perhaps you could make an appointment with them. They may be going to York. I was simply going to turn up at Newmarket early and trust to luck, but you won't want to do that."

"Definitely not," he said crisply. "I'll telephone straight away."

He bustled off to his own office, and I put the cassette into its small plastic box and handed it to Sir Thomas.

"I put it on tape because it's complicated, and you might want to hear it again."

"You're so right, Sid," said one of the administrators, ruefully. "All that about pigeons . . .!"

Lucas Wainwright came back. "The Caspars are at York, but went by air taxi and are returning tonight. George Caspar wants to see his horses work in the morning before flying back to York. I told his secretary chap that it was of the utmost importance I see Caspar, so we're due there at eleven. Suit you, Sid?"

"Yes, fine."

"Pick me up here, then, at nine?"

I nodded. "O.K."

"I'll be up in my office, checking the mail."

Eddy Keith gave me a final blank stare and without a word removed himself from the room.

Sir Thomas and all the administrators shook my hand

and also Chico's; and going down in the lift, Chico said, "They'll be kissing you next."

"It won't last."

We walked back to where I had left the Scimitar, which was where I shouldn't have. There was a parking ticket under the wiper blade. There would be.

"Are you going back to the flat?" Chico said, folding himself into the passenger's seat.

"No."

"You still think those boot men . . .?"

"Trevor Deansgate," I said.

Chico's face melted into half-mocking comprehension.

"Afraid he'll duff you up?"

"He'll know by now . . . from his brother." I shivered internally from a strong flash of the persistent horrors.

"Yeah, I suppose so." It didn't worry him. "Look, I brought that begging letter for you. . . ." He dug into a trouser pocket and produced a much-folded and slightly grubby sheet of paper. I eyed it disgustedly, reading it through. Exactly the same as the ones Jenny had sent, except signed with a flourish, "Elizabeth More," and headed with the Clifton address.

"Do you realize they may have to produce this filthy bit of paper in court?"

"Been in my pocket, hasn't it?" he said defensively.

"What else've you got in there? Potting compost?"

He took the letter from me and put it in the glove box, and let down the window.

"Hot, isn't it?"

"Mm."

I wound down my own side window, and started the car, and drove him back to his place in Finchley Road.

"I'll stay in the same hotel," I said. "And look . . . come to Newmarket with me tomorrow."

"Sure, if you want. What for?"

I shrugged, making light of it. "Bodyguard."

He was surprised. He said wonderingly, "You can't really be afraid of him—this Deansgate—are you?"

I shifted in my seat a bit, and sighed.

"I guess so," I said.

Chapter 17

I talked to Ken Armadale in the early evening. He wanted to know how my session with the Jockey Club had gone, but more than that, he sounded smugly self-satisfied, and not without reason.

"That erysipelas strain has been made immune to practically every antibiotic in the book," he said. "Very thorough. But I reckon there's an obscure little bunch he won't have bothered with, because no one would think of pumping them into horses. Rare, they are, and expensive. All the signs I have here are that they would work. Anyway, I've tracked some down."

"Great," I said. "Where?"

"In London, at one of the teaching hospitals. I've talked with the pharmacist there, and he's promised to pack some in a box and leave it at the reception desk for you to collect. It will have 'Halley' on it."

"Ken, you're terrific."

"I've had to mortgage my soul to get it."

I picked up the parcel in the morning and arrived at Portman Square to find Chico again waiting on the doorstep. Lucas Wainwright came down from his office and said he would drive us in his car, if we liked, and I thought of all the touring around I'd been doing for the past fortnight, and accepted gratefully. We left the Scimitar in the car park which had been full the day before, a temporary open-air affair in a cleared building site, and set off to Newmarket in a large, air-conditioned Mercedes.

"It's too darned hot," Lucas said, switching on the refrigeration. "Wrong time of year."

He had come tidily dressed in a suit, which Chico and I hadn't; jeans and sports shirts and not a jacket between us.

"Nice car, this," Chico said admiringly.

"You used to have a Merc, Sid, didn't you?" Lucas said.

I said yes, and we talked about cars half the way to Suffolk. Lucas drove well but as impatiently as he did everything else. A pepper-and-salt man, I thought, sitting beside him. Brown-and-gray speckled hair, brownish-gray eyes, with flecks in the iris. Brown-and-gray checked shirt, with a nondescript tie. Pepper and salt in his manner, in his speech patterns, in all his behavior.

He said, as in the end he was bound to, "How are you getting on with the syndicates?"

Chico, sitting in the back seat, made a noise between a laugh and a snort.

"Er . . ." I said. "Pity you asked, really."

"Like that, is it?" Lucas said, frowning.

"Well," I said, "there is very clearly something going on, but we haven't come up with much more than rumor and hearsay." I paused. "Any chance of us collecting expenses?"

He was grimly amused. "I suppose I could put it under the heading of general assistance to the Jockey

Club. Can't see the administrators quibbling, after yesterday."

Chico gave me a thumbs-up sign from behind Lucas's head, and I thought I would pile it on a bit while the climate was favorable, and recover what I'd paid to Jacksy.

"Do you want us to go on trying?" I said.

"Definitely." He nodded positively. "Very much so."

We reached Newmarket in good time and came to a smooth halt in George Caspar's well-tended driveway.

There were no other cars there: certainly not Trevor Deansgate's Jaguar. On that day he should, in the normal course of things, be at York, attending to his bookmaking business. I had no faith that he was.

George, expecting Lucas, was not at all pleased to see me, and Rosemary, coming downstairs and spotting me in the hall, charged across the parquet and rugs with shrill disapproval.

"Get out," she said. "How dare you come here?"

Two spots of color flamed in her cheeks, and she looked almost as if she was going to try to throw me out bodily.

"No, no, I say," Lucas Wainwright said, writhing as usual with naval embarrassment in the face of immodest female behavior. "George, make your wife *listen* to what we've come to tell you."

Rosemary was persuaded, with a ramrod-stiff back, to perch on a chair in her elegant drawing room, while Chico and I sat lazily in armchairs, and Lucas Wainwright did the talking, this time, about pig disease and bad hearts.

The Caspars listened in growing bewilderment and dismay, and when Lucas mentioned Trevor Deansgate, George stood up and began striding about in agitation.

"It isn't possible," he said. "Not Trevor. He's a friend."

"Did you let him near Tri-Nitro after that last training gallop?" I said.

George's face gave the answer.

"Sunday morning," Rosemary said, in a hard cold voice. "He came on the Sunday. He often does. He and George walked round the yard." She paused. "Trevor likes slapping horses. Slaps their rumps. Some people do that. Some people pat necks. Some people pull ears. Trevor slaps rumps."

Lucas said, "In due course, George, you'll have to give evidence in court."

"I'm going to looked a damned fool, aren't I?" he said sourly. "Filling my yard with guards and taking Deansgate in myself."

Rosemary looked at me stonily, unforgiving.

"I told you they were being nobbled. I told you. You didn't believe me."

Lucas looked surprised. "But I thought you understood, Mrs. Caspar. Sid did believe you. It was Sid who did all this investigating, not the Jockey Club."

Her mouth opened, and stayed open, speechlessly.

"Look," I said awkwardly, "I've brought you a present. Ken Armadale along at Equine Research has done a lot of work for you, and he thinks Tri-Nitro can be cured, by a course of some rather rare antibiotics. I've brought them with me from London."

I stood up and took the box to Rosemary, put it into her hands, and kissed her cheek.

"I'm sorry, Rosemary, love, that it wasn't in time for the Guineas. Maybe the Derby . . . but anyway the Irish Derby and the Diamond Stakes, and the Arc de Triomphe. Tri-Nitro will be fine for those."

Rosemary Caspar, that tough lady, burst into tears.

We didn't get back to London until nearly five, owing to Lucas's insisting on going to see Ken Armadale and

Henry Thrace himself, face to face. The Director of Security to the Jockey Club was busy making everything official.

He was visibly relieved when Ken absolved the people who'd done blood tests on the horses after their disaster races.

"The germ makes straight for the heart valves, and in the acute stage you'd never find it loose in the blood, even if you were thinking of illness and not merely looking for dope. It's only later, sometimes, that it gets freed into the blood, as it had in Zingaloo when we took that sample."

"Do you mean," Lucas demanded, "that if you did a blood test on Tri-Nitro at this minute you couldn't prove he had the disease?"

Ken said, "You would only find antibodies."

Lucas wasn't happy. "Then how can we prove in court that he has got it?"

"Well," Ken said. "You could do an erysipelas antibody count today and another in a week's time. There would be a sharp rise in the number present, which would prove the horse must have the disease, because he's fighting it."

Lucas shook his head mournfully. "Juries won't like this."

"Stick to Gleaner," I said, and Ken agreed.

At one point Lucas disappeared into the Jockey Club rooms in the High Street and Chico and I drank in the White Hart and felt hot.

I changed the batteries. Routine. The day crawled.

"Let's go to Spain," I said.

"Spain?"

"Anywhere."

"I could just fancy a señorita."

"You're disgusting."

"Look who's talking."

We reordered and drank and still felt hot.

"How much do you reckon we'll get?" Chico said.

"More or less what we ask."

George Caspar had promised, if Tri-Nitro recovered, that the horse's owner would give us the earth.

"A fee will do," I'd said dryly.

Chico said, "What will you ask, then?"

"I don't know. Perhaps five percent of his prize money."

"He couldn't complain."

We set off southward, finally, in the cooling car, and listened on the radio to the Dante Stakes at York.

Flotilla, to my intense pleasure, won it.

Chico, in the back seat, went to sleep. Lucas drove as impatiently as on the way up; and I sat and thought of Rosemary, and Trevor Deansgate, and Nicholas Ashe, and Trevor Deansgate, and Louise, and Trevor Deansgate.

Stab. Stab. *"I'll do what I said."*

Lucas dropped us at the entrance to the car park where I'd left the Scimitar. It would be like a furnace inside, I thought, sitting there all day in the sun. Chico and I walked over to it across the uneven stone-strewn ground.

Chico yawned.

A bath, I thought. A long drink. Dinner. Find a hotel room again . . . not the flat.

There was a Land-Rover with a two-horse trailer parked beside my car. Odd, I thought idly, to see them in central London. Chico, still yawning, walked between the trailer and my car to wait for me to unlock the doors.

"It'll be baking," I said, fishing down into my pocket for the keys, and looking downward into the car.

Chico made a choking sort of noise. I looked up,

and thought confusedly how fast, how very fast, a slightly boring hot afternoon could turn to stone cold disaster.

A large man stood in the space between the trailer and my car with his left arm clamped around Chico, who was facing me. The man was more or less supporting Chico's weight, because Chico's head lolled forward.

In his right hand the man held a small pear-shaped black truncheon.

The second man was letting down the ramp at the rear of the trailer.

I had no difficulty in recognizing them. The last time I'd seen them I'd been with a fortuneteller who hadn't liked my chances.

"Get in the trailer, laddie," the one holding Chico said to me. "The right-hand stall, laddie. Nice and quick. Otherwise I'll give your friend another tap or two. On the eyes, laddie. Or the base of the brain."

Chico, on the far side of the Scimitar, mumbled vaguely and moved his head. The big man raised his truncheon and produced another short burst of uncompromising Scottish accent.

"Get in the trailer," he said. "Go right in, to the back."

Seething with fury, I walked round the back of my car and up the ramp into the trailer. The right-hand stall, as he'd said. To the back. The second man stood carefully out of hitting distance, and there was no one else in the car park.

I found I was still holding my car keys, and put them back automatically into my pocket. Keys, handkerchief, money . . . and in the left-hand pocket, only a discharged battery. No weapon of any sort. A knife in the sock, I thought. I should have learned from Nicholas Ashe.

The man holding Chico came round to the back of the trailer and half dragged, half carried Chico into the left-hand stall.

"You make a noise, laddie," he said, putting his head round to my side of the central partition, "and I'll hit your friend here. On the eyes, laddie, and the mouth. You try and get help by shouting, laddie, and your friend won't have much face to speak of. Get it?"

I thought of Mason in Tunbridge Wells. A vegetable, and blind.

I said nothing at all.

"I'm traveling in here with your friend, all the way," he said. "Just remember that, laddie."

The second man closed the ramp, shutting out the sunlight, creating instant night. Where many trailers were open at the top at the back, this one was not.

Numb, I suppose, is how I felt.

The engine of the Land-Rover started, and the trailer moved, backing out of the parking lot. The motion was enough to rock me against the trailer's side, enought to show I wasn't going very far standing up.

My eyes slowly adjusted to a darkness which wasn't totally black owing to various points where the ramp fitted less closely than others against the back of the trailer. In the end I could see clearly, as if it mattered, the variations that had been done to turn an ordinary trailer into an escape-proof transport. The extra piece at the back, closing the gap usually left open for air, and the extra piece inside, lengthways, raising the central partition from head height to the roof.

Basically, it was still a box built to withstand the weight and kicks of horses. I sat helplessly on the floor, which was bare of everything except muddy dust, and thought absolutely murderous thoughts.

After all that unpredictable traveling around, I had agreed to go with Lucas and had stupidly left my car in plain vulnerable view all day. They must have picked me up at the Jockey Club, I thought. Either yesterday, or this morning. Yesterday, I thought, there had been no room in the car park, and I'd left my car in the street and got a ticket. . . .

I hadn't been to my flat. I hadn't been back to Aynsford. I hadn't been to the Cavendish, or to any routine place.

I had, in the end, gone to the Jockey Club.

I sat and cursed and thought about Trevor Deansgate.

The journey lasted for well over an hour: a hot, jolting, depressing time which I spent mostly in consciously not wondering what lay at the end of it. After a while I could hear Chico talking through the partition, though not the words. The flat, heavy, Glaswegian voice made shorter replies, rumbling like thunder.

A couple of pros from Glasgow, Jacksy had said. The one in with Chico, I thought, was certainly that. Not an average bashing mindless thug, but a hard man with brain power; and so much the worse.

Eventually the jolting stopped, and there were noises of the trailer being unhitched from the coupling; the Land-Rover drove away, and in the sudden quiet I could hear Chico plainly.

"What's happening?" he said, and sounded still groggy.

"You'll find out soon enough, laddie."

"Where's Sid?" he said.

"Be quiet, laddie."

There was no sound of a blow, but Chico was quiet.

The man who had raised the ramp came and lowered it, and six-thirty, Wednesday evening, flooded into the trailer.

"Out," he said.

He was backing away from the trailer as I got to my feet, and he held a pitchfork at the ready, the sharp tines pointing my way.

From deep in the trailer I looked out and saw where we were. The trailer itself, disconnected from the Land-Rover, was inside a building, and the building was the indoor riding school on Peter Rammileese's farm.

Timber-lined walls, windows in the roof, open because of the heat. No way that anyone could see in, casually, from outside.

"Out," he said again, jerking the fork.

"Do what he says, laddie," said the threatening voice of the man with Chico. "At once."

I did what he said.

Walked down the ramp onto the quiet tan-colored riding school floor.

"Over there." He jerked the fork. "Against the wall." His voice was rougher, the accent stronger, than the man with Chico. For sheer bullying power, there wasn't much to choose.

I walked, feeling that my feet didn't belong to me.

"Back to the wall. Face this way."

I turned with my shoulders lightly touching the wood.

Behind the man with the pitchfork, standing where from in the trailer I hadn't been able to see him, was Peter Rammileese. His face bore a nasty mixture of satisfaction, sneer, and anticipation, quite unlike the careful intentness of the two Scots. He had driven the Land-Rover, I supposed, out of my sight.

The man with Chico brought Chico to the top of the ramp and held him there. Chico half stood and half lay against him, smiling slightly and hopelessly disorganized.

"Hello, Sid," he said.

The man holding him lifted the hand with the truncheon, and spoke to me.

"Now listen, laddie. You stand quite still. Don't move. If you move, I'll finish your friend so quick you won't see it happen. Get it?"

I made no response of any kind, but after a moment he nodded sharply to the one with the pitchfork.

He came toward me slowly; warily. Showing me the prongs.

I looked at Chico. At the truncheon. At damage I couldn't risk.

I stood . . . quite still.

The man with the pitchfork raised it from pointing at my stomach to pointing at my heart, and from there, still higher. Slowly, carefully, one step at a time, he came forward until one of the prongs brushed my throat.

"Stand still," said the man with Chico, warningly.

I stood.

The prongs of the pitchfork slid past my neck, one each side below my chin, until they came to rest on the wooden surface behind me. Pushing my head back. Pinning me by the neck against the wall, unharmed. Better than through the skin, I thought dimly, but hardly a ball for one's self-respect.

When he'd got the fork aligned as he wanted it, he gave the handle a strong thrusting jerk, digging the sharp tines into the wood. After that he put his weight into pushing against the handle, so that I shouldn't dislodge what he'd done, and get myself free. I had seldom felt more futile or more foolish.

The man holding Chico moved suddenly as if released, carrying Chico bodily down the ramp and giving him a rough overbalancing shove at the bottom. As weak as a rag doll, Chico sprawled on the soft wood shavings, and the man strode over to me to feel for himself the force being applied in keeping me where I was.

He nodded to his partner. "And you keep your mind on your business," he said to him. "Never mind yon other laddie. I'll see to him."

I looked at their faces, to remember them forever.

The hard callous lines of cheekbone and mouth. The cold eyes, observant and unfeeling. The black hair and pale skin. The set of a small head on a thick neck, the ears flat. The heavy shape of a jaw blue with beard. Late thirties, I guessed. Both much alike, and both giving forth at great magnitude the methodical brutality of the experienced mercenary.

Peter Rammileese, approaching, seemed in comparison a matter of sponge. Despite his chums' disapproval, he too put a hand on the pitchfork handle and tried to give it a shake. It seemed to surprise him that he couldn't.

He said to me, "You'll keep your snotty nose out, after this."

I didn't bother to answer. Behind them, Chico got to his feet, and for one surging moment I thought that he'd been fooling them a bit with the concussed act, and was awake and on the point of some effective judo.

It was only a moment. The kick he aimed at the man who had been holding him wouldn't have knocked over a house of cards. In sick and helpless fury I watched the truncheon land again on Chico's head, sending him down onto his knees, deepening the haze in his brain.

The man with the pitchfork was doing what he'd been told and concentrating on keeping up the pressure on the handle. I tugged and wrenched at it with desperation to get free, and altogether failed, and the big man with Chico unfastened his belt.

I saw with incredulity that what he'd worn round his waist was not a leather strap but a length of chain, thin and supple, like the stuff in grandfather clocks. At one end he had fixed some sort of handle, which he grasped; and he swung his arm so that the free end fizzed through the air and wrapped itself around Chico.

Chico's head snapped up and his eyes and mouth opened wide with astonishment, as if the new pain had cleared away the mists like a flamethrower. The man swung his arm again and the chain landed on Chico, and I could hear myself shouting, "Bastards, bloody bastards . . ." and it made no difference at all.

Chico swayed to his feet and took some stumbling steps to get away, and the man followed him, hitting him all over with unvarying ferocity, taking a pride in his work.

I yelled incoherently . . . unconnected words, screaming at him to stop . . . feeling anger and grief and an agony of responsibility. If I hadn't taken Chico to Newmarket . . . if I hadn't been afraid of Trevor Deansgate . . . It was because of my fear that Chico was there . . . on that day. God . . . Bastard. Stop it . . . Stop . . . Wrenched at the pitchfork and couldn't get free.

Chico lurched and stumbled and finally crawled in a wandering circle round the riding school, and ended lying on his stomach not far away from me. The thin cotton of his shirt twitched when the chain landed, and I saw dotted red streaks of blood in the fabric here and there.

Chico . . . God . . .

It wasn't until he lay entirely still that the torment stopped. The man stood over him, looking down judiciously, holding his chain in a relaxed grasp.

Peter Rammileese looked if anything disconcerted and scared, and it was he who had got us there, he who had arranged it.

The man holding the pitchfork stopped looking at me

for the first time and switched his attention to where Chico lay. It was only a partial shift of his balance, but it make all the difference to the pressure on my neck. I wrenched at the handle with a force he wasn't ready for, and finally got myself away and off the wall; and it wasn't the man with Chico I sprang at in bloodlusting rage, but Peter Rammileese himself, who was nearer.

I hit him on the side of the face with all my strength, and I hit him with my hard left arm, two thousand quids' worth of delicate technology packed into a built-in club.

He screeched and raised his arms round his head, and I said "Bastard!" with savage intensity and hit him again, on the ribs.

The man with Chico turned his attention to me, and I discovered, as Chico had, that one's first feeling was of astonishment. The sting was incredible: and after the lacerating impact, a continuing fire.

I turned on the man in a rage I wouldn't have thought I could feel, and it was he who backed away from me.

I caught the next swing of his chain on my unfeeling arm. The free end wrapped itself twice round the forearm, and I tugged with such fierceness that he lost his grip on the handle. It swung down toward me, a stitched piece of leather; and if there had been just the two of us I would have avenged Chico and fought our way out of there, because there was nothing about cold blood in the way I went for him.

I grasped the leather handle, and as the supple links unwound and fell off my arm I swung the chain in a circle above my head and hit him an almighty crack around the shoulders. From his wide-opening eyes and the outraged Scottish roar I guessed that he was learning for the first time just what he had inflicted on others.

The man with the pitchfork at that point brought up

the reserves, and I might perhaps have managed one but it was hopeless against two.

He came charging straight at me with the wicked prongs, and though I dodged them like a bullfighter, the first man grabbed my right arm with both of his, intent on getting his chain back.

I swung round toward him in a sort of leap, and with the inside of my metal wrist hit him so hard on the ear and side of the head that the jolt shuddered up through my elbow and upper arm into my shoulder.

For a brief second I saw into his eyes at very close quarters: saw the measure of a hard fighting man, and knew he wasn't going to sit on the ramp of the trailer and wail, as Peter Rammileese was doing.

The crash on the head all the same loosened his grasp enough for me to wrench myself free, and I lunged away from him, still clutching his chain, and turned to look for the pitchfork. The pitchfork man, however, had thrown the fork away and was unfastening his own belt. I jumped toward him while he had both hands at his wrist and delivered to him too the realities of their chosen warfare.

In the half second in which both of the Scots were frozen with shock, I turned and ran for the door, where, somewhere outside, there had to be people and safety and help.

Running on wood shavings felt like running through treacle, and although I got to the door I didn't get through it, because it was a large affair like a chunk of wall which pushed to one side on rollers, and it was fastened shut by a bolt which let down into the floor.

The pitchfork man reached me there before I even got the bolt up, and I found that his belt wasn't leather either, nor grandfather clock innards, but more like the chain for tethering guard dogs. Less sting. More thud.

I still had the stinger, and I swung round low from

trying to undo the bolt and wrapped it round his legs. He grunted and rushed at me, and I found the other man right at my back, both of them clutching, and unfortunately I did them no more damage after that, though not for want of trying.

He got his chain back because he was stronger than I was and banged my hand against the wall to loosen my grasp, the other one holding on to me at the same time, and I thought, Well, I'm damned well not going to make it easy for you and you'll have to work for what you want; and I ran round that place, and made them run, round the trailer, and round by the walls and down again to the door at the end.

I picked up the pitchfork and for a while held them off, and threw it at one of them, and missed; and because one can convert pain into many other things so as not to feel it, I felt little except rage and fury and anger, and concentrated on those feelings to make them a shield.

I ended as Chico had, stumbling and swaying and crawling and finally lying motionless on the soft floor. Not so far from the door . . . but a long way from help.

They'll stop now I'm still, I thought; they'll stop in a minute; and they did.

Chapter 18

I lay with my face in the wood shavings and listened to them panting as they stood over me, both of them taking great gulps of breath after their exertions.

Peter Rammileese apparently came across to them, because I heard his voice quite close, loaded with spite, mumbling and indistinct.

"Kill him," he said. "Don't stop there. Kill him."

"Kill *him?*" said the man who'd been with Chico. "Are you crazy?" He coughed, dragging in air. "Yon laddie . . ."

"He's broken my jaw."

"Kill him yourself, then. We're not doing it."

"Why not? He's cut your ear half off."

"Grow up, mon." He coughed again. "We'd be grassed inside five minutes. We've been down here too long. Too many people've seen us. And this laddie, he's won money for every punter in Scotland. We'd be inside in a week."

"I want you to kill him," Peter Rammileese said, insisting.

"You're not paying," said the Scot flatly, still breathing heavily "We've done what was ordered, and that's that. We'll go into your house now for a beer, and after dark we'll dump these two, as arranged, and then we're finished. And we'll go straight up north tonight; we've been down here too long."

They went away, and rolled the door open, and stepped out. I heard their feet on the gritty yard, and the door closing, and the metal grate of the outside bolt, which was to keep horses in, and would do for men.

I moved my head a bit to get my nose clear of the shavings, and looked idly at the color of them so close to my eyes, and simply lay where I was, feeling shapeless, feeling pulped, and stupid, and defeated.

Jelly. A living jelly. Red. On fire. Burning, in a furnace.

There was a lot of romantic rubbish written about fainting from pain, I thought. One absolutely tended not to, because there was no provision for it in nature. The mechanics were missing. There were no fail-safe cut-offs on sensory nerves: they went right on passing the message for as long as the message was there to pass. No other system had evolved, because through millennia it had been unnecessary. It was only man, the most savage of animals, who inflicted pain for its own sake on his fellows.

I thought, I did manage it once, for a short time, after very much too long. I thought, This isn't as bad as that, so I'm going to stay here awake, so I may as well find something to think about. If one couldn't stop the message passing, one could distract the receptors from paying much attention, as in acupuncture; and over the years I'd had a lot of practice.

I thought about a night I'd spent once where I could see a hospital clock. To distract myself from a high state of awfulness, I'd spent the time counting. If I shut my eyes and counted for five minutes, five minutes would be gone: and every time I opened my eyes to check, it was only four minutes; and it had been a very long night. I could do better than that nowadays.

I thought about John Viking in his balloon, and imagined him scudding across the sky, his blue eyes blazing with the glee of breaking safety regulations like bubbles. I thought about Flotilla on the gallops at Newmarket, and winning the Dante Stakes at York. I thought about races I'd ridden in, and won, and lost; and I thought about Louise, a good deal about Louise and fourposter beds.

Afterward I reckoned that Chico and I had lain there without moving for over an hour, though I hadn't any clear idea of it at the time. The first sharp intrusion of the uncomfortable present was the noise of the bolt clicking open on the outside of the door, and the grinding noise as the door itself rolled partially open. They were going to dump us, they'd said, after dark; but it wasn't yet dark.

Footsteps made no sound on that soft surface, so that the first thing I heard was a voice.

"Are you asleep?"

"No," I said.

I shifted my head back a bit and saw little Mark squatting there on his heels, in his pajamas, studying me with six-year-old concern. Beyond him, the door, open enough to let his small body through. On the other side of the door, out in the yard, the Land-Rover.

"Go and see if my friend's awake," I said.

"O.K."

He straightened his legs and went over to Chico, and I'd got myself up from flat to kneeling by the time he returned with his report.

"He's asleep," he said, looking at me anxiously. "Your face is all wet. Are you hot?"

"Does your dad know you're down here?" I said.

"No, he doesn't. I had to go to bed early, but I heard a lot of shouting. I was frightened, I think."

"Where's your dad now?" I said.

"He's in the sitting room with those friends. He's hurt his face and he's bloody angry."

I practically smiled. "Anything else?"

"Mum was saying what did he expect, and they were all having drinks." He thought a bit. "One of the friends said his eardrum was burst."

"If I were you," I said, "I'd go straight back to bed and not let them catch you out here. Otherwise your dad might be bloody angry with you too, and that wouldn't be much fun, I shouldn't think."

He shook his head.

"Good night, then," I said.

"Good night."

"And leave the door open," I said. "I'll shut it."

"All right."

He gave me a trusting and slightly conspiratorial smile, and crept out of the doorway to sneak back to bed.

I got to my feet and staggered around a bit, and made it to the door.

The Land-Rover stood there about ten feet away. If the keys were in it, I thought, why wait to be dumped?

Ten steps. Leaned against the gray-green bodywork, and looked through the glass.

Keys. In the ignition.

I went back into the riding school and over to Chico, and knelt beside him because it was a lot less demanding than bending.

"Come on," I said. "Wake up. Time to go."

He groaned.

"Chico, you've got to walk. I can't carry you."

He opened his eyes. Still confused, I thought, but a great deal better.

"Get up," I said urgently. "We can get out, if you'll try."

"Sid . . ."

"Yeah," I said. "Come on."

"Go away. I can't."

"Yes, you damned well can. You just say 'Sod the buggers,' and it comes easy."

It came harder than I'd thought, but I half lugged him to his feet, and put my arm round his waist, and we meandered waveringly to the door like a pair of drunken lovers.

Through the door, and across to the Land-Rover. No furious yells of discovery from the house; and as the sitting room was at the far end of it, with a bit of luck they wouldn't even hear the engine start.

I shoveled Chico onto the front seat and shut the door quietly, and went around to the driving side.

Land-Rovers, I thought disgustedly, were made for left-handed people. All the controls, except the indicators, were on that side; and whether it was because I myself was weak, or the battery was flat, or I'd damaged the machinery by using it as a club, the fingers of my left hand would scarcely move.

I swore to myself and did everything with my right hand, which meant twisting, which would have hurt if I hadn't been in such a hurry.

Started the engine. Released the brake. Shoved the gear lever into first. Did the rest thankfully with my feet, and set off. Not the smoothest start ever, but enough. The Land-Rover rolled to the gate, and I turned out in the opposite direction from London, thinking instinctively that if they found we'd gone and chased after us, it would be toward London that they would go in pursuit.

The "sod the buggers" mentality lasted me well for two or three miles and through some dicey one-handed gear changing, but suffered a severe setback when I looked at the petrol gauge and found it pointing to nearly empty.

The question of where we were going had to be sorted out, and immediately; and before I'd decided, we came round a bend and found in front of us a large garage, still open, with attendants by the pumps. Hardly believing it, I swerved untidily into the forecourt, and came to a jerking halt by the two-star.

Money in right-hand pocket, along with car keys and handkerchief. I pulled all of them out in a handful and separated the crumpled notes. Opened the window beside me. Gave the attendant who appeared the money and said I'd have that much petrol.

He was young, a school kid, and he looked at me curiously.

"You all right?"

"It's hot," I said, and wiped my face with the handkerchief. Some wood shavings fell out of my hair. I must indeed have looked odd.

The boy merely nodded, however, and stuck the petrol nozzle into the Land-Rover's filling place, which was right beside the driver's door. He looked across me to Chico, who was half lying on the front seat with his eyes open.

"What's wrong with him, then?"

"Drunk," I said.

He looked as if he thought we both were, but he simply finished the filling, and replaced the cap, and turned away to attend to the next customer. I went again through the tedious business of starting right-handedly, and pulled out onto the road. After a mile I turned off the main road into a side road, and went round a bend or two, and stopped.

"What's happening?" Chico said.

I looked at his still wuzzy eyes. Decide where to go, I thought. Decide for Chico. For myself, I already knew. I'd decided when I found I could drive without hitting things, and at the garage which had turned up so luckily, and when I'd had enough money for the petrol, and when I hadn't asked the boy to get us help in the shape of policemen and doctors.

Hospitals and bureaucracy and questions and being prodded about: all the things I most hated. I wasn't going near any of them, unless I had to for Chico.

"Where did we go today?" I said.

After a while he said, "New market."

"What's twice eight?"

Pause. "Sixteen."

I sat in a weak sort of gratitude for his returning wits, waiting for strength to go on. The impetus which had got me into the Land-Rover and as far as that spot had ebbed away and left room for a return of fire and jelly. Power would come back, I thought, if I waited. Stamina and energy always came in cycles, so that what one couldn't do one minute, one could the next.

"I'm burning," Chico said.

"Mm."

"That was too much."

I didn't answer. He moved on the seat and tried to sit upright, and I saw the full awareness flood into his face. He shut his eyes tight and said, "*Jesus,*" and after a while he looked at me through slits, and said, "You too?"

"Mm."

The long hot day was drawing to dusk. If I didn't get started, I thought vaguely, I wouldn't get anywhere.

The chief practical difficulty was that driving a

Land-Rover with one hand was risky, if not downright dangerous, as I had to let go of the steering wheel and lean to the left every time I changed gear: and the answer to that was to get the left-hand fingers to grip the knob just once, and tightly, so that I could switch off the current, and the hand would stay there on the gear lever, unmoving, until further notice.

I did that. Then I switched on the side lights, and the headlights, dipped. Then the engine. I'd give anything for a drink, I thought, and set off on the long drive home.

"Where are we going?" Chico said.

"To the Admiral's."

I had taken the southern route round Sevenoaks and Kingston and Colnbrook, and there was the M-4 motorway stretch to do, and the cross at Maidenhead to the M-40 motorway just north of Marlow, and then round the north Oxford ring road and the last leg to Aynsford.

Land-Rovers weren't built for comfort and jolted the passengers at the best of times. Chico groaned now and then, and cursed, and said he wasn't getting into a mess like that again, ever. I stopped twice briefly on the way from weakness and general misery, but there wasn't much traffic, and we rolled into Charles's drive in three and a half hours, not too bad for the course.

I switched the Land-Rover off and my left hand on, and couldn't get the fingers to move. That was all it needed, I thought despairingly, the final humiliation of that bloody evening, if I had to detach myself from the socket end and leave the electric part of me stuck to the gears. Why, *why*, couldn't I have two hands, like everyone else?

"Don't struggle," Chico said, "and you'll do it easy."

I gave a cough that was somewhere between a laugh

and a sob, and the fingers opened a fraction, and the hand fell off the knob.

"Told you," he said.

I laid my right arm across the steering wheel and put my head down on that, and felt spent and depressed . . . and punished. And someone, somehow, had to raise the strength to go in to tell Charles we were there.

He solved that himself by coming out to us in his dressing gown, the light streaming out behind him from his open front door. The first I knew, he was standing by the window of the Land-Rover, looking in.

"Sid?" he said incredulously. "Is it you?"

I dragged my head off the steering wheel and opened my eyes, and said, "Yeah."

"It's after midnight," he said.

I got a smile at least into my voice. "You said I could come any time."

An hour later, Chico was upstairs in bed and I sat sideways on the gold sofa, shoes off, feet up, as I often did.

Charles came into the drawing room and said the doctor had finished with Chico and was ready for me, and I said no, thanks very much, and tell him to go home.

"He'll give you some knockout stuff, like Chico."

"Yes, and that's exactly what I don't want, and I hope he was careful about Chico's concussion, with those drugs."

"You told him yourself about six times, when he came." He paused. "He's waiting for you."

"I mean it, Charles," I said. "I want to think. I want just to sit here and think, so would you please say goodbye to the doctor and go to bed?"

"No," he said. "You can't."

"I certainly can. In fact, I have to, while I still feel . . ." I stopped. While I still feel *flayed,* I thought: but one couldn't say that.

"It's not sensible."

"No. The whole thing isn't sensible. That's the point. So go away and let me work it out."

I had noticed before that sometimes when the body was injured the mind cleared sharply and worked for a while with acute perception. It was a time to use, if one wanted to; not to waste.

"Have you seen Chico's skin?" he said.

"Often," I said flippantly.

"Is yours in the same state?"

"I haven't looked."

"You're exasperating."

"Yeah," I said. "Go to bed."

When he'd gone I sat there, deliberately and vividly remembering in mind and body the biting horror I'd worked so hard to blank out.

It had been too much, as Chico said.

Too much.

Why?

Charles came downstairs again at six o'clock, in his dressing gown, and with his most impassive expression.

"You're still there, then," he said.

"Yuh."

"Coffee?"

"Tea," I said.

He went and made it, and brought two big steaming mugs, naval fashion. He put mine on the table that stood along the back of the sofa, and sat with his in an armchair. The empty-looking eyes were switched steadily my way.

"Well?" he said.

I rubbed my forehead. "When you look at me . . ." I said, hesitatingly. "Usually, I mean. Not now. When you look at me, what do you see?"

"You know what I see."

"Do you see a lot of fears and self-doubts, and feelings of shame and uselessness and inadequacy?"

"Of course not." He seemed to find the question amusing, and then sipped the scalding tea, and said more seriously, "You never show feelings like that."

"No one does," I said. "Everyone has an outside and an inside, and the two can be quite different."

"Is that just a general observation?"

"No." I picked up the mug of tea, and blew across the steaming surface. "To myself, I'm a jumble of uncertainty and fear and stupidity. And to others . . . Well, what happened to Chico and me last evening was because of the way others see us." I took a tentative taste. As always when Charles made it, the tea was strong enough to rasp the fur off your tongue. I quite liked it, sometimes. I said, "We've been lucky, since we started this investigating thing. In other words, the jobs we've done have been comparatively easy, and we've been getting a reputation for being successful, and the reputation has been getting bigger than the reality."

"Which is, of course," Charles said dryly, "that you're a pair of dim-witted layabouts."

"You know what I mean."

"Yes, I do. Tom Ullaston rang me here yesterday morning, to arrange about stewards for Epsom, he said, but I gathered it was mostly to tell me what he thought about you, which was, roughly speaking, that if you had still been a jockey it would be a pity."

"It would be great," I said, sighing.

"So someone lammed into you and Chico yesterday to stop you chalking up another success?"

"Not exactly," I said.

I told him what I had spent the night sorting out; and his tea got cold.

When I'd finished he sat for quite a while in silence, simply staring at me in his best give-away-nothing manner.

Then he said, "It sounds as if yesterday evening was . . . terrible."

"Well, yes, it was."

More silence. Then, "So what next?"

"I was wondering," I said diffidently, "if you'd do one or two jobs for me today, because I . . . er . . ."

"Of course," he said. "What?"

"It's your day for London. Thursday. So could you bear to drive the Land-Rover up instead of the Rolls, and swap it for my car?"

"If you like," he said, not looking enchanted.

"The battery charger's in it, in my suitcase," I said.

"Of course I'll go."

"Before that, in Oxford, could you pick up some photographs? They're of Nicholas Ashe."

"Sid!"

I nodded. "We found him. There's a letter in my car too, with his new address. A begging letter, same as before."

He shook his head at the foolishness of Nicholas Ashe. "Any more jobs?"

"Two, I'm afraid. The first's in London, and easy. But as for the other . . . would you go to Tunbridge Wells?"

When I told him why, he said he would, even though it meant canceling his afternoon's board meeting.

"And would you lend me your camera, because mine's in the car . . . and a clean shirt?"

"In that order?"

"Yes, please."

Wishing I didn't have to move for a couple of

thousand years, I slowly unstuck myself from the sofa some time later and went upstairs, with Charles's camera, to see Chico.

He was lying on his side, his eyes dull and staring vaguely into space, the effect of the drugs wearing off. Sore enough to protest wearily when I told him what I wanted to photograph.

"Sod off."

"Think about barmaids."

I peeled back the blanket and sheet covering him and took pictures of the visible damage, front and back. Of the invisible damage there was no measure. I put the covers back again.

"Sorry," I said.

He didn't answer, and I wondered whether I was really apologizing for disturbing him at that moment or more basically for having tangled his life in mine, with such dire results. A hiding to nothing was what he'd said we were on with those syndicates, and he'd been right.

I took the camera out onto the landing and gave it to Charles.

"Ask for blown-up prints by tomorrow morning," I said. "Tell him it's for a police case."

"But you said no police . . ." Charles said.

"Yes, but if he thinks it's already for the police, he won't go trotting round to them when he sees what he's printing."

"I suppose it's never occurred to you," Charles said, handing over a clean shirt, "that it's your view of you that's wrong, and Thomas Ullaston's that's right?"

I telephoned to Louise and told her I couldn't make it that day after all. Something's come up, I said, in the classic evasive excuse, and she answered with the disillusion it merited.

"Never mind, then."

"I do mind, actually," I said. "So how about a week tomorrow? What are you doing after that for a few days?"

"Days?"

"And nights."

Her voice cheered up considerably. "Research for a thesis."

"What subject?"

"Clouds and roses and stars, their variations and frequency in the life of your average liberated female."

"Oh, Louise," I said, "I'll . . . er . . . help you all I can."

She laughed and hung up, and I went to my room and took off my dusty, stained, sweaty shirt. Looked at my reflection briefly in the mirror and got no joy from it. Put on Charles's smooth Sea Island cotton and lay on the bed. I lay on one side, like Chico, and felt what Chico felt; and at one point or other, went to sleep.

In the evening I went down and sat on the sofa, as before, to wait for Charles, but the first person who came was Jenny.

She walked in, saw me, and was immediately annoyed. Then she took a second look, and said, "Oh, no, not again."

I said merely, "Hello."

"What is it this time? Ribs again?"

"Nothing."

"I know you too well." She sat at the other end of the sofa, beyond my feet. "What are you doing here?"

"Waiting for your father."

She looked at me moodily. "I'm going to sell that flat in Oxford," she said.

"Are you?"

"I don't like it any more. Louise McInnes has left, and it reminds me too much of Nicky. . . ."

After a pause I said, "Do I remind you of Nicky?"

With a flash of surprise she said, "Of course not." And then, more slowly, "But he . . ." She stopped.

"I saw him," I said. "Three days ago, in Bristol. And he looks like me, a bit."

She was stunned, and speechless.

"Didn't you realize?" I said.

She shook her head.

"You were trying to go back," I said. "To what we had at the beginning."

"It's not true." But her voice said that she saw it was. She had even told me so, more or less, the evening I'd come to Aynsford to start finding Ashe.

"Where will you live?" I said.

"What do you care?"

I supposed I would always care, to some extent, which was my problem, not hers.

"How did you find him?" she said.

"He's a fool."

She didn't like that. The look of enmity showed where her instinctive preference still lay.

"He's living with another girl," I said.

She stood up furiously, and I remembered a bit late that I really didn't want her to touch me.

"Are you telling me that to be beastly?" she demanded.

"I'm telling you so you'll get him out of your system before he goes on trial and to jail. You're going to be damned unhappy if you don't."

"I hate you," she said.

"That's not hate, that's injured pride."

"How dare you!"

"Jenny," I said, "I'll tell you plainly, I'd do a lot for you. I've loved you a long time, and I do care what happens to you. It's no good finding Ashe and getting him convicted of fraud instead of you, if you don't wake up and see him for what he is. I want to make you angry with him. For your own sake."

"You won't manage it," she said fiercely.

"Go away," I said.

"What?"

"Go away. I'm tired."

She stood there looking as much bewildered as annoyed, and at that moment Charles came back.

"Hello," he said, taking a disapproving look at the general atmosphere. "Hello, Jenny."

She went over and kissed his cheek, from long habit.

"Has Sid told you he's found your friend Ashe?" he said.

"He couldn't wait."

Charles was carrying a large brown envelope. He opened it, pulled out the contents, and handed them to me: the three photographs of Ashe, which had come out well, and the new begging letter.

Jenny took two jerky strides and looked down at the uppermost photograph.

"Her name is Elizabeth More," I said slowly. "His real name is Norris Abbott. She calls him Ned."

The picture, the third one I'd taken, showed them laughing and entwined, looking into each other's eyes, the happiness in their faces sharply in focus.

Silently, I gave Jenny the letter. She opened it and looked at the signature at the bottom, and went very pale. I felt sorry for her, but she wouldn't have wanted me to say so.

She swallowed, and handed the letter to her father.

"All right," she said after a pause. "All right. Give it to the police."

She sat down again on the sofa with a sort of emotional exhaustion slackening her limbs and curving her spine. Her eyes turned my way.

"Do you want me to thank you?" she said.

I shook my head.

"I suppose one day I will."

"There's no need."

With a flash of anger she said, "You're doing it again."

"Doing what?"

"Making me feel guilty. I know I'm pretty beastly to you sometimes. Because you make me feel guilty, and I want to get back at you for that."

"Guilty for what?" I said.

"For leaving you. For our marriage going wrong."

"But it wasn't your fault," I protested.

"No, it was yours. Your selfishness, your pigheadedness. Your bloody determination to win. You'll do anything to win. You always have to win. You're so hard. Hard on yourself. Ruthless to yourself. I couldn't live with it. No one could live with it. Girls want men who'll come to them for comfort. Who say, I need you, help me, comfort me, kiss away my troubles. But you . . . you can't do that. You always build a wall and deal with your own troubles in silence, like you're doing now. And don't tell me you aren't hurt, because I've seen it in you too often, and you can't disguise the way you hold your head, and this time it's very bad, I can see it. But you'd never say, would you, Jenny, hold me, help me, I want to cry?"

She stopped, and in the following silence made a sad little gesture with her hand.

"You see?" she said. "You can't say it, can you?"

After another long pause I said, "No."

"Well," she said, "I need a husband who's not so rigidly in control of himself. I want someone who's not afraid of emotion, someone uninhibited, someone weaker. I can't live in the sort of purgatory you make of life for yourself. I want someone who can break down. I want . . . an ordinary man."

She got up from the sofa and bent over and kissed my forehead.

"It's taken me a long time to see all that," she said. "And to say it. But I'm glad I have." She turned to her father. "Tell Mr. Quayle I'm cured of Nicky, and I won't be obstructive from now on. I think I'll go back to the flat now. I feel a lot better."

She went with Charles toward the door, and then paused and looked back, and said, "Goodbye, Sid."

"Goodbye," I said; and I wanted to say, Jenny, hold me, help me, I want to cry; but I couldn't.

Chapter 19

Charles drove himself and me to London the following day in the Rolls, with me still in a fairly droopy state and Charles saying we should put it off until Monday.

"No," I said.

"But even for you this is daunting . . . and you're dreading it."

Dread, I thought, was something I felt for Trevor Deansgate, who wasn't going to hold off just because I had other troubles. Dread was too strong a word for the purpose of the present journey; and reluctance too weak. Aversion, perhaps.

"It's better done today," I said.

He didn't argue. He knew I was right, otherwise he wouldn't have been persuaded to drive me.

He dropped me at the door of the Jockey Club in Portman Square, and went and parked the car, and walked back again. I waited for him downstairs, and we went up in the lift together: he in his city suit, and I in trousers and a clean shirt, but no tie and no jacket. The weather was still hot. A whole week of it we'd had, and it seemed that everyone except me was bronzed and healthy.

There was a looking glass in the lift. My face stared out of it, grayish and hollow-eyed, with a red streak of a healing cut slanting across near the hairline on my forehead, and a blackish bruise on the side of my jaw. Apart from that I looked calmer, less damaged, and more normal than I felt, which was a relief. If I concentrated, I should be able to keep it that way.

We went straight to Sir Thomas Ullaston's office, where he was waiting for us. Shook hands, and all that.

To me he said, "Your father-in-law told me on the telephone yesterday that you have something disturbing to tell me. He wouldn't say what it was."

"No, not on the telephone," I agreed.

"Sit down, then. Charles . . . Sid . . ." He offered chairs, and himself perched on the edge of his big desk. "Very important, Charles said. So here I am, as requested. Fire away."

"It's about syndicates," I said. I began to tell him what I'd told Charles, but after a few minutes he stopped me.

"No. Look, Sid, this is not going to end here simply between me and you, is it? So I think we must have some of the others in, to hear what you're saying."

I would have preferred him not to, but he summoned the whole heavy mob; the Controller of the Secretariat, the Head of Administration, the Secretary to the Stewards, the Licensing Officer, who dealt with the registration of owners, and the Head of Rules Department, whose province was disciplinary action. They came into the room and filled up the chairs, and for the second time in four days turned their serious civilized faces my way, to listen to the outcome of an investigation.

It was because of Tuesday, I thought, that they would listen to me now. Trevor Deansgate had given me an authority I wouldn't otherwise have had, in that company, in that room.

I said, "I was asked by Lord Friarly, whom I used to ride for, to look into four syndicates, which he headed. The horses were running in his colors, and he wasn't happy about how they were doing. That wasn't surprising, as their starting prices were going up and down like yo-yos, with results to match. Lord Friarly felt he was being used as a front for some right wicked goings on, and he didn't like it."

I paused, knowing I was using a light form of words because the next bit was going to fall like lead.

"On the same day, at Kempton, Commander Wainwright asked me to look into the same four syndicates, which I must say had been manipulated so thoroughly that it was a wonder they weren't a public scandal already."

The smooth faces registered surprise. Sid Halley was not the natural person for Commander Wainwright to ask to look into syndicates, which were the normal business of the Security Service.

"Lucas Wainwright told me that all four syndicates had been vetted and O.K.'d by Eddy Keith, and he asked me to find out if there was any unwelcome significance in that."

For all that I put it at its least dramatic, the response from the cohorts was one of considerable shock. Racing might suffer from its attraction for knaves and rogues, as it always had, but corruption within the headquarters itself? Never.

I said, "I came here to Portman Square to make notes about the syndicates, which I took from Eddy Keith's files, without his knowledge. I wrote the notes in Lucas's office, and he told me about a man he'd sent out on the same errand as myself, six months ago. That man, Mason, had been attacked, and dumped in the streets of Tunbridge Wells, with appalling head injuries, caused by kicks. He was a vegetable, and blind. Lucas told me also that the man who had formed the syndicates, and who had been doing the manipulating, was a Peter Rammileese, who lived at Tunbridge Wells."

The faces were all frowningly intent.

"After that I . . . er . . . went away for a week, and I also lost the notes, so I had to come back here and do them again, and Eddy Keith discovered I'd been seeing his files, and complained to you, Sir Thomas, if you remember?"

"That's right. I told him not to fuss."

There were a few smiles all around, and a general loosening of tension. Inside me, a wilting fatigue.

"Go on, Sid," Sir Thomas said.

Go on, I thought. I wished I felt less weak, less shaky, less continuously sore. Had to go on, now I'd started. Get on with it. Go on.

I said, "Well, Chico Barnes, who was here with me on Tuesday"—they nodded—"Chico and I, we went down to Tunbridge Wells, to see Peter Rammileese. He was away, as it happened. His wife and little son were there, but the wife had fallen off a horse and Chico went to the hospital with her, taking the little boy, which left me, and an open house. So I . . . er . . . looked around."

Their faces said, "Tut-tut," but none of their voices.

"I looked for any possible direct tie-in with Eddy, but actually the whole place was abnormally tidy and looked suspiciously prepared for any searches any tax men might make."

They smiled slightly.

"Lucas warned me at the beginning that as what I

was doing was unofficial, I couldn't be paid, but that he'd give me help instead, if I needed it. So I asked him to help me with the business of Trevor Deansgate, and he did."

"In what way, Sid?"

"I asked him to write to Henry Thrace, to make sure that the Jockey Club would hear at once if Gleaner died, or Zingaloo, and to tell me, so that I could get a really thorough post-mortem done."

They all nodded. They remembered.

"And then," I said, "I found Peter Rammileese on my heels with two very large men who looked just the sort to kick people's heads in and leave them blinded in Tunbridge Wells."

No smiles.

"I dodged them that time, and I spent the next week rolling around England in unpredictable directions so that no one could really have known where to find me, and during that time, when I was chiefly learning about Gleaner and heart valves and so on, I was also told that the two big men had been imported especially from Scotland for some particular job with Peter Rammileese's syndicates. There was also a rumor of someone high up in the Security Service who would fix things for crooks, if properly paid."

They were shocked again.

"Who told you that, Sid?" Sir Thomas asked.

"Someone reliable," I said, thinking that maybe they wouldn't think a suspended jockey like Jacksy as reliable as I did.

"Go on."

"I wasn't really making much progress with those syndicates, but Peter Rammileese apparently thought I was, because he and his two men laid an ambush for Chico and me, the day before yesterday."

Sir Thomas reflected. "I thought that was the day

you were going to Newmarket with Lucas to see the Caspars. The day after you were here telling us about Trevor Deansgate."

"Yes, we did go to Newmarket. And I made the mistake of leaving my car in plain view near here all day. The two men were waiting beside it when we got back. And . . . er . . . Chico and I got abducted, and where we landed up was at Peter Rammileese's place at Tunbridge Wells."

Sir Thomas frowned. The others listened to the unemotional relating of what they must have realized had been a fairly violent occurrence with a calm understanding that such things could happen.

There had seldom been, I thought, a more silently attentive audience.

I said, "They gave Chico and me a pretty rough time, but we did get out of there, owing to Peter Rammileese's little boy opening a door for us by chance, and we didn't end up in Tunbridge Wells streets; we got to my father-in-law's house near Oxford.

They all looked at Charles, who nodded.

I took a deep breath. "At about that point," I said, "I . . . er . . . began to see things the other way round."

"How do you mean, Sid?"

"Until then, I thought the two Scotsmen were supposed to be preventing us from finding what we were looking for in those syndicates."

They nodded. Of course.

"But supposing it was exactly the reverse . . . Supposing I'd been pointed at those syndicates in order to be led to the ambush. Suppose the ambush itself was the whole aim of the exercise."

Silence.

I had come to the hard bit, and needed the reserves I didn't have, of staying power, of will. I was aware of Charles sitting steadfastly beside me, trying to give me his strength.

I could feel myself shaking. I kept my voice flat and cold, saying the things I didn't like saying, that had to be said.

"I was shown an enemy, who was Peter Rammileese. I was given a reason for being beaten up, which was the syndicates. I was fed the expectation of it, through the man Mason. I was being given a background to what was going to happen; a background I would accept."

Total silence and blank, uncomprehending expressions.

I said, "If someone had savagely attacked me out of the blue, I wouldn't have been satisfied until I had found out who and why. So I thought, supposing someone wanted to attack me, but it was imperative that I didn't find out who or why. If I was given a false who, and a false why, I would believe in those, and not look any further."

One or two very slight nods.

"I did believe in that who and that why for a while," I said. "But the attack, when it came, seemed out of all proportion . . . and from something one of our attackers said, I gathered it was not Peter Rammileese himself who was paying them, but someone else."

Silence.

"So after we had reached the Admiral's house, I began thinking, and I thought, if the attack itself was the point, and it was not Peter Rammileese who had arranged it, then who had? Once I saw it that way, there was only one possible who. The person who had laid the trail for me to follow."

The faces began to go stiff.

I said, "It was Lucas himself who set us up."

They broke up into loud, jumbled, collective protest, moving in their chairs with embarrassment, not meeting my eye, not wanting to look at someone who was so mistaken, so deluded, so pitiably ridiculous.

"No, Sid, really," Sir Thomas said. "We've a great regard for you"—the others looked as if the great regard was now definitely past tense—"but you can't say things like that."

"As a matter of fact," I said slowly, "I would much rather have stayed away and not said it. I won't tell you any more, if you don't want to hear it." I rubbed my fingers over my forehead from sheer lack of inner energy, and Charles half made, and then stopped himself from making, a protective gesture of support.

Sir Thomas looked at Charles and then at me, and whatever he saw was enough to calm him from incredulity to puzzlement.

"All right," he said soberly. "We'll listen."

The others all looked as if they didn't want to, but if the Senior Steward was willing, it was enough.

I said, with deep weariness and no satisfaction, "To understand the *why* part, it's necessary to look at what's been happening during the past months; during the time Chico and I have been doing . . . what we have. As you yourself said, Sir Thomas, we've been successful. Lucky . . . tackling pretty easy problems . . . but mostly sorting them out. To the extent that a few villains have tried to stop us dead as soon as we've appeared on the skyline."

The disbelief still showed like snow in July, but at least they seemed to understand that too much success invited retaliation. The uncomfortable shiftings in the chairs grew gradually still.

"We've been prepared for it, more or less," I said.

"In some cases it's even been useful, because it's shown us we're nearing the sensitive spot. . . . But what we usually get is a couple of rent-a-thug bullies in or out of funny masks, giving us a warning bash or two and telling us to lay off. Which advice," I added wryly, "we have never taken."

They had all begun looking at me again, even if sideways.

"So then people begin to stop thinking of me as a jockey, and gradually see that what Chico and I are doing isn't really the joke it seemed at first. And we get what you might call the Jockey Club Seal of Approval, and all of a sudden, to the really big crooks, we appear as a continuing, permanent menace."

"Do you have proof of that, Sid?" Sir Thomas said.

Proof . . . Short of getting Trevor Deansgate in there to repeat his threat before witnesses, I had no proof. I said, "I've had threats . . . only threats, before this."

A pause. No one said anything, so I went on.

"I understand on good authority," I said, with faint amusement, "that there would be some reluctance to solve things by actually killing us, as people who had won money in the past on my winners would rise up in wrath and grass on the murderers."

Some tentative half smiles amid general dislike of such melodrama.

"Anyway, such a murder would tend to bring in its trail precisely the investigation it was designed to prevent."

They were happier with that.

"So the next best thing is an ultimate deterrent. One that would so sicken Chico and me that we'd go and sell brushes instead. Something to stop us investigating anything else, ever again."

It seemed all of a sudden as if they did understand what I was saying. The earlier, serious attention came right back. I thought it might be safe to mention Lucas again, and when I did there was none of the former vigorous reaction.

"If you could just imagine for a moment that there *is* someone in the Security Service who can be bribed, and that it is the Director himself, would you, if you were Lucas, be entirely pleased to see an independent investigator making progress in what had been exclusively your territory? Would you, if you were such a man, be pleased to see Sid Halley right here in the Jockey Club being congratulated by the Senior Steward and being given carte blanche to operate wherever he liked throughout racing?"

They stared.

"Would you, perhaps, be afraid that one of these days Sid Halley would stumble across something you couldn't afford for him to find out? And might you not, at that point, decide to remove the danger of it once and for all? Like putting weedkiller on a nettle before it stings you."

Charles cleared his throat. "A preemptive strike," he said smoothly, "might appeal to a retired commander."

They remembered Charles had been an admiral, and looked thoughtful.

"Lucas is only a man," I said. "The title Director of Security sounds pretty grand, but the Security Service isn't that big, is it? I mean, there are only about thirty people in it full time, aren't there, over the whole country?"

They nodded.

"I don't suppose the pay is a fortune. One hears about bent policemen from time to time, who've taken bribes from crooks. Well . . . Lucas is constantly in contact with people who might say, for instance, how about a quiet thousand in readies, Commander, to smother my little bit of trouble?"

The faces were shocked.

"It does happen, you know," I said mildly. "Backhanders are a flourishing industry. I agree that you wouldn't want the head of racing security to be shutting his eyes to skulduggery, but it's more a breach of trust than anything aggressively wicked."

What he'd done to Chico and me was indeed aggressively wicked, but that wasn't the point I wanted to make.

"What I'm saying," I said, "is that in the wider context of the everyday immoral world, Lucas's dishonesty is no great matter."

They looked doubtful, but that was better than negative shakes of the head. If they could be persuaded to think of Lucas as a smallish-scale sinner, they would believe more easily that he'd done what he had.

"If you start from the idea of a deterrent," I said, "you see everything from the other side." I stopped. The inner exhaustion didn't. I'd like to sleep for a week, I thought.

"Go on, Sid."

"Well . . ." I sighed. "Lucas had to take the slight risk of pointing me at something he was involved in, because he needed a background he could control. He must have been badly shocked when Lord Friarly said he'd asked me to look into those syndicates, but if he had already toyed with the idea of getting rid of me, I'd guess he saw at that point how to do it."

One or two of the heads nodded sharply in comprehension.

"Lucas must have been sure that a little surface digging wouldn't get me anywhere near him—which it didn't—but he minimized the risk by specifically directing my attention to Eddy Keith. It was safe to set me investigating Eddy's involvement with the shady side of the syndicates, because of course he wasn't involved. I could look forever, and find nothing." I paused. "I don't think I was supposed to have much time to find out anything at all. I think that catching us took much longer than was intended in the original plan."

Catching us . . . catching me. They'd have taken me alone, but both had been better for them . . . and far worse for me. . . .

"Took much longer? How do you mean?" Sir Thomas said.

Concentrate, I thought. Get on with it.

"From Lucas's point of view, I was very slow," I said. "I was working on the Gleaner thing, and I didn't do anything at all about the syndicates for a week after he asked me. Then directly I'd been told about Peter Rammileese and Mason, and could have been expected to go down to Tunbridge Wells, I went away somewhere else entirely, for another week; during which time Lucas rang Chico four times to ask him where I was."

Silent attention, as before.

"When I came back, I'd lost the notes, so I did them again in Lucas's office, and I told him Chico and I would go down to Peter Rammileese's place the following day, Saturday. I think it's likely that if we had done so, the . . . er . . . deterring would have been done then, but in fact we went the same afternoon that I'd been talking to Lucas, on the Friday, and Peter Rammileese wasn't there."

Weren't they all thirsty? I wondered. Where was the coffee? My mouth was dry, and a good deal of me hurt.

"It was on that Friday morning that I asked Lucas to

write to Henry Thrace. I also asked him—entreated him, really—not to mention my name at all in connection with Gleaner, as it might get me killed."

A lot of frowns awaited an explanation.

"Well . . . Trevor Deansgate had warned me in those sort of terms to stop investigating those horses."

Sir Thomas managed to raise his eyebrows and imply a frown at one and the same time.

"Are those the threats you mentioned before?" he said.

"Yes, and he repeated them when you . . . er . . introduced us, in your box at Chester."

"Good God."

"I wanted to get the investigation of Gleaner done by the Jockey Club so that Trevor Deansgate wouldn't know it had anything to do with me."

"You did take those threats seriously," Sir Thomas said thoughtfully.

I swallowed. "They were . . . seriously given."

"I see," said Sir Thomas, although he didn't. "Go on."

"I didn't actually tell Lucas about the threats themselves," I said. "I just begged him not to tie me in with Gleaner. And within days, he had told Henry Thrace that it was I, not the Jockey Club, who really wanted to know if Gleaner died. At the time I reckoned that he had just been careless or forgetful, but now I think he did it on purpose. Anything which might get me killed was to him a bonus, even if he didn't see how it could do."

They looked doubtful. Doubts were possible.

"So then Peter Rammileese—or Lucas—traced me to my father-in-law's house, and on the Monday Peter Rammileese and the two Scots followed me from there to a horse show, where they had a shot at abduction, which didn't come off. After that I kept out of their way for eight more days, which must have frustrated them no end."

The faces waited attentively.

"During that time I learned that Peter Rammileese was manipulating not four, but nearer twenty syndicates, bribing trainers and jockeys wholesale. It was then also that I learned about the bribable top man in the Security Service who was turning a blind eye to the goings on, and I regret to say I thought it must be Eddy Keith."

"I suppose," Sir Thomas said, "that that was understandable."

"So anyway, on Tuesday Chico and I came here, and Lucas at last knew where I was. He asked to come to Newmarket with us on Wednesday, and he took us there in his own super four-liter air-conditioned highly expensive Mercedes, and although he's usually so keen to get on with the next thing, he wasted hours doing nothing in Newmarket, during which time I now think he was in fact arranging and waiting for the ambush to be properly set up, so that this time there should be no mistakes. Then he drove us to where the Scots were waiting for us, and we walked straight into it. The Scots did the special job they had been imported for, which was deterring Chico and me, and I heard one of them tell Peter Rammileese that now that they had done what was ordered, they were going north straight away, they'd been down in the south too long."

Sir Thomas was looking slightly strained.

"Is that all, Sid?"

"No. There's the matter of Mason."

Charles stirred beside me, uncrossing and recrossing his legs.

"I asked my father-in-law to go to Tunbridge Wells yesterday, to ask about Mason."

Charles said, in his most impressive drawl, "Sid asked me to see if Mason existed. I saw the police fellows in Tunbridge Wells. Very helpful, all of them. No one called Mason, or anything else for that matter, has been found kicked near to death and blinded in their streets, ever."

"Lucas told me about Mason's case in great detail," I said. "He was very convincing, and of course I believed him. But have any of you ever heard of anyone called Mason who was employed by the Security Service, that was so badly injured?"

They silently, bleakly, shook their heads. I didn't tell them that I'd finally had doubts about Mason because there was no file for him in "Personnel." Even in a good cause, our breaking and entering wouldn't please them.

A certain amount of gloom had settled on their faces, but there were also questions they wanted to ask. Sir Thomas put their doubts into words.

"There's one obvious flaw in your reverse view of things, Sid, and that is that this deterrent . . . hasn't deterred you."

After a pause I said, "I don't know that it hasn't. Neither Chico nor I could go on, if it meant . . . if we thought . . . anything like that would happen again."

"Like exactly what, Sid?"

I didn't reply. I could feel Charles glancing my way in his best noncommittal manner, and it was he, eventually, who got quietly to his feet, and walked across the room, and gave Sir Thomas the envelope which contained the pictures of Chico.

"It was a chain," I said matter-of-factly.

They passed the photographs around in silence. I didn't particularly look to see what they were thinking; I was just hoping they wouldn't ask what I knew they would; and Sir Thomas said it baldly. "Was this done to you as well?"

I reluctantly nodded.

"Will you take your shirt off, then, Sid?"

"Look," I said, "what does it matter? I'm not laying any charges of assault or grievous bodily harm, or anything like that. There's going to be no police, no court case, nothing. I've been through all that once, as you know, and I'm not, absolutely not, doing it again. This time there's to be no noise. All that's necessary is to tell Lucas I know what's been happening, and if you thought it right, to get him to resign. There's nothing to be gained by anything else. You don't want any public scandal. It would be harmful to racing as a whole."

"Yes, but . . ."

"There's Peter Rammileese," I said. "Perhaps Eddy Keith might really sort out those syndicates now. It would only get Rammileese deeper in if he boasted that he'd bribed Lucas, so I shouldn't think he would. I doubt if he'd talk about Chico and me, either."

Except perhaps, I thought sardonically, to complain that I'd hit him very hard.

"What about the two men from Glasgow?" Sir Thomas said. "Are they just to get away with it?"

"I'd rather that than go to court again as a victim," I said. I half smiled. "You might say that the business over my hand successfully deterred me from that sort of thing for the rest of my life."

A certain amount of urbane relief crept into both the faces and the general proceedings.

"However," Sir Thomas said, "the resignation of the Director of Security cannot be undertaken lightly. We must judge for ourselves whether or not what you have said is justified. The photographs of Mr. Barnes aren't enough. So please . . . take off your shirt."

Bugger it, I thought. I didn't want to. And from the distaste in their faces, they didn't want to see. I hated the whole damned thing. Hated what had happened to us. Detested it. I wished I hadn't come to Portman Square.

"Sid," Sir Thomas said seriously, "you must."

I undid the buttons and stood up and slid the shirt off. The only pink bit of me was the plastic arm, the rest being mottled black with dark red crisscrossed streaks. It looked, by that time, with all the bruising coming out, a lot worse than it felt. It looked, as I knew, appalling. It also looked, on that day, the worst it would. It was because of that that I'd insisted on going to Portman Square on that day. I hadn't wanted to show them the damage, yet I'd known they would insist, and I would have to: and if I had to, that day was the most convincing. The human mind was deviously ambivalent when it wanted to defeat its enemies.

In a week or so, most of the marks would have gone, and I doubted whether there would be a single permanent external scar. It had all been quite precisely a matter of outraging the sensitive nerves of the skin, transient, leaving no trace. With such a complete lack of lasting visible damage, the Scots would know that even if they were brought to trial, they would get off lightly. For a hand, all too visible, the sentence had been four years. The going rate for a few days' surface discomfort was probably three months. In long robbery-with-violence sentences it was always the robbery that stretched the time, not the violence.

"Turn round," Sir Thomas said.

I turned round, and after a while I turned back. No one said anything. Charles looked his most unruffled. Sir Thomas stood up and walked over to me, and inspected the scenery more closely. Then he picked up my shirt from the chair, and held it for me to put on again.

I said, "Thank you," and did up the buttons. Pushed the tails untidily into the top of my trousers. Sat down.

It seemed quite a long time before Sir Thomas lifted the interoffice telephone and said to his secretary, "Would you ask Commander Wainwright to come here, please?"

If the administrators still had any doubts, Lucas himself dispelled them. He walked briskly and unsuspectingly into a roomful of silence, and when he saw me sitting there, he suddenly stopped moving, as if his brain had given up transmitting to his muscles.

The blood drained from his face, leaving the gray-brown eyes staring from a barren landscape. I had an idea that I must have looked like that to Trevor Deansgate in the stewards' box at Chester. I thought that quite likely, at that moment, Lucas couldn't feel his feet on the carpet.

"Lucas," Sir Thomas said, pointing to a chair, "sit down."

Lucas fumbled his way into the chair with his gaze still fixedly on me, as if he couldn't believe I was there, as if by staring hard enough he would make me vanish.

Sir Thomas cleared his throat. "Lucas, Sid Halley, here, has been telling us certain things which require explanation."

Lucas was hardly listening. Lucas said to me, "You can't be here."

"Why not?" I said.

They waited for Lucas to answer, but he didn't.

Sir Thomas said eventually, "Sid has made serious charges. I'll put them before you, Lucas, and you can answer as you will."

He repeated more or less everything I'd told them, without emphasis and without mistake. The judicial mind, I thought, taking the heat out of things, reducing passion to probabilities. Lucas appeared to be listening, but he looked at me all the time.

"So you see," Sir Thomas said finally, "we are waiting for you to deny—or admit—that Sid's theories are true."

Lucas turned his head away from me and looked vaguely round the room.

"It's all rubbish, of course," he said.

"Carry on," said Sir Thomas.

"He's making it all up." He was thinking again, fast. The briskness in some measure returned to his manner. "I certainly didn't tell him to investigate any syndicates. I certainly didn't tell him I had doubts about Eddy. I never talked to him about this imaginary Mason. He's invented it all."

"With what purpose?" I asked.

"How should I know?"

"I didn't invent coming here twice to copy down notes of the syndicates," I said. "I didn't invent Eddy complaining because I'd seen those files. I didn't invent you telephoning Chico at my flat four times. I didn't invent you dropping us at the car park. I didn't invent Peter Rammileese, who might be persuaded to . . . er . . . talk. I could also find those two Scots, if I tried."

"How?" he asked.

I'd ask young Mark, I thought. He would have learned a lot about the friends in all that time: little Mark and his accurate ears.

I said, "Don't you mean, I invented the Scots?"

He glared at me.

"I could also," I said slowly, "start looking for the real reasons behind all this. Trace the rumors of corruption to their source. Find out who, besides Peter Rammileese, is keeping you in Mercedeses."

Lucas Wainwright was silent. I didn't know that I could do all I'd said, but he wouldn't want to bet I couldn't. If he hadn't thought me capable, he'd have seen no need to get rid of me in the first place. It was his own judgment I was invoking, not mine.

"Would you be prepared for that, Lucas?" Sir Thomas asked.

Lucas stared my way some more, and didn't answer.

"On the other hand," I said, "I think if you resigned, it would be the end of it."

He turned his head away from me and stared at the Senior Steward instead.

Sir Thomas nodded. "That's all, Lucas. Just your resignation, now, in writing. If we had that, I would see no reason to proceed any further."

It was the easiest let-off anyone could have had, but to Lucas, at that moment, it must have seemed bad enough. His face looked strained and pale, and there were tremors round his mouth.

Sir Thomas produced from his desk a sheet of paper, and from his pocket a gold ballpoint pen.

"Sit here, Lucas."

He rose and gestured to Lucas to sit by the desk.

Commander Wainwright walked over with stiff legs and shakily sat where he'd been told. He wrote a few words, which I read later. *I resign from the post of Director of Security to the Jockey Club. Lucas Wainwright.*

He looked around at the sober faces, at the people who had known him well, and trusted him, and had worked with him every day. He hadn't said a word, since he'd come into the office, of defense or appeal. I thought, How odd it must be for them all, facing such a shattering readjustment.

He stood up, the pepper-and-salt man, and walked toward the door.

As he came to where I sat, he paused, and looked at me blankly, as if not understanding.

"What does it take," he asked, "to stop you?"

I didn't answer.

What it took rested casually on my knee. Four strong fingers, and a thumb, and independence.

Chapter 20

Charles drove us back to Aynsford.

"You'll get a bellyfull of courtrooms anyway," he said. "With Nicholas Ashe, and Trevor Deansgate."

"It's not so bad just being an ordinary witness."

"You've done it a good few times now."

"Yes," I said.

"What will Lucas Wainwright do after this, I wonder?"

"God knows."

Charles glanced at me. "Don't you feel the slightest desire to gloat?"

"Gloat?" I was astounded.

"Over the fallen enemy."

"Oh, yes?" I said, "And in your war at sea, what did you do when you saw an enemy drowning? Gloat? Push him under?"

"Take him prisoner," Charles said.

After a bit I said, "His life from now on will be prison enough."

Charles smiled his secret smile, and ten minutes farther on he said, "And do you forgive him, as well?"

"Don't ask such difficult questions."

Love thine enemy. Forgive. Forget. I was no sort of Christian, I thought. I could manage not to hate Lucas himself. I didn't think I could forgive; and I would never forget.

We rolled on to Aynsford, where Mrs. Cross, carrying a tray upstairs to her private sitting room, told me that Chico was up, and feeling better, and in the kitchen. I went along there and found him sitting alone at the table, looking at a mug of tea.

"Hello," I said.

"Hello."

There was no need, with him, to pretend anything. I filled a mug from the pot and sat opposite him.

"Bloody awful," he said, "wasn't it?"

"Yeah."

"And I was dazed, like."

"Mm."

"You weren't. Made it worse."

We sat for a while without talking. There was a sort of stark dullness in his eyes, and none of it, any longer, was concussion.

"Do you reckon," he said, "they let your head alone for that?"

"Don't know."

"They could've."

I nodded. We drank the tea, bit by bit.

"What did they say today?" he asked. "The brass."

"They listened. Lucas resigned. End of story."

"Not for us."

"No."

I moved stiffly on the chair.

"What'll we do?" he asked.

"Have to see."

"I couldn't . . ." He stopped. He looked tired and sore, and dispirited.

"No," I said. "Nor could I."

"Sid . . . I reckon . . . I've had enough."

"What, then?"

"Teach judo."

And I could make a living, I supposed, from equities, commodities, insurance, and capital gains. Some sort of living . . . not much of a life.

In depression we finished the tea, feeling battered and weak and sorry for ourselves. I couldn't go on if he didn't, I thought. He'd made the job seem worthwhile. His naturalness, his good nature, his cheerfulness: I needed them around me. In many ways I couldn't function without him. In many ways, I wouldn't bother to function if I didn't have him to consider.

After a while I said, "You'd be bored."

"What, with Wembley and not hurting, and the little bleeders?"

I rubbed my forehead, where the stray cut itched.

"Anyway," he said, "it was you, last week, who was going to give up."

"Well . . . I don't like being . . ." I stopped.

"Beaten," he said.

I took my hand away and looked at his eyes. There was the same thing there that had suddenly been in his voice. An awareness of the two meanings of the word. A glimmer of sardonic amusement. Life on its way back.

"Yeah." I smiled twistedly. "I don't like being beaten. Never did."

"Sod the buggers, then?" he said.

I nodded. "Sod 'em."

"All right."

We went on sitting there, but it was a lot better after that.

Three days later, on Monday evening, we went back to London, and Chico, humoring the fears he didn't take seriously, came with me to the flat.

The hot weather had gone back to normal, or in other words, warm-front drizzle. Road surfaces were slippery with the oily patina left by hot dry tires, and in west London every front garden was soggy with roses. Two weeks to the Derby . . . and perhaps Tri-Nitro would run in it, if the infection cleared up. He was fit enough, apart from that.

The flat was empty and quiet.

"Told you," Chico said, dumping my suitcase in the bedroom. "Want me to look in the cupboards?"

"As you're here."

He raised his eyebrows to heaven and did an inch-by-inch search.

"Only spiders," he said. "They've caught all the flies."

We went down to where I'd parked at the front and I drove him to his place.

"Friday," I said, "I'm going away for a few days."

"Oh, yes? Dirty weekend?"

"You'll never know. I'll call you when I get back."

"Just the nice gentle crooks from now on, right?"

"Throw all the big ones back," I said.

He grinned, waved, and went in, and I drove away, with lights going on everywhere in the dusk. Back at the flats, I went round to the lock-up garages to leave the car in the one I rented there, out of sight.

Unlocked the roll-up door, and pushed it high. Switched the light on. Drove the car in. Got out. Locked the car door. Put the keys in my pocket.

"Sid Halley," a voice said.

A voice. *His* voice.

Trevor Deansgate.

I stood facing the door I'd just locked, as still as stone.

"Sid Halley."

I had known it would happen, I supposed. Sometimes, somewhere, as he'd said. He had made a serious threat. He had expected to be believed. I had believed him.

Oh, God, I thought. It's too soon. It's always too soon. Let him not see the terror I feel. Let him not know. Dear God . . . give me courage.

I turned slowly toward him.

He stood a step inside the garage, in the light, the thin drizzle like a dark gray-silver sheet behind him.

He held the shotgun, with the barrels pointing my way.

I had a brick wall on my left and another behind me, and the car on my right; and there were never many people about at the back of the flats, by the garages. If anyone came, they'd hardly dawdle around in the rain.

"I've been waiting for you," he said.

He was dressed, as ever, in city pin stripes. He brought, as always, the aura of power.

With eyes and gun facing unwaveringly my way, he stretched up behind him quickly with his left hand and found the bottom edge of the roll-up door. He gave it a sharp downward tug, and it rolled down nearly to the ground behind him, closing us in. Both hands, clean, manicured, surrounded by white cuffs, were back on the gun.

"I've been waiting for you, on and off, for days. Since last Thursday."

I didn't say anything.

"Last Thursday two policemen came to see me.

George Caspar telephoned. The Jockey Club warned me they were going to take proceedings. My solicitor told me I'd lose my bookmaking license. I would be warned off from racing, and might well go to jail. Since last Thursday, I've been waiting for you."

His voice, as before, was a threat in itself, heavy with the raw realities of the urban jungle.

"The police have been to the lab. My brother is losing his job. His career. He worked hard for it."

"Let's all cry," I said. "You both gambled. You've lost. Too bloody bad."

His eyes narrowed and the gun barrels moved an inch or two as his body reacted.

"I came here to do what I said I would."

Gambled . . . lost. . . . So had I.

"I've been waiting in my car around these flats," he said. "I knew you'd come back, sometime or other. I knew you would. All I had to do was wait. I've spent most of my time here since last Thursday, waiting for you. So tonight you came back . . . with that friend. But I wanted you on your own. . . . I went on waiting. And you came back. I knew you'd come, in the end."

I said nothing.

"I came here to do what I promised. To blow your hand off." He paused. "Why don't you beg me not to? Why don't you go down on your bloody knees and beg me not to?"

I didn't answer. Didn't move.

He gave a short laugh that had no mirth in it at all. "It didn't stop you, did it, that threat? Not for long. I thought it would. I thought no one could risk losing both their hands. Not just to get me busted. Not for something small like that. You're a bloody fool, you are."

I agreed with him, on the whole. I was also trembling inside, and concerned that he shouldn't see it.

"You don't turn a hair, do you?" he said.

He's playing with me, I thought. He must know I'm frightened. No one could possibly, in these circumstances, not be frightened to death. He's making me sweat . . . wanting me to beg him . . . and I'm not . . . *not* . . . going to.

"I came here to do it," he said. "I've been sitting here for days, thinking about it. Thinking of you with no hands, with just stumps . . . with two plastic hooks."

Sod you, I thought.

"Today," he said, "I started thinking about myself. I shoot off Sid Halley's right hand, and what happens to me?" He stared at me with increased intensity. "I get the satisfaction of fixing you, making you a proper cripple instead of half a one. I get revenge . . . hideous, delightful revenge. And what else do I get? I get ten years, perhaps. You can get life for G.B.H., if it's bad enough. Both hands . . . that might be bad enough. That's what I've been sitting here today, thinking. And I've been thinking of the feeling there'd be against me in the slammer, for shooting your other hand off. Yours, of all people. I'd be better off killing you. That's what I thought."

I thought numbly that I wasn't so sure, either, that I wouldn't rather be dead.

"This evening," he said, "after you'd come back for ten minutes, and gone away again, I thought of rotting away in jail year after year wishing I'd had the bloody sense to leave you alone. I reckoned it wasn't worth years in jail, just to know I'd fixed you. Fixed you alive, or fixed you dead. So I decided, just before you came back, not to do that, but just to get you down on the ground squealing for me not to. I'd have my revenge that way. I'd remind you of it all your life. I'd tell people I'd had you crawling. Make them snigger."

Jesus, I thought.

"I'd forgotten," he said, "what you're like. You've no bloody nerves. But I'm not going to shoot you. Like I said, it's not worth it."

He turned abruptly, and stooped, putting one hand under the garage door. Heaved; rolled it upward and open.

The warm drizzle in the dark outside fell like shoals of silver minnows. The gentle air came softly into the garage.

He stood there for a moment, brooding, holding his gun; and then he gave me back what in the straw barn he'd taken away.

"Isn't there *anything,*" he said bitterly, "that you're afraid of?"